Praise for James Swain
and
The Night Monster

"Starts on an adrenaline high and never loses steam. Swain excels at sturdy storytelling and intelligent plotting."

—*The Sacramento Bee*

"James Swain is the real thing, a writer of pure, athletic prose, capable of bringing alive characters as original and three-dimensional as our best novelists."

—JAMES W. HALL

"Spock-like logic and a bullet-train-paced plot drive Swain's third thriller to feature Florida PI Jack Carpenter. This installment grabs you by the throat and doesn't let go until the last page."

—*Publishers Weekly*

D1053531

BY JAMES SWAIN

The Night Stalker
Midnight Rambler
Grift Sense
Funny Money
Sucker Bet
Loaded Dice
Mr. Lucky
Deadman's Poker
Deadman's Bluff

THE NIGHT MONSTER

A NOVEL OF SUSPENSE

JAMES SWAIN

BALLANTINE BOOKS • NEW YORK

2010 Ballantine Books Mass Market Edition

Copyright © 2009 by James Swain

Published in the United States by Ballantine Books, an imprint of The Random House Publishing Group, a division of Random House, Inc., New York.

BALLANTINE and colophon are registered trademarks of Random House, Inc.

Originally published in hardcover in the United States by Ballantine Books, an imprint of The Random House Publishing Group, a division of Random House, Inc., in 2009.

ISBN 978-0-345-51547-6

Printed in the United States of America

www.ballantinebooks.com

9 8 7 6 5 4 3 2 1

To Michael Connelly

Whoever fights monsters should see
to it that in the process he does not become
a monster. And when you look into an abyss,
the abyss also looks into you.

— NIETZSCHE

PART 1

THE RABBIT HOLE

PROLOGUE

Cops aren't supposed to get frightened. The badge and the uniform and the gun strapped to a cop's side are intended to ward off the normal fears that most people experience when confronted by unspeakable horror and evil.

But it doesn't always work out that way. Cops get scared, just like everyone else. Sometimes they get so scared, they run for their lives. Other times, they get shaken to the core and never forget the things they've seen. It happened to me, two years into the job.

I was going home in my cruiser when I got the distress call. A woman was being assaulted at the Sunny Isle apartment complex, and a neighbor had called 911. Sunny Isle was a mile from where I lived, so I took the call.

According to the dispatcher, a college student named Naomi Dunn was being assaulted by a man inside her apartment. It had sounded like a domestic disturbance, something I'd dealt with many times as a cop. When the dispatcher had asked if I wanted backup, I'd said no, I could handle the situation. The dispatcher had told me to proceed with caution.

I arrived at Sunny Isle a few minutes later. Four orange stucco buildings made up the complex, with entrances from each apartment facing a courtyard containing a pool and a children's play area. It had started to rain, and there were white caps on the water.

I searched for a place to park. The lot was filled with junkers, many with student tags. Several had bumper stickers that said Clinton in '92! I'd read about the Arkansas governor's run for president, and didn't think he had a chance.

I parked and got out of my cruiser. There was a yellow rain slicker in the trunk, but I didn't bother to retrieve it. I was a native, and was used to getting drenched by the occasional downpour.

Walking into the courtyard, I scanned the unmarked stucco buildings. They were quiet, and I saw nothing out of the ordinary. I walked around for a few minutes, then decided to leave. It had been a long day, and I wanted to eat dinner with my wife and two-year-old daughter, then hit the books. I was studying to become a detective, and the lengthy test was weighing heavily on my mind.

"Officer! Officer!"

A ghostlike woman materialized by the pool. Dressed in a simple black housedress, her soaking wet hair was plastered to her head.

"Did you call the police?" I asked.

"That was me."

Her voice was trembling, and she was shaking from head to toe. I couldn't tell if there was something wrong with her, or if she was just plain scared.

"What's the problem?" I asked.

"Earlier I saw a large man lurking around the complex. Then I heard noises from Naomi Dunn's apartment. She was screaming, so I called nine-one-one."

"Is Naomi Dunn still in her apartment?"

"Yes." The woman pointed at the last building, on the ground floor. "He's still in there, hurting her."

"Do you know who he is?"

"No, but he was huge."

I started to walk toward the building, and the ghostly woman called after me.

"Take your gun out," she said.

The words made me freeze. I'd been trained not to draw my weapon unless my life was being threatened. The tone of her warning said that it was. Unstrapping my holster, I rested my hand on my gun's handle.

"Please go inside your apartment and lock your door," I said.

"Yes, Officer."

I waited until the woman was in her apartment before I approached Dunn's apartment, and put my ear to the door. There was banging and shoving inside, the sounds loud enough to be heard over the rain. I knocked and stepped back.

When no one answered, I went to the window, and peeked through the flimsy curtains. The apartment's interior was a disaster area, with furniture uplifted and an upside down TV set on the floor with Dan Rather's smiling face. A bloodstain on the wall made me shudder, a bloody hand dragged across the wall. It didn't look like any domestic disturbance I'd ever seen.

Movement in the rear of the apartment caught my eye. Down the hallway and through an open door, a twenty-something woman stood inside a bedroom. Blond and powerfully built, she was throwing vicious kicks and punches at a person I could not see. The rapidity of the blows told me that she was schooled in self-defense, and made me wonder if the blood I'd seen had come from the person she was hitting.

I instinctively relaxed. I assumed this was Naomi Dunn, and could see that she was holding her own with her assailant. I had arrived just in time.

I drew my weapon and approached the door. I'd joined the police force because I thought I could make a difference. Twenty-four months into the job, and that still hadn't happened. But tonight was going to be different. I was going to save a young woman before something awful happened to her. I had never been more ready in my life.

I tested the door's handle. It was locked, and I lifted my leg and kicked three inches above the knob. The door splintered but did not come down. As I lifted my leg to kick it again, the door opened into my face. I heard my nose break, and flew backward to the ground.

I lay on my back with raindrops splashing on my face. My gun had left my hand and was lying somewhere nearby. Fighting the urge to pass out, I lifted my head, and saw a giant emerge from the apartment carrying an unconscious Dunn over his shoulder. From my vantage point it was hard to tell exactly how big he was. What registered was how small Dunn looked in comparison. She was a big woman, yet looked tiny slung over his shoulder.

"Police," I muttered. "You're under arrest."

The giant gazed down at me, his face round and bloodied. He had wild eyes and pursed lips, and reminded me of the crazies that I often encountered on the mean streets of Fort Lauderdale. When he spoke, the words only confirmed my suspicion.

"Pigs don't come to the party," he said.

"Let her go."

"No. She's mine."

Laughing, he walked around the corner of the apartment building and disappeared. I pulled myself up to a sitting position and looked for my gun. In the distance I heard tires squealing on wet asphalt.

I wiped away the blood coming out of my nose. I was hurting, yet none of that really mattered. I'd failed to stop him. I hadn't made a difference at all.

"Officer! Officer!" The ghostly woman had appeared again, and was kneeling beside me. "He got away. I saw him throw Naomi into the back of a green van."

"Did you get a license number?" I asked.

She brought her hand to her mouth. "No."

I pulled myself to my feet and leaned against the open doorway. The world was spinning, and I felt ready to pass out. "Go to your apartment, and call nine-one-one. Tell them to hurry."

The woman hurried away. Soon sirens pierced the air. They snapped me back to reality, and to the sad fact of how miserably I'd failed to do my job. Because I'd let my guard down, a young woman was lying unconscious in the back of a van.

I went to the parking lot to meet the responding officers. What had just happened would haunt me, and I promised myself that I would track this crazy bastard down.

I hadn't known how long that would take.

CHAPTER 1

THE CEILING of my rented room was spinning.

My pillow was soaked with sweat, as were the sheets, and my heart was racing a hundred miles an hour. Next to me, my dog Buster was licking my face.

Sitting up, I leaned against the cool plaster wall behind my bed. Sunlight streamed through the slats in the windows, and I listened to the cawing of seagulls scrapping for food on the beach.

I looked at the night table beside my bed. Lying on it was a stack of missing person reports. After becoming a detective, I'd run the Broward County Sheriff's Department's brand-new Missing Persons Unit. I'd run the unit for sixteen years before being kicked off the force two years ago. The reports were copies of files that had gone unsolved during my tenure. Every few months I reread them, just to see if there was something I'd missed.

Before going to bed, I'd reread Naomi Dunn's report. It had been the first case I'd worked when I'd joined Missing Persons, and was the reason that I'd chosen to work that unit, and not Homicide or Vice, which had also been available at the time. I considered myself responsible for what had happened to Dunn, yet now, eighteen years later, I knew no more about her disappearance than I did back then.

The file contained a profile of Dunn's abductor written by the CSI team who'd examined the crime scene. Based on the abductor's shoe prints, and the neighbor's and my own eyewitness accounts, he was six feet ten inches tall, and weighed three hundred pounds. He was also crazy. This was based upon my own observations, and the fact that Dunn, a second-degree black belt, had knocked out two of his front teeth, which had been found in her apartment. A person in his right mind would have run away from Dunn, yet her attacker had not.

Dunn's abductor should have been easy to find, only the opposite had been true. No crazed giants existed on the books of any Florida police departments, nor any hospitals or mental wards. Over time, I'd extended my search, and contacted police departments and mental hospitals around the country.

I'd found only one match.

His name was Ed Kemper. Kemper was a giant and a sociopath. He'd shot his grandparents at fourteen, then murdered his mother, her best friend, and six other women. By the time I found him, Kemper was serving seven consecutive life sentences in a Vacaville, California, prison and could not have abducted Dunn.

Eighteen years of looking, all dead ends.

I opened Dunn's file on my lap. Its pages were dog-eared from use. Nearly every page had my handwritten notes scribbled in the margins. Although we'd never met, I had developed a bond with Dunn, and felt like I knew her.

I studied the crime scene photos taken at the apartment. Blood from the abductor's wounds had been found in every room. I'd sent the DNA to the FBI, who'd stored it in CODIS, a computer system that contained the DNA of a quarter million known violent criminals. Hopefully a match would someday be made, and Dunn's abductor would be brought to justice.

Jimmy Buffett's "Cheeseburger in Paradise" floated across my room. It was the ring tone to my cell phone, a birthday present from my daughter, Jessie. I grabbed the phone off the night table. Caller ID said CANDY.

Detective Candice Burrell now ran Missing Persons, and was a friend. I made my living these days finding missing kids for police departments, and I was hoping she was calling with a job.

"Hello Detective Burrell," I said.

"Am I glad you answered," Burrell said. "I'm in a real jam. Are you busy?"

"My calendar's wide open."

"I'm at the courthouse waiting to give testimony in a trial, and I just got a call that an eight-year-old autistic boy has gone missing from Lakeside Elementary School. I need you to go find him."

I slipped out of bed. A rumpled pair of cargo pants and a Tommy Bahama shirt lay on the floor. Within seconds they were hanging from my body.

"The boy's name is Bobby Monroe, and he disappeared from his classroom about a half hour ago," Burrell went on. "Four uniforms are at Lakeside now, and don't have a clue as to where this kid went. They think he might have been abducted."

As a cop, I'd dealt with many missing autistic kids. They were seldom targets for abductors, and I had a feeling something else was going on.

"Is the school locked down?" I asked.

"Yes. That was the first thing the principal did."

"Good. Is Bobby Monroe in a special class for autistic children, or is he mainstreamed?"

"I don't know what that is."

"Many schools in Broward have autistic kids sit in regular classes with nonautistic kids. It helps develop them socially."

"I think he's in a regular class."

"What's his teacher saying?"

"The regular teacher is sick. There's a substitute teacher today, and she's freaking out."

Autistic children often became distressed by simple changes in their daily routine, such as a change in classrooms or teachers, or even moving something on their desk, like a pencil or an eraser. The picture was getting clearer.

"Here's what I'm thinking," I said. "The appearance of the substitute upset Bobby, so he took off. Most autistic kids go to confined spaces to vent their anger. Bobby could be hiding in a closet, or maybe squeezed himself into a refrigerator."

"Oh, Jesus—"

"Tell the uniforms at the school to start looking in every hidden space they can find. Also tell them not to call out Bobby's name. He'll hear them, and only make himself harder to find."

"How soon can you be there?"

I grabbed my gun off the night table, and slipped it into the concealed holster in my pants pocket.

"Give me fifteen minutes," I said.

"You're a lifesaver," Burrell said.

CHAPTER 2

INTERSTATE 595 was the asphalt spine of Broward County, and ran from the ocean's sandy beaches to the Everglades' swampy marshes. Soon I was hurtling down it with the wind blowing in my face and Buster hanging out the passenger window.

I was waved through by a guard at the front gate of Lakeside Elementary. The school consisted of three mustard-colored buildings connected by covered walkways. It sat on a barren tract of land, surrounded by a six-foot-high chain-link fence that encompassed the entire property. Leashing Buster, I hurried inside.

A uniformed cop stood outside the principal's office. His nameplate said D. Gordon. His tanned face bore more lines than a roadmap.

"You must be Jack Carpenter," Officer Gordon said. "It's good to meet you."

I might have left the force under a dark cloud after beating up a suspect, but I still had my fans in the department. I asked Gordon for an update.

"Two groups of teachers and all of the maintenance men have turned the school upside down," Gordon said. "We haven't found a trace of Bobby Monroe. I'm beginning to think he's not here."

"Do you think he left the grounds?"

"That's what my gut's telling me."

"There was a guard at the front entrance when I drove in. How would Bobby have gotten past him?"

"I don't know. I just don't think Bobby's here. We've looked everywhere."

Gordon looked about fifty. Age counted for something when you were a cop. If Gordon's gut was telling him that Bobby Monroe wasn't here, he was probably right.

"I want to speak with the kids in his class," I said.

"Follow me. What's with the pooch?"

"He helps me find things."

"Good. We could use some help."

Gordon led me down a hallway to a classroom doorway. We passed a number of rooms filled with kids that were in lockdown mode. Until Bobby Monroe's whereabouts were determined, none of the children in Lakewood were going anywhere. Gordon put his hand on the doorknob and glanced at me.

"Be careful what you say to the substitute teacher. She's a nervous wreck, and I don't want to send her over the edge."

"What's her name?"

"Ms. Rosewater."

We entered the classroom. Ms. Rosewater stood at the blackboard, a plump, pale, bespectacled young woman with her hair tied in a bun. About thirty kids sat at their desks, facing her. Seeing my dog, they stood up in their chairs and started chattering loudly.

"Class, be quiet," she said.

Her voice sounded ready to crack. I introduced myself.

"I'd like to speak to the children," I said.

"By all means," she replied.

I faced the kids and made Buster lie on the floor. My dog was a brown, pure-bred Australian Shepherd with a docked tail—not a common breed. The kids stared at him like he was some exotic animal in the zoo.

"Good morning. My name is Jack Carpenter, and this is my dog Buster. We're going to help the police find your missing classmate. Before we do that, I need to ask you some questions. Who was the last person to see Bobby Monroe?"

A little girl in pigtails sitting in the front row raised her hand.

"What's your name?"

"Missy."

"Tell me what happened, Missy."

"We were going to gym. Miss Rosewater had us line up by the door. Bobby was right behind me. We went into the hall, and I asked Bobby if he was feeling okay. He didn't say nothing. I turned around, and he was gone."

"Did he run back into the classroom? Or down the hall?"

"I don't know where he went."

"Why did you ask Bobby if he was okay?"

"He was banging his desk and making really weird noises. I thought maybe he had a bellyache."

I glanced at Ms. Rosewater. "Which desk is Bobby's?"

The substitute teacher led me to an empty desk in the room's center. Over the back of the chair hung a blue knapsack, which I opened and quickly searched. A crumbled candy wrapper caught my eye. It was for a bag of peanut M&Ms, and had Harrison Ford's photo splashed across the wrapper promoting the new Indiana Jones movie. Walking to the front of the room, I held the wrapper in the air.

"Does everyone know what this is?" I asked.

The children nodded as one.

"Good. Which one of you gave this bag of candy to Bobby?"

Their faces turned expressionless. I scanned the room, and settled on a little boy with curly blond hair who wasn't making eye contact with me. His desk was adjacent to Bobby's, and I decided he was the culprit. I didn't like traumatizing kids, but I had to get to the truth. Crossing the room, I knelt down in front of his desk.

"What's your name?"

"Stuart," he said, staring at his desk.

"Look at me, Stuart."

Stuart lifted his eyes, which were moist and met my gaze.

"Did you give this bag of candy to Bobby?"

Stuart hesitated, then nodded reluctantly.

"Didn't your regular teacher tell you not to do that?"

"Yeah."

"Then why did you?"

"Bobby saw the candy in my lunch bag, and got all excited. He said that if I gave him the candy, he'd recite all the lines from the latest Indiana Jones movie during lunch."

"Can Bobby do that?"

"Bobby knows all the lines from the Indiana Jones

movies and from Star Wars and a bunch of TV shows. He's super smart."

It was not uncommon for autistic children to have amazing memories, and I could see Bobby pressuring Stuart to give him the M&Ms.

"Did you see Bobby eat the candy?" I asked.

"Uh-huh," Stuart whispered.

"Is that when Bobby started acting strange?"

"Yeah. I'm sorry if I made Bobby sick. I didn't mean to."

In order for autistic children to mainstream, their parents often removed sugar and dairy products from their diets, which helped calm them down. Stuart's bag of M&Ms had hit Bobby's nervous system like a bomb, and Bobby had gone on sensory overload and decided to run. Grabbing Bobby's knapsack from his desk, I walked to the front of the classroom where Buster lay on the floor. I placed the knapsack in front of my dog's face, and let him get a good whiff. Buster rose from the floor and walked to the back of the classroom. I was right behind him.

Buster stuck his face against one of the windows that faced the playground. The latch was unlocked, and I pushed the window open. The opening didn't look large enough for a child to climb through, but I knew from past experience that autistic children were capable of just about anything when they were on tilt. I turned to face Officer Gordon.

"How big is the school property?"

"Twenty acres," Gordon replied.

"What does it back up on to?"

"Mostly woods."

"I'm going outside to look around. I'd suggest you

round up the teachers and maintenance men who are searching for Bobby, and do the same."

I headed for the door. Scaling a fence was not difficult for most young boys, and Bobby could have gone just about anywhere. Our chances of finding him grew slimmer by the minute. A thought flashed through my mind, and I turned back to Gordon.

"Do the woods have any freestanding water?" I asked.

"Yes, there's a large pond."

"Is it visible from the school grounds?"

"In some spots, yes."

My shoulder banged the door as I raced from the classroom.

CHAPTER 3

WATER HAS a magical effect on autistic children. It calls to them like a siren's song. I found this out the hard way when an autistic little boy who'd disappeared from his home was found on the bottom of his next-door neighbor's swimming pool. It was a lesson I'd never forgotten.

I ran across the playground with Buster on my heels. The morning air was still and hot, and sweat poured down my face and burned my eyes. As I came to the fence that encompassed the property, I noticed a piece of torn fabric hanging in the twisted barbs across the top, and felt myself shudder.

I scaled the fence, and landed on the other side. Buster began digging at the ground in an attempt to join me. I couldn't wait, and plunged into the woods.

There was no discernible path, the underbrush thick with weeds and exposed tree roots. More than once I nearly fell, only to right myself as I began to go down. In the distance I heard a thrashing sound accompanied by a boy's muted screams.

"Bobby! I'm coming!" I shouted.

I charged toward the sound, the tree branches tearing

at my face and arms. On the ground I spotted a child's sneaker, and it gave me an adrenaline burst that propelled me through the dense trees and into a small clearing fronting the pond.

The pond was several acres in size, its water dark and menacing. Twenty yards from where I stood, a boy's head bobbed up and down. Bobby Monroe appeared to be sitting down in the water, his arms thrashing helplessly. Something beneath the water had latched on to him, and was pulling him down.

Knowing what had gotten him, I dove in.

Back when I was growing up, there had been as many alligators in south Florida as there had been people. Over the years the gator population had thinned out, but there were still plenty around, and every once in a while they attacked someone.

"Bobby!"

Bobby twisted his head at the sound of my voice. His eyes were filled with terror, and he was swallowing water. He was trying with all his might to stop from being pulled to the murky depths. If the gator got him down to the bottom of the pond, he'd roll the boy until he drowned, then turn him into a meal.

"I'm coming! Hold on!"

I'd swam competitively as a kid, and still swam whenever I could. I powered my body across the water, my eyes never leaving Bobby's face.

"Keep fighting!"

Bobby's head dropped beneath the surface, then came back up. He spit out a mouthful of brackish water while staring at me helplessly. His arms were no longer thrashing, his body rigid and still. He had given up. I lunged through the water and shot out my arm, only to see him vanish before my eyes.

I am part Seminole Indian. I tell you this because as a kid I visited my relatives on the reservation, and watched men in the tribe wrestle alligators in front of tourists. I'd seen enough of these battles to know that there was an art to grappling with a gator, and it centered around getting your hands around its jaws and not letting go.

I dove beneath the water and swam straight down. The water was dark and I couldn't see a thing, but I could feel the gator's tail thrashing the water. I followed the thrashing until I had the tail in my hands. Grabbing a gator by the tail wasn't very smart, but I knew the gator was preoccupied and wasn't about to let Bobby go.

I got both my hands on the gator's tail and pulled it close to me. Then I put the gator into a bear hug. The scales on its back were rough, and tore through my clothes and into my skin. From tail to nose it felt about six feet long, maybe two hundred pounds. He was a big one, and filled with fight.

I squeezed him hard and got nowhere. Then I released one of my arms, and with my fingers tried to poke him in the eye. I'd seen this on the reservation once, and knew it was a surefire way to get a gator to open its mouth.

But that didn't work this time. I could stay underwater for over a minute, but I doubted Bobby could. He was drowning and I needed to do something fast. With my free hand, I drew the Colt 1908 Hammerless resting in my pants pocket, and shoved its barrel against the gator's side. I'd never shot my gun underwater before, and had no idea if it would work. Only I was desperate and willing to give anything a try.

I squeezed the trigger and heard the gun discharge. The gator twisted violently in my grasp, and then the fight started to leave its body. Shoving the Colt back into my pocket, I used both hands to remove Bobby's leg from the gator's jaws. The boy had gone limp, and I prayed I wasn't too late.

I came out of the water with Bobby draped in my arms. Officer Gordon was standing at the edge of the pond with Buster by his side. Gordon had his walkie-talkie out and was calling for an ambulance. My dog was covered in dirt—he had dug his way beneath the fence.

"For the love of Christ," Gordon said.

I laid Bobby facedown on the ground. He was still breathing, and I whacked him on the back until he spit up the water trapped in his lungs. Then I rolled him over.

"Hey, kiddo," I said.

Bobby looked anxiously at me. He had curly black hair and the wholesome good looks every parent wishes for their child. His right foot was bleeding, and I removed his sneaker and sock to have a look. His sneaker had done a good job of protecting his foot, and although he was cut in several places, none of the cuts were very deep, and he still had all his toes. I grabbed his big toe and gave it a wiggle, and drew a smile out of him.

"Hi, Bobby," I said. "My name's Jack, and this is Officer Gordon, and this is my dog Buster. We're going to take you to the hospital. Okay?"

Bobby did not respond. He was a hard kid to read. I glanced at Gordon.

"Want to do the honors?" I asked.

"You do it. He trusts you."

Kneeling, I gathered Bobby into my arms. As I started to lift him, the boy screamed, and pushed me away. I laid him back down.

"Everything's going to be okay," I said.

Bobby screamed again and punched me with his fists.

"I hear you like Indiana Jones movies. I do, too."

The boy kept screaming. I heard Gordon swear under his breath.

"Sweet Jesus, would you look at that."

I turned around and looked into the pond. The dead alligator had risen to the surface, and was lying on top of the water a few yards from us.

"Watch him." I waded into the water and lifted the gator's head up. He was bigger than I'd thought, and looked almost prehistoric. "Look, Bobby. He's dead."

Bobby's eyes grew as big as silver dollars, and he stopped screaming. I came out of the water and went to where he lay. This time when I picked him up, he did not resist, but burrowed his head into my chest and held me tight. I kissed the top of his wet head and headed back toward the school.

CHAPTER 4

"HAVE NO FEAR, Jack Carpenter is here," a familiar voice said.

Detective Candy Burrell slipped through the filmy white curtain that surrounded my bed in the emergency ward of Broward General Hospital. I'd followed Bobby Monroe's ambulance to the hospital, then decided to have the cuts and bruises on my body examined by a doctor.

Burrell knelt down to pet Buster, who lay dutifully beside my bed. Burrell got along famously with my dog, a rare member of an exclusive club.

"Who taught you to wrestle alligators?" she asked.

"It's an old family tradition."

"I hear you're pretty good at it."

"How's Bobby doing?"

"He's going to be okay. How are *you* doing?"

"I'll live."

"Has anyone looked at your cuts yet?"

I shook my head. The emergency ward was filled with people with problems far worse than mine, and I'd been lying on the bed for thirty minutes.

"I need to ask a favor," Burrell said.

I moved my legs and patted the bed. Burrell sat down and smiled. Since getting my old job running Missing Persons, she'd started wearing pantsuits that showed off her trim, athletic figure. She was of Italian descent, small-boned and pretty, with slate-blue eyes that electrified her tanned face.

"Name it," I said.

She started to speak, then glanced at the opening in the curtain. Down the hall, a man was talking in a loud, argumentative voice.

"Wait. Who's that?" I asked.

"Frank Yonker."

"What's that jerk doing here?"

"He showed up in the emergency room with Bobby Monroe's parents. He wants to get a statement from you."

"About what?"

"He wants to know what happened at Lakeside Elementary this morning."

When kids get injured or traumatized during rescues, their parents sometimes sued the police for negligence. Frank Yonker was a local attorney who chased ambulances for a living, and had caused the department plenty of grief over the years.

"What's his beef?" I asked. "Bobby ran off school property and jumped into a pond. How can the police be liable for that?"

"Yonker is claiming that no one from Missing Persons was at the school, and that we sent you instead of sending a qualified detective to handle the search."

"I'm not qualified?"

"You were thrown off the force."

"Not to split hairs, but I resigned."

"You left under a dark cloud, and the newspapers called you bad names. Yonker wants to know why you were sent to Lakeside. Once he gets a statement from you, he'll probably file his lawsuit."

I leaned back on my pillow. "So what's the favor?"

"I was wondering if you'd slip out the back door of the hospital and get your cuts tended to someplace else. The department will pick up the tab."

"What about Yonker?"

"I'll deal with him."

"You want me to turn into the invisible man."

"That's one way to put it."

"For you, anything."

Burrell patted my leg. "That's my Jack."

"Can I give you some advice about dealing with Yonker?"

She started to reply, then simply nodded.

"Yonker is a tough character," I said. "If he can't get to me, he'll work on you, and try to prove that you were negligent in the way you handled the case. You need to establish a timeline in case this goes to court. Write down everything you did this morning, starting from what time you got to work, when you got to the court-house, and when you got the call that Bobby Monroe was missing. Have the other detectives in Missing Persons do the same."

"What will that prove?"

"That you were doing your job when the call came, and acted appropriately. Do it now, while it's fresh in your memory. When Yonker goes to interview you, hand him the timelines, and let him see what he's up against. More than likely, he'll go away."

"You think so?"

"He doesn't make money when he loses."

Burrell rose from the bed and planted a kiss on my cheek. "By the way, Chief Moody wants you to join him for a drink after work. He really appreciates what you did."

I climbed out of bed. Chief Moody was the reason I was no longer a cop, and I couldn't see clinking glasses with him while reminiscing about the good old days.

"Tell him I'll take a rain check," I said. "My daughter's in town playing in a college basketball tournament tonight."

"Couldn't you just have a drink with him?"

"Why should I?"

"You should mend fences. It's healthy."

I pulled back the curtain beside my bed. The hospital bed next to mine was unoccupied. I'd found my escape route. I snapped my fingers for Buster, who rose from the floor.

"Tell Moody to meet me at the Bank Atlantic Center at seven o'clock," I said. "We can have a couple of cold ones in the parking lot before the game."

Burrell rolled her eyes. "Right."

I slipped through the curtain with my dog.

"See you later," I said.

CHAPTER 5

I GOT OUT of Broward General without Frank Yonker spotting me, and drove to a nearby walk-in clinic. Parking in a shady spot, I rolled down the windows. Buster took the hint, and went to sleep in the back.

The clinic was filled with screaming kids and moaning old people. I was put into an examination room and told by a nurse that a doctor would be in shortly. Having nothing better to do, I took apart my Colt on the examining table, and used a Q-tip and some cotton balls I filched from a medicine cabinet to clean it.

I'd started carrying a 1908 Colt Pocket Hammerless my first day as a detective, and I considered it the best concealment weapon in the world. It was thinner than most handguns, and because there was no hammer to catch on my clothing, it was an easy draw. It had gotten me out of many tight situations, and had never let me down. They say you are in love with a gun when you see one dropped on TV and are afraid it might get scratched. That was how I felt about my Colt.

I had my guy reassembled and back in my pocket by the time a doctor entered the room. He looked Middle Eastern and spoke with a heavy British accent. I removed my shirt and pants, and showed him the cuts on my body. He asked me how I'd gotten them.

"Wrestling with an alligator," I replied.

The doctor rolled his eyes.

"Now I've heard everything," he said.

I left the clinic covered in Band-Aids. Walking to my car, I powered up my cell phone and found a message waiting from my daughter, Jessie. She'd called from the Bank Atlantic Center, where she and her teammates were practicing for tonight's basketball game. There was urgency to her voice, and I called her back.

"Thanks for calling me back so fast," my daughter said.

"Anything for you," I said.

"Are you coming to the game tonight? A bunch of the girls' fathers said they'll be there."

"Of course I'm coming to the game. Now tell me what's going on."

"There's been a creepy guy with a video camera lurking around the court during practice. He kept shooting closeups of the team, even when we were just standing around listening to Coach. He's got a press badge, but something tells me he's a stalker. I asked one of the security guards to talk to him, but the guy disappeared."

Bad guys trying to get close to young women often posed as TV reporters or fashion photographers. I said, "What did he look like?"

"He was white, kinda short and thin, in his late forties. He was wearing dirty Bermuda shorts, a faded blue T-shirt, and a baseball cap. During the break, I tried to snap a photo of him with my cell phone, but he took off running."

"You might have scared him away."

"He'll be back, Daddy."

"You think so?"

"I'd bet money on it."

Intuition was the messenger of fear. Jessie's gut was telling her that this guy was a threat. It was time to stop questioning and start helping.

"I'll look for him at the game tonight," I said.

"Thank you, Daddy."

I drove east, to the beach, and pulled into the parking lot of the Sunset Bar and Grill, a ramshackle building that sat with one half in the sand and the other half over the ocean. I lived in a rented room above the bar with a spectacular view of the water. One day a hurricane would come and blow it all away, but for now, I called it home.

I showered and put on my best clothes, then headed downstairs. Behind the bar was a shaven-headed, heavily tattooed ex-convict named Sonny. I'd leaned on Sonny after my life had fallen apart, and he'd never let me down. He gave me a plate of table scraps, which I placed on the floor for my dog.

"How did you get all those Band-Aids on your arms?" Sonny asked.

"Wrestling with an alligator," I replied.

"Yeah, and I'm Peter Pan."

"You've put on weight."

"Up yours."

"I need to go out later. Can you babysit Buster for me?"

"Hot date?"

"My daughter's basketball game."

"The place won't be the same without you."

"I bet you say that to all the boys."

At six o'clock I left the Sunset and drove to the Bank Atlantic Center on the west side of the county. Built ten years ago with taxpayer money, the Center is a concrete and glass arena that hosts rock concerts and sporting events. Inside, I bought a cold beer and a couple of hot dogs, and sat in the stands with a group of fathers whose daughters were also on the team. It was the second round of an NCAA regional tournament, the Lady Seminoles of Florida State vs. the Lady Cougars of Ole Miss, and the game was expected to be close. I started yelling at the opening tip-off. By the half, I was so hoarse I could hardly speak.

The game was just as advertised, and hotly contested. I'd been watching women's hoops since my daughter had started playing in high school, and knew the names of every player on both teams. With two minutes left in the game, Sara Long, the Lady Seminole's leading scorer, sunk a three-pointer that put her team firmly ahead. I rose from my seat along with the rest of the fathers and cheered.

That's when I spotted the stalker.

He stood with a group of photographers beneath a basket. Small and thin, he wore green shorts, a ratty T-shirt, and a Marlin's baseball cap pulled down low. His sole interest was the Lady Seminoles, and his video camera never stopped filming.

I hustled down the aisle toward the floor. Every security guard in the Center was a retired cop, and there wasn't one who didn't know me. I was going to ask one of the guards to pull this creep off the floor and check his credentials. Chances were, they were fake, which would be grounds for having him arrested.

I hopped over the restraining gate, and started moving around the court toward the basket. The game was winding down, the eyes of everyone in the stands on the players. When I was a few feet away from the stalker, I stopped. A plastic reporters' pass hung around his neck, the ID portion turned around. I didn't think that was a coincidence.

"Hey buddy, don't I know you?" I asked.

It was a line I'd used often as a cop. It tended to scare the crap out of bad guys.

The stalker lowered his camera. His chin was covered in gray stubble, and his teeth hadn't seen a dentist in years.

"I don't think so," the stalker said.

I grabbed the ID, and flipped it over. It was blank.

"Where's your press pass?" I asked.

"I must have left it in my car."

I pointed at the exit. "Let's go."

"You a cop?"

"Used to be."

His shoulders sagged. Body language could tell you a lot about a person's intentions. This guy was guilty as charged.

A roar shook the arena, and I looked at the court. Jessie had stolen the ball out of an opponent's hands. She dribbled effortlessly down the court, planted her feet and took a shot, the ball arcing perfectly through the basket.

"That a girl," I shouted.

Something hard hit me in the chest. Losing my balance, I fell backward, and hit the floor on my backside.

It took a moment for me to get my wits. The stalker's video camera lay beside me. Looking up, I saw him sprinting toward the exit.

I jumped to my feet. In my experience, only guys who were wanted by the police ever ran away.

I'd hooked a live one.

CHAPTER 6

THE TEMPERATURE dropped ten degrees as I ran into the parking lot. It was a perfect night, with a soft breeze blowing off the ocean and a pale full moon. I lived in paradise, although it often got spoiled by guys like this.

The stalker had vanished. I climbed onto the bumper of a pickup truck, and tried to find him. When that didn't work, I shut my eyes, hoping to hear where he'd gone. The hiss of traffic on the Sawgrass Expressway sounded like steam escaping out of a pipe, and drowned out all sound.

I hopped off the pickup and trotted up and down the aisles. I was guessing my stalker had jumped into a car and was hiding from me. A maroon Ford minivan with fast-food wrappers lying by the driver's door caught my eye. Something told me that the scumbag with the video camera had dropped them there. As I approached the vehicle, my cell phone rang. Caller ID said JESSIE.

"Hey honey," I said.

"Where are you?" my daughter asked.

"I had to run outside. Did you win?"

"We beat them by eight points. One of the fathers

said you were chasing somebody. Did you find the stalker I told you about?"

"Yes, but he gave me the slip. Let me call you right back."

"We're heading back to the motel. Call me if you find him, will you?"

"You bet."

I closed my phone and slipped it into my pocket. Then I approached the minivan, and stuck my face to the tinted windshield. I couldn't see inside, and I went around to the back and tried to look through the back window. It was covered in duct tape. I considered peeling the tape back, then decided I was overstepping whatever rights I had as a pissed-off father. I dialed the sheriff's department on my cell phone and heard an operator pick up.

"This is Jack Carpenter. Who's this?"

"Hey Jack, it's Gloria," the operator said. "How you been? I heard you were working solo these days."

"That's right. Who's on duty tonight?"

Gloria passed along the names of the cops working the night shift. One was a detective named Bob Smith who'd worked for me in Missing Persons, and who knew how to get things done. I asked to speak to him, and Gloria patched me through.

"This is Detective Smith," he answered.

"Jack Carpenter here."

"Hey, pal, what's up?"

"I need for you to run a license through the system."

"I can do that."

I started to read the license off the minivan. My eyes weren't what they used to be, and I stepped forward to get a clearer look. As I did, there was a loud ripping sound, and I lifted my eyes to see an enormous arm spring through the duct-taped window, and grab the front of my shirt.

"Hey!" I shouted.

I went straight up in the air, my feet no longer touching the ground. I am a big guy—six foot one, a hundred ninety pounds soaking wet—and the giant arm shook me like a rag doll. I had never felt so helpless.

The minivan started up and backed out of the spot. I was afraid the driver would back up into another car and crush me to death. I drew my Colt and aimed at the back door. I didn't like shooting at someone I couldn't see, but there was no other choice. Before I could get off a shot, the giant arm tossed me through the air.

I landed on my back, my skull snapping against the pavement. The Colt and cell phone left my hands, and I heard them skip away. The sickening taste of blood filled my mouth. The minivan braked in front of me, its gears shifting. I rolled to my left just as it backed up, and watched the tires missing my head by inches.

The minivan's rear door slid back, and I heard someone get out. A dirty work boot appeared by my face. It was the biggest foot I'd ever seen.

The boot came down square on my head, pinning me to the ground. Struggling to free myself, I envisioned my brains being ground out of my skull.

"Get back in the van," someone said.

I recognized the voice. It was the stalker I'd been chasing.

"Nuh-uh," the owner of the giant foot grunted.

"People are coming!"

"I want to kill him."

"There's no time."

"There's always time to kill."

"Do as I say, before someone sees us."

"But I want . . ."

"Get in the fucking van!"

The foot left my head. It was like the weight of the world had been lifted from me. I tried to rise, but a fist crashed down on my skull.

"Hey buddy, are you okay?"

Opening my eyes, I saw a pear-shaped man wearing the traditional maroon colors of Florida State standing over me. He had a rolled-up program in his hand, and wore a concerned look on his face.

"I think so," I said.

"Had too much to drink, huh?"

"Guess so."

"Would you mind moving? I need to get into my car."

I was lying next to the driver's door of the guy's car. I rolled out of the way and heard him get into his vehicle and drive off.

I slowly got to my feet. The parking lot was nearly empty. I looked at my watch and realized I'd been out cold for nearly ten minutes.

I worked my jaw back and forth and tilted my head from side to side. Nothing felt broken, and I was thankful that I was still alive. I tried to remember the minivan's license plate, but the letters and numbers had gotten jumbled in my brain.

I searched for my Colt and my cell phone. I found my phone first. It had been stepped on, and the face was cracked. It refused to power up.

My handgun took longer to locate. It had followed Murphy's Law and landed beneath one of the few remaining vehicles in the lot. I crawled on my belly like a snake to retrieve it.

My aging Acura Legend was parked on the other side of the lot. Reaching the street, I traveled several blocks until I found a service station with a pay phone. Pulling in, I called Bob Smith back.

"I was starting to worry about you," Smith said.

"I got mugged while we were talking. Someone inside the minivan jumped me."

"You hurt?"

"Just my pride."

"Give me the license again."

"I whacked my head, and can't remember it. I don't think it will do any good anyway. Something tells me the minivan was stolen."

"What was the make?"

"Maroon Ford, about ten years old."

I listened to Smith's fingers bang on a keyboard.

"You're right," Smith said. "A 1998 maroon Ford mini-van belonging to a house painter named Terry Williams was stolen from his driveway in Lauderdale Lakes last night. Williams told the uniform who responded to the call that he was surprised the vehicle was taken, because it didn't have any seats."

"Why didn't it have seats?"

"Williams said he used the vehicle to transport his painting equipment, and he took the seats out."

A pair of guys stalking a women's basketball game had purposely stolen a minivan with the seats ripped out. It sounded like a perfect vehicle for a kidnapping.

"That's not good," I said. "I need you to send a cruiser to the Day's Inn on State Road 84. The Florida

State women's basketball team is staying there, and I think these guys have their eye on one of the players."

"Will do. Are you heading there now?"

"Yep. Tell the cruiser to meet me behind the motel. That's where the players stay."

"Got it."

I ended the call and jumped into my car. The average response time for a police cruiser in Fort Lauderdale was eight and a half minutes. I knew from experience that a lot of bad stuff could happen in that amount of time. I punched the gas pulling out of the service station and started running red lights.

CHAPTER 7

THE DAY'S INN on State Road 84 was a time warp. Hot pink stucco and a flashing neon vacancy sign, it had been there for as long as I could remember. The Lady Seminoles usually rented a row of rooms in the back, away from the highway.

I drove behind the motel, tasting the salty ocean breeze. Coming around the corner, a pair of shiny animal eyes flashed back at me from the swamp behind the motel.

The team bus was parked in back. I parked behind it and got out.

Peels of laughter and loud dance music floated through the air. My daughter's team was celebrating their hard-earned win over Ole Miss. Everything looked fine, but looks could be deceiving. I decided to find Jessie and make sure she was okay.

I started to cross the lot, and stopped in my tracks. A vehicle was parked in the grass between the team bus and the swamp. It looked like a Ford minivan, and I approached for a closer look.

It *was* a Ford minivan, the rear window covered in

duct tape. It was the same vehicle from the Bank Atlantic Center. I drew my Colt.

I approached the driver's door. Through the tinted side window glowed the orange ember of a cigarette. Grabbing the handle, I jerked the door open.

Behind the wheel sat the stalker. Headbanger music blared out of his car radio, his fingers tapping out the beat on the wheel. He shot me a startled look.

"Remember me?" I asked.

The stalker nodded stiffly, his eyes never leaving my Colt.

"Get out, and keep your hands where I can see them."

He hopped out of the minivan, tossing his butt to the ground. Enough light was coming from the motel for me to get a good look at him. Small of build, with rotting teeth and a crooked nose, his darting eyes made him look feral.

"What's your name?" I asked.

"Mouse," he mumbled.

"Is that your first or last name?"

"Just Mouse."

"Okay, Mouse, put your hands in the air."

Mouse lifted his arms into the air. There was something childlike about the way he acted that made me think he was not all there. But that didn't make him any less dangerous. I stuck my head into the open door and peered inside the minivan. The interior had been stripped and reeked of paint remover. I pulled my head back out.

"Where's your partner?" I asked.

"I don't have a partner," Mouse replied.

"Stop lying. Which girl on the basketball team are you after?"

Mouse's mouth opened, but no words came out. *Guilty as charged.*

I decided to frisk him, but I didn't do it the old-fashioned way. Instead, I made Mouse turn his pockets inside-out, and when I saw that he wasn't carrying a weapon, I had him unbutton his shorts, and drop them to his knees. Then I made him do a slow three-sixty spin. It was a great way to humiliate a person, and often led to a suspect opening up. Seeing that he was clean, I let him pull his pants back up.

"Where's your partner?" I asked again.

Mouse hesitated, then pointed at the row of rooms where the Lady Seminoles were staying. "There."

"Show me," I said.

Mouse started toward the motel. When asked, criminals often led people of authority to places where they'd committed crimes. I'd never fully understood the reason, and guessed the answer was rooted in the subconscious.

Mouse stopped at the last room in the row. The door was closed, the shades on the window tightly drawn.

"Is your partner in there?" I asked.

"Maybe," he said.

I ripped the baseball cap from his head, and used it to slap him in the face. I couldn't do that as a cop, but I wasn't a cop anymore.

"Stop hitting me," Mouse protested.

"Is he in there or not?"

"He's in there."

"Knock on the door. When he answers, tell him everything is okay, that you were just checking up on him."

"Okay."

Mouse rapped loudly on the door, then took a step back. I should have taken that as a warning that something bad was about to happen, but my adrenaline was pumping and I felt in control of the situation. From the other side of the door came a woman's muffled scream. A smile crossed Mouse's lips.

"What's so funny?" I said.

"You'll see," he replied.

The door banged open, and I found myself staring at a huge man dressed in a black sweatshirt and black pants, his face covered by a ski mask. He was so big, he had to duck beneath the door frame as he came out. Even though I was holding a gun, his presence scared the daylights out of me, and I stepped back.

"Stop right there," I said.

The giant stopped. Slung over his shoulder was a young woman wearing gray sweats. She lifted her head, and I saw that it was Sara Long, the top scorer on Jessie's team. Sara's mouth was taped shut, her wrists hog-tied with rope. Seeing me, she let out a muffled scream.

"Put her down," I said.

The giant grunted something unintelligible under his breath.

"I mean business," I said.

"She's mine," the giant said.

The giant patted the bottom of Sara's behind. It was a strange gesture, almost affectionate, and I knew that he wasn't going to comply.

Mouse shot his arm out, and grabbed my wrist. Considering his size, he was unusually strong. He twisted the Colt's barrel so it pointed at the ground.

"Got him," Mouse said.

The giant struck me in the head with his free hand.

The blow felt like a baseball bat. My knees buckled, and the Colt fell from my hand.

Still holding Sara, the giant lifted me off the ground by my shirt, carried me across the lot, and slammed my head into the side of the team bus. The smart thing would have been to not fight back, but it wasn't in my genes to quit.

I punched the giant in the face. The blow snapped his head, and his ski mask slipped off. He snarled at me like a dog.

"That was a no-no," the giant said.

His face was round and childlike. It was the same crazy bastard who'd abducted Naomi Dunn from her apartment. After eighteen years of looking, I'd finally found him, and now he was about to abduct another young woman right out from under me.

It was my last thought just before I passed out.

CHAPTER 8

Two HOSPITAL VISITS on the same day was a record, even for me.

I awoke in a private room with uneven plaster walls and a window facing a parking lot filled with cars. It was starting to get light. I'd been unconscious all night.

I squeezed my fingers, and moved my arms and legs. Nothing felt broken, and I wasn't wearing any casts, nor were there pulleys hanging from the ceiling above my bed. I just had a splitting headache, and my mouth tasted like dried blood.

"Hi, Daddy."

Jessie sat beside my bed playing with my cell phone. Her cheeks were red and puffy. If I'd accomplished anything as a cop, it was shielding my family from my work, and it killed me to see her upset like this. She rose and kissed my cheek.

"How are you feeling?" she asked. "I got your cell phone to work."

"I'll live. What happened?"

"Someone threw you into the swamp behind the motel. You were lucky you didn't drown. Coach Daniels pulled you out and gave you CPR."

"Coach Daniels is kind of cute, isn't she?"

"Daddy!"

"I need some water. My throat is killing me."

Jessie filled a plastic cup from a jug sitting on the nightstand. I took it away from her and sucked it down.

"You were in pain, so the doctor gave you a sedative," she said. "He said the only reason your skull wasn't broken is because you have a thick head."

I found the strength to laugh.

"Have you talked to your mother?" I asked.

"I called Mom's cell, but she didn't pick up. Then I tried her at the hospital, and the receptionist told me there was a huge pile-up on the interstate, and all the nurses and doctors were working the emergency room."

"So your mother doesn't know."

"No, Daddy."

My wife had left me and moved away to Tampa after I'd gotten kicked off the force. I'd tried every trick in the book to get her to come back. So far, none of them had worked. I needed to tell her what had happened, not Jessie.

"Let me call your mother," I said.

"Are you sure?"

"Positive."

"There are two detectives in the hall who want to talk to you." Jessie fished their business cards out of the pocket of her jeans and read their names aloud. "Detectives Boone and Weaver. Sounds like a comedy team."

"First tell me what's going on," I said.

"You mean about Sara?"

"Yes."

My daughter rested her elbows on the arm of my bed.

A tear fell from her eye, and ran down the side of her face. "Sara's gone. The police are conducting a manhunt across south Florida. I was watching it on TV earlier. They've closed down all the highways and are looking for the kidnappers' minivan with helicopters."

"I need to see this."

Jessie switched on the TV that hung over my bed. Sara Long's abduction was the lead story on the local news channel. While a smiling newscaster explained what had happened, photographs of a bikini-clad Sara from a college edition of *Sports Illustrated* flashed across the screen. The segment ended, and Jessie killed the picture.

"Who else saw Sara's abductors at the motel?" I asked.

"The desk clerk saw them drive away, but didn't see their faces. That's why the detectives want to talk to you. They're hoping you saw what the men looked like. *Did* you see them, Daddy?"

Jessie's voice was filled with pleading. Although I loved my daughter more than anything in the world, telling her what had happened would only compromise the police investigation, and I wasn't about to do that.

"They were bad men," I said.

Jessie waited for me to continue. When I didn't, she let out a sigh.

"Should I get the detectives now?" she asked.

"That would be a good idea."

Detectives Boone and Weaver actually did look like a comedy team. Larry Boone was as round as a beach ball and prematurely balding, while Rob Weaver was built like a toothpick and had a thick mane of black hair. I wasn't sure which was the straight man and which was the comic, but that would become apparent once they started grilling me. Both were homicide detectives, and were on loan to help with the investigation. They sat with their knees pressed against my bed and opened spiral notebooks in their laps.

"Start from the beginning, and tell us what happened," Boone said.

I explained how I'd chased Mouse at Jessie's basketball game, and ended with me describing the giant who'd tried to crush my skull. Boone and Weaver traded glances and put their pens down.

"How big was this guy?" Boone asked.

"Scary big," I said.

"Be specific."

"Six-ten, three hundred pounds. And strong. He picked me up with one arm and carried me across the parking lot while holding Sara. I punched him in the face, and it didn't faze him."

"You make him sound like Superman," Weaver said.

"I've never encountered someone that strong."

Both detectives loosened the knots in their ties. The gesture was not lost on me. They didn't believe me.

"I know it sounds crazy, but that's what happened," I said.

"How much did you have to drink at the game?" Boone asked.

"A couple of beers."

"Just a couple?"

"I drank a Budweiser during the first half, got a refill during halftime, and didn't finish it. I wasn't drunk, if that's what you're implying."

Boone looked down at his notebook and read from it. "The cashier at the concession stand said you purchased a half dozen sixteen-ounce Bud drafts during halftime. That's a lot of beer."

"I bought those for the other dads," I explained. "We were sitting together in the stands, and I offered to get the beer."

"What other dads?"

"The fathers of the girls on the team. We sit together during the games and root for our daughters. I'm guessing you didn't bother talking to them."

Boone shook his head and flipped his notebook closed. He had rings beneath his eyes and his clothes stank of cigarettes. His body language told me that he didn't want to hear any more of what I had to say. I folded my hands and waited him out.

"Here's the skinny, Jack," Boone said. "We have a suspect named Tyrone Biggs cooling his heels down at the county lockup. Biggs is Sara Long's ex-boyfriend. He also plays basketball at Florida State, and is a really big dude. My partner and I think you saw *him* in the parking lot at the Day's Inn."

I followed college basketball, and knew Tyrone Biggs. He was the Florida State center, and was headed for a pro career in the NBA if his knees held up. He *was* big, but he wasn't the monster I'd seen stealing Sara Long out of her motel room.

"It wasn't Tyrone Biggs," I said.

"The evidence says it was," Boone said.

"What evidence is that?"

"Sara Long's abductor didn't break into her motel room. She opened the door, and let him in. Chances are, she wouldn't let in the guy you just described."

"Did the room have a peephole in the door?"

"Yes. We talked to Sara's teammates, and they said that

she's extremely cautious, and wouldn't have opened her door without first looking outside."

"You're sure she let him in?"

"Positive."

That didn't make sense, but it still didn't change what I'd seen.

"Are you holding Biggs based solely on that?" I asked.

"There's more," Weaver said. "Sara and Biggs recently split up, and Sara considered having a restraining order placed on him. It seems Biggs called her and threatened her if she wouldn't get back together with him. Sara decided not to pursue it because she didn't want to hurt his chances of playing pro ball."

"It wasn't Tyrone Biggs," I repeated.

Boone rested his elbows on the rail of my bed and looked me squarely in the eye. I had more to say, but shut my mouth instead.

"All we're asking is that you drive over to the lockup with us, and take a look at this guy," Boone said. "Maybe it will clear your head."

"My head is fine," I said.

"Come on, Jack. Play ball with us. This guy Biggs is a real jerk."

The worst thing that could happen during a missing person investigation was that the police followed the wrong leads and went down a rabbit hole. Boone and Weaver were going down a rabbit hole right now. If I didn't convince them they were wrong, they'd take the rest of the detectives working the investigation down with them.

"Okay," I said.

Boone slapped his hands on his knees. "Great. I'll go

find your doctor, and get you cleared out of here. Do you want us to wheel you out?"

"I can make it on my own."

I got out of bed and found my clothes hanging in the closet. I started to dress. "Where's my gun?" I asked.

"Down at headquarters. It's being held as evidence."

"How do I get it back?"

"Talk to Burrell. She has it."

The detectives went to find a doctor. I dressed while staring at the TV. The channel I'd been watching had an update about Sara. The stolen Ford minivan had been found in the elevated parking garage across the street from the Broward County Library. In the back of the minivan were Sara's clothes.

I shivered. I knew what had happened inside that van. Sara had been drugged, and her abductors had changed her clothes. They'd also stuck a wig on her, just to play it safe. They'd stolen another car, and driven to a motel, where they'd rented a room with double beds, and tied Sara to one of them. Now they were waiting for the dust to settle. Once the police removed their roadblocks, which they'd eventually have to do, they'd move Sara to another location.

Every crime had a signature, and this crime's signature was very distinct. I was dealing with a pair of serial abductors who'd done this many times before. If Sara was going to have a chance, I needed to move fast.

CHAPTER 9

I FINISHED DRESSING and headed for the door. A doctor came into my room holding a clipboard. He had me sign a form, and handed me a vial of pills to deal with the pain. The label on the vial said *May cause drowsiness*. I tossed them into the trash.

In the hall I found Jessie slumped in a chair, fast asleep. I woke her up and explained that I was leaving with the detectives.

"Don't you have practice this morning?" I asked.

"I was going to skip it," my daughter said.

"You need to go. It will take your mind off things."

"Okay. Can you lend me some money for a cab? I'm kind of broke."

"Not a problem."

Jessie called for a cab. Ten minutes later, it pulled up in front of the hospital. Before climbing in, my daughter hugged me, and I felt her heart pounding against my chest. She was like me, and tended to hold things in. I could only imagine what all this was doing to her.

The cab drove away. Detectives Boone and Weaver

stepped out from the side of the building. They'd been smoking cigarettes, waiting for me.

"Ready when you are," Boone said.

They drove me to the Days Inn. My Legend was still parked in the back. I'd had the car for sixteen years and had almost forgotten what the original color was. But it still drove, and that's all I cared about.

I followed the detectives to the county jail on SE 1st Avenue, which everyone called the Inn on the River because of its proximity to the New River. While Boone arranged to have Tyrone Biggs put in a lineup, I chatted with Captain Mike, who'd been processing criminals into the jail for as long as I'd been a cop.

"Who are you here to see?" Captain Mike asked.

"A suspect named Tyrone Biggs," I replied.

"The basketball player? I processed him through this morning."

"What's he like?"

"He's one of those white guys who thinks he's a black gangsta. I told him I had Florida State in the office college basketball pool this year, and he growled at me."

"Mister Personality."

"He's an asshole, if you ask me."

Boone appeared and had me follow him. We walked down a hallway to a small room with a two-way mirror. We went inside and Boone shut the door. I stood next to the mirror, my breath fogging the glass.

Standing in a lineup in the next room were seven white males. Each was extremely tall, and ranged in height between six-five and six-ten. I recognized several as longtime perps, and I guessed Boone had pulled them out of the lockup.

Tyrone Biggs stood in the center of the line wearing a sleeveless black athletic shirt—what cops called a "wife-beater"—and ragged blue jeans with a gaping hole in each leg. His arms were covered in tattoos, one of which snaked up his neck and stopped just below his ear. I'd admired his play on the basketball court, but I didn't like what I was seeing now. Biggs's eyes glinted with hostility and both hands were clenched into fists. I understood why Boone and Weaver were so certain he'd abducted Sara Long. His body language suggested he was guilty of *something*.

"What do you think?" Boone asked.

"The guy I saw was more muscular," I said.

Boone let out an exasperated breath.

"I'm just telling you what I saw."

"You got knocked out," Boone said. "Did it ever occur to you that your imagination might have distorted what you saw?"

"My imagination didn't distort anything."

"But it *could* have."

"Not here."

"You suffered a concussion and were unconscious for most of the night. What if your imagination turned Tyrone Biggs into someone else, and substituted him into your memory? Stranger things have happened."

I wasn't changing my story. Boone needed to see the light.

"Here's an idea," I said. "Grill Biggs, and let me be in the room with you. See how Biggs reacts when he sees me. If he's guilty, you'll know it soon enough."

"I can't do that."

"Why not?"

"It's against procedure."

"Come on. I was a detective for sixteen years."

"So what?"

"There is no procedure."

Boone looked at the lineup. The seven men were growing uneasy, their bodies slick and shiny with sweat. Of the group, Biggs looked the most uncomfortable.

"What the hell," Boone said.

The interrogation cells were in the basement of the jail. Each was small and windowless, with sophisticated eavesdropping equipment wired into the ceiling light fixtures. Boone led me into one and had me stand in the corner.

A few minutes later, Tyrone Biggs was brought into the cell by a pair of guards. Biggs was tall and rangy, but the body mass wasn't there. This wasn't the same person who'd snatched Sara and beaten me up.

Boone had Biggs sit in a plastic chair that was bolted to the floor. Biggs dropped his huge frame into the chair and nearly broke it. Boone pointed at me.

"Recognize him?" Boone asked.

Biggs glanced at me. "No. Should I?"

"This is Jack Carpenter," Boone said. "Jack used to be a detective. You beat him up when you were abducting Sara Long at the Day's Inn last night."

"That's bullshit."

"Watch your language," Boone snapped.

"If he says I beat him up, he's lying."

"He's not lying," Boone said. "*You're* lying."

Biggs fell silent and stared at the floor. He wasn't acting the way innocent people acted. I pushed myself off the wall.

"What are you doing in Fort Lauderdale?" I asked.

"I drove down to see Sara play," Biggs replied.

"Are you two back together?"

"We're working on it."

"Did you see the whole game?"

"Most of it."

I'd been sitting in the Florida State rooting section during the game, and had not seen Biggs in the stands. I could have missed him, only he was too big to miss.

"Where did you watch the game from?" I asked.

Biggs hesitated, and I knew I'd caught him.

"A bar?" I asked.

His mouth tightened.

"Or did you go to a strip club?"

His face reddened. *Busted.*

"Here's what I'm guessing," I said. "You came to see Sara, only temptation got the better of you, and you went to a strip club instead of the game. Things must have gotten out of hand, because now you don't want to talk about it. And because you won't talk, you're screwing up the police's ability to find Sara."

Biggs leaned back in his chair, looked at the ceiling and blew out his lungs. "I went to a tittie bar, and a chick gave me a hand job in the VIP lounge for fifty bucks."

"What was her name?"

"Sky."

"Why didn't you tell the police?"

"I didn't want it making the newspapers."

"Afraid it would ruin your NBA chances?"

"Fuck you."

"Watch it!" Boone cautioned.

There was a sweet smell coming off Biggs that I'd

thought was aftershave, but now realized was cheap perfume from the stripper who'd jerked him off. Sara Long deserved better than this loser.

"Did you call Sara after the game?" I asked.

"Yeah, I called her," Biggs replied.

"What did you say?"

"I told her I'd come by, and we'd go out and celebrate."

"Did she agree?"

"Yes."

"You were going to pick her up at the motel?"

"That's right."

Now I understood what had happened. Sara had been expecting Biggs to pick her up. She had looked through the peephole and seen a giant figure standing outside in the dark; she'd assumed it was Biggs and unlocked the door.

Now I was pissed. Biggs had unwittingly aided in Sara's abduction. I pointed my finger at him and saw him squirm in his chair.

"What?" Biggs said.

"You know what," I said.

"No, I don't."

"It's time for you to come clean. Otherwise, the police will continue to think that you did this, and not focus on catching the real abductors."

"Come clean how?"

"I want you to tell us everything that happened at the strip club, starting with the time you got there, till the time you left."

A line of sweat appeared above Biggs's upper lip. Liar's sweat. Biggs had gotten more than a hand job from Sky. If it came out, his career would be finished.

No NBA contract, or lucrative sneaker endorsements, or beautiful girls waiting in every town he played in. He wasn't prepared for that, even if it meant harming Sara. He was a selfish prick, and nothing I could say was going to change him.

"I want to talk to my lawyer," Biggs said.

CHAPTER 10

I WANTED TO BE a detective for just ten minutes. That was all the time I'd need to put the fear of God into Biggs, and make him start telling the truth. Boone pulled me into the hallway.

"So, what do you think?" Boone asked.

"Biggs is a scumbag, but he didn't abduct Sara Long."

"Then why won't he talk to us?"

The hallway was filled with men wearing tailored suits and silk neckties. They looked like defense lawyers who happened to have better hearing than most dogs. I pulled Boone into a corner where no one could eavesdrop.

"Biggs had sex with a stripper and doesn't want the NBA to find out. That's why he's keeping his mouth shut."

"I think he did it," Boone said. "I'm going to ask the DA to press charges. Are you sure you don't want to change your story?"

Boone had made up his mind. He disliked Biggs so much that it had tainted his reasoning. Cops called it personalizing a case. It had ruined more criminal investigations than anything I knew of. Shaking my head, I watched Boone walk away.

I trudged up the stairwell to the main floor, turned over my visitor's pass to the desk sergeant, and started to sign myself out.

"Not so fast," the desk sergeant said.

"What did I do?" I asked.

"Detective Burrell wants to see you. She's in her office on the second floor."

I reclaimed my visitor's pass and went upstairs. The second-floor receptionist waved me through, and I walked down the hall. Burrell occupied my old corner office with its depressing view of the employee parking lot. I'd never liked looking at the cars cops drove; they were usually aging pieces of junk and had always reminded me how poorly cops were paid. I stuck my head into Burrell's office, and caught her gazing through the window.

"Good morning," I said.

Burrell spun around in her chair. She still wore yesterday's blue pantsuit, her hair disheveled, her eyes ringed from lack of sleep. I didn't need a crystal ball to figure out what was going on. The search for Sara had gone cold.

"Have a seat," she said.

I sat across from her. You could tell a lot about people by the photographs that sat on their desks. The photos on Burrell's desk were of her father, her uncle, and her two brothers—all rank-and-file cops. I supposed it was in her genes to carry a shield.

"Boone let me question Tyrone Biggs," I said. "He didn't abduct Sara Long."

"How can you be positive? Strange things happen to people's memories when they get knocked out."

I had hired and trained Burrell, and it felt strange to hear her question me. Only that was what the job required. You had to question everyone.

"And it was dark," Burrell added.

"I know what I saw," I said. "It wasn't Biggs."

"Then who was it?"

"I don't know who he is."

Lying on the desk was a green Pendaflex file. Burrell picked the file up and handed it to me. I opened it and started to read.

"Those are the records of eleven men of unusual height who've committed crimes against women in south Florida in the past five years," she said. "Maybe one of them is the guy you saw abducting Sara Long."

Burrell was giving me the benefit of the doubt, which was more than Boone and Weaver had done. I removed the records and spread them across her desk. The mug shots of eleven hardened criminals stared up at me. Five were white, three black, three Hispanic. I studied their faces, then put the records back into the file.

"It's none of these guys," I said.

"You're sure about that?"

"Yes. I know this is going to sound strange, but I've seen the guy before."

Burrell's mouth dropped open. "You have? When?"

"Eighteen years ago. I was a patrolman, and went to an apartment complex in Fort Lauderdale on a call. A college student named Naomi Dunn was being assaulted by an unknown male. I responded and tried to get into the apartment. The guy opened a door in my face and knocked me down. I saw him leave with Dunn thrown over his shoulder. It was the same person I saw abduct Sara Long."

"What else do you remember about him?"

"He looked crazy," I said.

"Did you write this up in your report?"

"I did, but my supervisor made me change it."

An uneasy silence filled the office. Burrell put her elbows on her desk and gave me a hard look.

"Why did he do that?"

"I was studying to become a detective. My supervisor said that if I wrote in my report that this guy was a crazy giant, people would think I was making excuses, and I might not get promoted. He made me change my report to say that Dunn's abductor was a big guy who was high on something."

"Only he wasn't."

I felt my face burn, and shook my head.

"You shouldn't have done that," Burrell said.

"I made up for it."

"How so?"

"I had a choice of units when I became a detective. Missing Persons was brand-new, just a cubicle and a desk. I took over, and immediately started looking for Dunn. I've never stopped looking."

"Where did you look?"

"I contacted every police department in the state, and every hospital. When that didn't pan out, I contacted police departments and hospitals in other states. Nothing turned up."

The red button on her desk phone lit up. It was the office's private line, and only a few select people had the number. Burrell answered it.

"Excuse me, Mayor Dawson, but I have someone sitting in my office," she said. "If you don't mind, I'm going to put you on hold. I'll be right back."

Burrell put the call on hold and nestled the receiver into the cradle. Her eyes had not left my face the whole time.

"Let me see if I get this straight," she said. "You think Sara Long's abduction is connected to an eighteen-year-old case, and the culprit is some big guy with mental problems that there are no records of."

"I know it sounds stupid, but yes."

"You once told me that criminals don't operate in vacuums. They live in regular neighborhoods and shop for groceries and do other normal stuff. If this guy has been running around for that long, how come there's no record of him?"

"I don't know," I said. "He works with a partner called Mouse, so maybe Mouse is the visible one, while he stays undercover."

"A mouse and a giant."

"That's right."

Burrell drummed her desk. The sound gave a nice beat to the blinking light on her phone. I could tell she was growing exasperated with me.

"The mayor wants me to formally arrest Tyrone Biggs," she said.

"Why is the mayor involved?"

"Because the case has become political. If I don't make an arrest soon, the city stands to lose the women's NCAA basketball tournament next month. We're talking millions of dollars of tourism revenue and lots of TV exposure."

"But Tyrone Biggs is innocent. Someone else did this."

"Jack, be reasonable. You got hit in the head, and your mind is playing tricks on you. What other explanation is there?"

I rose from my chair. I had told my story to three detectives, and none had believed me. I needed to find more evidence to prove my case. If I didn't, Sara Long would end up like Naomi Dunn.

"Who's got my gun?" I asked.

"I do."

"Can I have it back? Or do I need to take a sanity test first?"

Burrell removed my Colt from her desk. There was a slight hesitation as she handed it to me. Like she thought I might have gone off my rocker, and could hurt someone with it. I slipped it into the holster in my pocket and went to the door.

"Tell the mayor I said hello," I said.

CHAPTER 11

I DROVE to the Bank Atlantic Center where my daughter's team was practicing. Entering through a service entrance, I walked to the arena without seeing a single cop or security guard. Had I still been running Missing Persons, I would have assigned a pair of cops to every practice until Sara Long was found.

I stood beneath a basket and canvassed the arena. The Lady Seminoles were at the far end of the court, practicing their jump shots. I waved to my daughter and also to her coach, who I owed a dinner. Then I looked in the stands to see if any suspicious characters were hanging around.

Satisfied that Jessie and her teammates were safe, I went to the lobby and tagged a maintenance man mopping the floor. Maintenance men were good sources of information, and had helped me many times during investigations. I handed him my business card, which identified me as a retired detective with the Broward County police.

"My name's Jack Carpenter," I said. "I was wondering if you were working the basketball game last night."

The maintenance man studied my card. He was pushing

sixty, with snow-white hair worn in a buzz cut, and
bloodshot eyes that said he was no stranger to the bottle.
Stitched in red above his shirt pocket was the name
Frank.

"Is this about the girl that was abducted?" Frank
asked.

"That's right. I was wondering if anyone found a
video camera courtside last night, and turned it in. It's
linked to the case."

"Didn't hear about any video camera getting turned
in," Frank said.

"Do you have a lost and found?"

"Yeah. We keep stuff we find in a locked room in the
back."

"Who runs the lost and found?"

"I do."

"Would you check to see if the camera is there?"

Frank leaned on his mop and gave me a hard look. I
felt a confrontation coming on, and pulled a crisp
twenty from my wallet. I tucked the money into his shirt
pocket.

"I'd really appreciate it," I said.

Frank went to look for the missing video camera. He
returned empty-handed and with whiskey on his breath.
I had expected more for my money.

"The camera's not in lost and found," he said.

"Was it ever?" I asked.

Frank gave me a look and shrugged.

"Did you pawn it?" I asked.

He winced like I'd slapped him in the face. I'd made a
study of body language, and everything about Frank's
body had told me that he was lying through his teeth. I
decided to vent my anger on him.

"I could get you in a lot of trouble," I said.

"I didn't—"

"Withholding evidence is a serious crime."

"You can't prove—"

"You could go to jail. Ever been to jail before? It's murder on old guys. They make you clean the toilets and mop the floors."

His chest sunk and his mouth dropped open. He whispered the word *shit*.

"Tell me where the camera is," I said.

Frank blinked. Then he blinked again. Being busted was like being in a car wreck, with everything turning to slow motion. Frank was in slow motion right now. When he spoke, his words were barely a whisper. "There's a fence in my neighborhood. I dropped by his place this morning, and sold him the camera. He moves the stuff fast."

"Any chance of retrieving it?" I asked.

Frank shook his head.

"Did you watch the film on the camera before you fenced it?"

"Yeah."

"Remember any of it?"

"It was of Sara Long and another girl on the team. I didn't know that the Long girl had been abducted until I picked up the paper at lunch. By then it was too late to get the camera back."

"Would you have tried to?"

"Of course. I'm just trying to make ends meet."

"Who was the other girl on the tape?"

"One of the forwards. About five-ten, wore her hair in a ponytail. On the film she was practicing shooting three-pointers. She had a sweet shot."

An icy finger ran down the length of my spine.

"Was she wearing number sixteen?" I asked.

Frank closed his eyes and plumbed his memory.

"I think so," he said.

The other girl on the tape was Jessie. Sara Long's abductors had been profiling two members of the Lady Seminoles, and had picked Sara over my kid.

God had spared me.

I returned to the arena. The Lady Seminoles were working on their layups, their exertion echoing across the hardwood floor. Their coach was pushing them hard, trying to make them forget the loss the team had suffered. More than once I saw a player go to the sidelines to cry into a towel, then go back to the floor, and resume practicing.

A voice snapped my head. A man sat in the bleachers, talking on a cell phone. The one and only Karl Long, Sara's father.

Karl Long was a well-known real estate developer with a penchant for ruthless deals and expensive toys. He was pushing fifty, a tall, good-looking guy with a hundred-dollar haircut and perfect teeth. He never sat with the other fathers during the games, but sequestered himself in a private box. I waved to him and climbed the bleachers.

"Jack Carpenter," I said.

I offered my hand. Long snapped his phone shut and glared at me.

"I know who you are," Long said. "You were at the Days Inn when Sara was abducted last night."

There was a hint of accusation in his voice. It was common for parents of missing kids to take out their grief on the people around them. It was part of coping, and I'd experienced it many times working cases.

"I just wanted to tell you how sorry I am," I said. "I know how hard this must be for you."

"You've got a lot of nerve," he replied.

It was rare for me to be speechless. This was one of those times.

"You're an ex-detective," Long went on. "You carry a gun. You were *right there* in the parking lot when it happened. Why didn't you stop that son-of-a-bitch from taking my daughter? What the hell is wrong with you, man?"

I wanted to ask Long where he'd gotten his information, since the victim's families were often the last to know the details. Instead, I tried to calm him down.

"I didn't want to risk shooting Sara," I said. "Then I got knocked out. I would have saved her if I could have. You have to believe that."

"You should have done more."

"I spent the night in the hospital."

"I don't want to hear your excuses."

"I'm sorry, Karl. I truly am."

"Don't take that personal tone with me."

Long gave me a murderous look. Behind the icy demeanor was real pain. He had everything money could buy, and now someone had taken from him the one thing his money couldn't buy back. His baby.

"I want to help," I said.

"How do you propose doing that?"

"I'm an expert at finding missing kids. It's how I make my living."

"I've hired the best detective agency in town to find Sara. They're wired into the police and also the criminal underground. They're professionals, which is more than I can say about you."

Private detective agencies were good at staking out motel rooms and digging up dirt, and little else. Long had probably paid the agency a big retainer, and in return, gotten a lot of promises. The agency had also probably told him some unpleasant things about me. I was the bad guy in all this, just like I'd been the bad guy for saving Bobby Monroe's life.

But none of that fazed me. I guess you could say I was used to it. Taking out my wallet, I removed my business card. Long acted astonished when I gave it to him.

"You've got to be joking," he said.

"Take it," I said.

"Why should I?"

"Because you're going to need all the help you can get."

"You think so?"

"Yes, I do. These guys are pros."

Long tore my business card in two and let the pieces flutter from his hands.

"Get lost," he said.

I walked down the bleachers toward the arena. The Lady Seminoles had taken a break, and I spotted Jessie standing by the sidelines, waving to me. There was a pleading look in her eyes that told me she had something important to tell me.

I put Karl Long out of my mind and hurried toward her.

CHAPTER 12

JESSIE WAS BREATHING hard as I approached.

"How's practice going?" I asked.

"Horrible. I can't stop thinking about Sara, and neither can anyone else."

"You need to focus on the game tonight."

"I'm trying, Daddy."

Jessie glanced over her shoulder at her coach, who was standing nearby, then dropped her voice. "A couple of the girls on the team want to talk to you."

"About Sara?"

My daughter wiped the sweat from her face with a towel. "Yeah."

"Why the secrecy?"

"Some of the girls broke curfew the other night, and Sara was with them," Jessie explained. "I don't think they want Coach to hear what they have to say."

"Have they told the police about this?"

"No. I overheard them talking in the locker room earlier. I cornered them, and told them they should tell you, and that you wouldn't rat them out. You won't, will you?"

Keeping secrets from the police during a criminal

investigation wasn't just wrong, it was against the law. If I spoke to Jessie's teammates and didn't tell the police, I'd be committing a crime myself. I vehemently shook my head.

"But Daddy—"

"If it's important, then I'll have to tell the police."

"Can't you leave their names out of it?"

I wasn't going to make promises I couldn't keep. "Tell your friends to meet me in the lobby near the concession stands after practice. If they tell me something that will help the police find Sara, then they'll have to come forward and give a statement to the police. Otherwise, I won't use their names. Deal?"

My daughter was squirming. It reminded me of how young she still was. The same went for the rest of the girls on the team. The coach's whistle cut through the air.

"All right," Jessie said. "Did you call Mom?"

"Not yet."

"Daddy! Call her!"

I parked myself by the hot-dog stand in the lobby and contemplated calling my wife. Rose worked as a nurse in Tampa, and I knew her break times by heart. She was on one now, and I would have enjoyed hearing her voice.

I decided against it. I was trying to convince Rose to move back to Fort Lauderdale, but I still didn't have anything for her to come home to. Not a house, nor a bank account, just a business finding missing kids that was making enough money for me to feed me and my dog and pay my rent. The last thing she needed to be hearing was my tales of wrestling with alligators and getting knocked unconscious in motel parking lots.

A thunderclap broke my concentration. The lobby was lined with tinted windows that stretched to the ceiling, and outside a heavy rain was falling between golden rays of sunshine. In south Florida, it could be storming and be sunny at the same time, the good and the bad joined at the hip.

Two girls from the team appeared dressed in street clothes with their hair still wet from a shower. Amber Woodward, a tall, lanky redhead, was one of the team's forwards, while Holly Masterson, a short, compact brunette, excelled in defense. Neither looked ready to talk, and I extracted a pack of chewing gum from my pocket and offered both girls a stick. They accepted, and the three of us chewed in silence.

"Maybe I should go first," Holly finally said.

"Please," I said.

"We came to Fort Lauderdale two days ago for the tournament. The first day we practiced, had dinner, and went to the motel. Right when we were going to bed, Sara came to our room and asked me and Suzie if we wanted to visit the Hard Rock Casino.

"At first we both said no. Coach is strict about curfew, and she'll bench us if we break it. But Sara wanted to see the celebrities who hung out there. She even offered to pay the cabfare. So we caved and said okay.

"We got to the Hard Rock around eleven. The place was packed, and we walked around the casino floor and people-watched for a while. It was fun, and we didn't feel like we were doing anything wrong, you know?"

"Sure," I said.

"Then things got ugly," Amber chimed in.

I gave Amber my full attention. Despite her size, she was a scrapper, and I'd seen her mix it up with lots of players bigger than her, and usually come out on top.

"What happened?" I asked.

"A man was filming us with his cell phone, and wouldn't stop," Amber said. "He approached Sara, and started asking her weird questions, like how were her classes going, and things like that. He seemed to know stuff about her."

"Can you describe him?"

"He was in his late forties, kind of short and thin. He hadn't bathed in a while, and his clothes were dirty. Finally I had enough of his questions, and told him to leave us alone. That was when I realized I'd seen him before."

"You had? Where?"

"He was on the sidelines with a video camera during last week's game against Georgia. He stuck out because he was dressed so crummy."

"You're sure it was the same man?"

"Yes. It was him."

"Where was the game played?"

"At home in Tallahassee."

Her answer gave me pause. Tallahassee housed the state's capital, and as a result, had more cops and law enforcement people than most Florida cities. I found myself wondering if Sara's abductors had purposely waited to abduct Sara in Fort Lauderdale, where there were fewer cops and a lot more places to get lost.

"Is there anything else you want to tell me?" I asked.

Both girls shook their heads. I took out my wallet and handed them my business cards. "That's my cell phone. Call me anytime if you think of something else."

"We will," they both said.

Outside it had stopped raining and the sun had come out. The team bus pulled up to the front door and the driver honked his horn. I escorted Amber and Holly outside, and waited for Jessie to come out with the rest of the team. She appeared moments later, and we hugged.

"Did you learn anything?" she asked.

"Yes. Thanks for coming through."

Jessie got on the bus, and I watched it leave. I went to my car and got behind the wheel. I had information that the police desperately needed to hear, only a nagging question kept running through my mind. Would they listen to what I had to say?

The answer, I quickly discovered, was no.

I called Boone, Weaver, and Burrell. After I told them what I'd learned, each detective told me an arrest in Sara's case was imminent and hung up. They had almost sounded like they were reading from a script.

My next call was to Chief Black Cloud, leader of the Seminole Indian nation. The Seminoles owned the Hard Rock Casino and were one of the richest tribes in the country. Chief Black Cloud had single-handedly built the casino and made his people rich. Recently he'd been forced to step down as president, but his smiling photograph remained on the tribe's website, and I knew that he still ran things.

I had visited the Hard Rock plenty of times as a cop. Its glittering casino was a magnet for runaways, and I'd pulled many off the casino floor and returned them to their parents. I had done this without disrupting the casino's business, or alerting the press. I'd respected the tribe, and as a result, I had a good relationship with Black Cloud.

A secretary patched me through, and Black Cloud picked up on the first ring.

"Good afternoon, Jack," Black Cloud said.

"Good afternoon, Chief," I replied.

"Che-Han-Tah-Mo, Ah-hee-tho-sta."

"Shtongo, edama-he-do."

The Seminoles had two traditional languages. The chief had greeted me in Creek, and I had responded in Miccosukee, a few lines of which I'd learned growing up.

"Not bad for a half breed," Black Cloud said.

I would have taken offense, only I knew Black Cloud was a half breed himself.

"So what can I do for you today?" the chief asked.

"I'm calling to ask a favor."

"Are you looking for a job? I heard you were no longer a policeman. I could set you up right now to run our security team. You would fit in well here. Say yes, and I'll make the call."

Black Cloud had offered me several jobs over the years, all of which I'd turned down. It had nothing to do with the money, which was excellent, or the people, whom I liked. His casino had no windows, and being stuck inside a building without sunshine for eight hours a day was for me the equivalent of going straight to hell.

"Thanks for the offer, but I'm on my own now," I said.

"Still finding missing kids?"

"Yes."

"You were good at that. What can I do for you?"

"Two nights ago, a man was spotted in your casino stalking three women from the Florida State women's basketball team. One of those women was later abducted from her motel room. With your permission, I'd like to visit the casino's surveillance control room, and see if I can spot this man on your surveillance tapes. If I can identify him, it might lead me to the missing girl."

"I don't know, Jack," the chief said. "The surveillance control room is off-limits to everyone but a handful of people. Even I have a hard time getting in there."

"I need for an exception to be made. A girl's life is at stake."

"How soon would you like to come in?"

"Right now."

"Will you be bringing any policemen with you?"

"No, I'll be by myself."

"Do the police know about this man who was in our casino?"

"The police have another suspect in custody who they're going to charge with the crime. I told the police about the man in your casino, but they refused to listen."

"This sounds personal, Jack. Is it?"

Through my mind flashed Sara Long's abduction and the beating I'd taken, the police's unwillingness to listen to my story, and finally Karl Long's blistering accusations that I was lousy at my work.

"Yes, it's personal," I said.

"I will see what I can do. Give me a number where you can be reached."

I gave the chief my cell phone number and thanked him for his help.

CHAPTER 13

I DECIDED to grab lunch while waiting for Black Cloud to call me back. A number of fast-food restaurants were located around the arena, and I opted for a McDonald's Value Meal, a twelve-hundred-calorie artery-clogging feast for a mere six bucks. Normally, I tried to stay away from fast food, except when I was on a case. Then it was practically all I ate.

As I was pulling out of the drive-through with my grub, my cell phone played its familiar song. The caller ID said SUNSET. It was Sonny.

"How's it going?" I answered.

"Not so good," Sonny said. "You need to get over here on the double."

"Can it wait? I'm working."

"It's your dog."

Something hard dropped in the pit of my stomach.

"Is Buster okay?"

"Oh, he's just dandy."

Buster wasn't hurt, and I felt myself relax.

"What did he do?"

"The bar got busy, so I stuck him upstairs in your

room. The next thing I know, it sounds like World War Three is going on up there. He was going bonkers."

"Did you leave him something to chew on?" I asked.

"No, was I supposed to?"

Buster was a herding dog, not a house dog, and would gnaw clean through a table leg if locked up for too long. I said, "How serious are the damages?"

"Catastrophic."

The bad feeling returned to my stomach.

"Throw him a bone. I'll be right there," I said.

I took the Sawgrass Expressway south, then got onto 595, and raced east toward the ocean. Of all the dogs I could have rescued from the pound, Buster hadn't been the nicest, nor the prettiest dog sitting on death row. But he'd tugged at my heartstrings, so I'd adopted him. The fact that he occasionally gnawed on a bad person didn't bother me, but when he started destroying furniture, I got concerned. My room at the Sunset had come furnished, and I wasn't looking forward to replacing the things he'd ruined.

I pulled into the Sunset's parking lot with a rubbery squeal and hopped out of my car. I ran up the staircase beside the bar to my room.

I opened the door expecting the worst. Buster sat in the center of the floor, surrounded by fluffy white mattress stuffing. He had pulled the mattress off the bed, eaten a hole through its center, and distributed the stuffing across the room. He'd also attacked the dresser and night table, and chewed on the legs so viciously that they now resembled toothpicks. Seeing me, he howled happily, and ran into my arms.

"You stupid dog," I said.

"Holy shit," a voice said.

I glanced over my shoulder. Sonny stood in the door-way, wearing his trademark Guns & Roses T-shirt with holes in the armpits. His face was white.

"I thought I asked you to give him a bone," I said.

"I gave him a knuckle bone. He must have eaten it."

I quickly assessed the damage. Had I still been a cop, I would have strung yellow crime-scene tape across the door, the place was such a disaster. Along with ruining my bed, plus the dresser and night table, Buster had chewed a hole in the wall through which the ocean air was now blowing. All of the furniture would have to be replaced, the wall fixed, and the room repainted.

"How much do you think this is going to cost?" I asked.

"A couple of grand, easy," Sonny replied.

"I've got nine hundred bucks to my name. Can you lend me the rest? I'll pay you back. You know I'm good for it."

Sonny shook his head from side to side. "I'd give you the money if I thought it would do any good."

"What do you mean?"

"It's over, Jack."

"What's over?"

"Ralph's in town for his monthly visit. He's coming by later to check up on things. He's going to see this and go ape shit."

Ralph was the Sunset's long-distance owner, a nasty New York banker who enjoyed yanking Sonny's chain. Ralph had not wanted to rent me the room because of Buster, but had decided that having an ex-cop living above the bar was a good insurance policy.

"Can't you hide the damage from him?" I asked.

"How am I going to do that?"

"I don't know, say you're having the room fumigated."

"Ralph always checks the building, Jack. He's going to see this, and then he'll explode. You know how he is."

"There must be something we can do."

"Like what? Join the Foreign Legion?"

My cell phone chimed. It was Black Cloud calling me back. I answered.

"I've gotten clearance for you to visit the Hard Rock's surveillance control room," Black Cloud said. "The surveillance director said you can come in, and he'll help you find the guy who was stalking the college students. How soon can you get over here?"

I hesitated. I needed to clean up Buster's mess, and salvage my situation with the Sunset. But at the same time, if I didn't get over to the Hard Rock, I'd lose my chance to learn the identity of one of Sara Long's abductors.

"I'm on my way," I said.

"Call me when you're near, and I'll come downstairs to greet you."

"I will. Thanks, Chief."

I said good-bye and folded my phone. Sonny had grabbed the mattress and was struggling to pull it back onto the bed. I went to the doorway and saw him glare at me.

"Don't tell me you're leaving," Sonny said.

"I have to. I'm on a case."

"You're not going to help me clean this place up?"

"I'm sorry, but I can't."

Sonny pulled the mattress onto the bed and began shoving the stuffing back into it.

"Take your stuff," he said.

I froze in the doorway. "Are you evicting me?"

"No, but Ralph will, and then you'll have to come back and get your things. Take them now, Jack. It will be easier."

"You don't know what Ralph will do. He might just laugh it off."

"Fat chance. Take your stuff, or Ralph will throw it in the Dumpster."

The finality in his voice was unmistakable, and I realized that this was the end. I had lived above the Sunset for over a year. Sonny and the good-natured drunks who supported the bar had always been there for me. The Sunset was my home, and they were my friends, and it had just gone up in flames. I grabbed my clothes out of the closet along with a cardboard box that contained my old cop stuff and headed for the stairwell.

"Wait," Sonny said.

From the night table he picked up the stack of missing person files that had been my bedtime reading. Then he went into the bathroom and grabbed my shaving kit.

"Don't forget these," he said.

Sonny crossed the room and handed the items to me. His eyes mirrored the pain that I was feeling. I wasn't just losing a friend; I was losing one of my best friends. Sonny patted Buster, then gave me a bear hug.

"Good luck, man," he said.

CHAPTER 14

I THREW my worldly possessions into my car and drove to the Hard Rock. Traffic on 595 was the usual madness, and I darted between lanes while trying to focus on the task at hand. My wife believed that everything happened for a reason, and I wondered what was the reason behind this sudden turn of events in my life.

Exiting on 441, I headed south into Hollywood, the massive casino looming in the distance. Back when I was a kid, the Seminoles had made money giving airboat rides to tourists and putting on rinky-dink rodeos with the headlights of their pickups used to light up the ring. Now they were on top of the world and worth billions.

Entering the casino grounds, I called Black Cloud on my cell. He was there to greet me when my car was taken by the valet. He was a big man, with jet-black hair that cascaded onto his shoulders and a chiseled face that looked like something you'd see on a statue in a park. He'd done two tours of duty in Vietnam and come home with shrapnel in one of his legs. He walked with a limp but refused to carry a cane.

"It's been too long," Black Cloud said, pumping my hand.

"You look good," I said.

"You're lying. I look old and tired. What's with the dog?"

"He's my partner. Can I bring him inside?"

"Sure. We don't have a problem with dogs."

I followed him into the bustling casino. Everywhere I looked, little old ladies with arms like Popeye were yanking on slot machines, while men chomping on cigars were risking hundreds of dollars on the turn of a card. I couldn't look at it without remembering the cow pasture that had been here not that long ago.

Once inside an elevator, Black Cloud activated the control panel with a special key, and we were delivered to the fourth floor where the surveillance control room was located.

"Welcome to the inner sanctum," he said.

We walked down a short hallway to an unmarked steel door with a surveillance camera perched above it. Black Cloud knocked loudly, then faced me.

"We have a small problem," he said.

"What's that?" I asked.

"There's a sting going on inside the casino. Our security team is trying to nab a group of cheaters. You're going to have to wait until they're done."

"Any idea how long?"

"Could be awhile. These people have stolen a lot of money from us. We need to catch them before they do it again."

I didn't like the sound of that. I'd already wasted most of the day, and every lost hour increased the chance that I'd never find Sara Long. Before I could reply, the steel door swung in and a short man wearing a black turtleneck greeted us.

"Hey, Chief," the man in the turtleneck said.

"Hey, Harry," Black Cloud replied. "Any luck catching those cheaters?"

"Not yet."

Harry ushered us into the room and shut the door. Dark and chilly, the surveillance control room was crammed with sophisticated surveillance equipment that watched the action in the casino. A gang of technicians sat in front of a row of computers, staring intently at the flickering screens.

"Harry, I want you to meet Jack Carpenter and his dog," Black Cloud said. "Jack is an ex-Broward detective and a friend of the casino. He's also part Seminole, so watch what you say around him."

The man in the turtleneck pumped my hand. Beads of sweat dotted his brow, and I could tell that something was bothering him.

"Nice to meet you," Harry said.

"Same here," I replied.

"I need to run," Black Cloud said. "Good luck in your search."

"What can I do for you?" Harry asked when Black Cloud had left.

"I'm looking for a missing college girl that was in your casino two nights ago," I replied. "There was a man stalking her. I'm hoping one of your surveillance cameras took a photo of him."

"We're dealing with a situation inside the casino right now," Harry said. "Once we're done, I'll do what I can to help you."

I followed Harry to the back of the room. Five men were huddled around a high-resolution monitor showing a blackjack game. The game consisted of seven players, a dealer wearing a tuxedo, and some bystanders watching the action.

"This is Jack Carpenter and his dog," Harry said to the group.

None of the men took their eyes from the monitor.

"You'll go blind doing that," I said.

One man turned his head, a thin smile on his face. He was in his early sixties and Italian, with salt and pepper hair and a nose that had been broken a few times but hadn't lost its character. His face was best described as intense.

"You a cop?" the man asked.

"Ex-detective," I replied. "I used to run the Missing Persons Unit of the Broward sheriff's department."

"My name's Tony Valentine," the man said. "I'm a consultant. I help casinos catch cheaters. Do you know what grift sense is?"

"Never heard of it."

"It's the ability to spot a con or someone who's a crook. Think you can spot a crook in a crowd of people?"

"Sure," I replied.

Valentine turned to the others. "Want to give him a shot, guys?"

"Why not?" one of the men replied.

Valentine turned back to me. "Here's the deal, Jack. The guys on the monitor are a gang of professional cheaters. They've been swindling the Hard Rock for a month, and have stolen over three hundred thousand bucks."

I whistled through my teeth. The seven guys at the table wore baseball caps and colorful T-shirts and were swigging bottles of beer. They looked like a bunch of regular Joes, and did not fit the image that I had of professional cheaters.

"What are they doing?" I asked.

"They're using paper."

"What's that?"

"They marked the casino's cards, and put them back into play."

"Can I see them?"

Valentine removed a worn deck of playing cards from his pocket and gave it to me. The deck had a red diamond design along with the Hard Rock's distinctive logo.

"The casino subjects its dealers to polygraph tests every month," Valentine said. "One of the dealers got tripped up in a lie, and confessed to taking several dozen decks out of the casino, giving them to the gang to be marked, and slipping them back in."

"Is this one of the decks?" I asked.

"Yes."

I examined the cards but saw nothing out of the ordinary.

"How are they marked?"

"They've been stained with drops of water," Valentine said. "The gang only stained the high value cards, which are the most important cards in blackjack. The stains let the cheaters know the value of the cards the dealer is holding. That knowledge gives the cheaters a fifteen percent edge over the house."

I removed the ace of spades from the deck, and held it up to the dim overhead light. When viewed from the right angle, the stain on the card was plainly visible.

"Why don't you arrest them?" I asked.

The men fell silent, as did Valentine.

"Did I say something wrong?"

"The dealer who snitched was found in the trunk of his car with his throat slit," Valentine said. "Without his testimony, we don't have a case."

"So you're letting the cheaters play in the hopes of catching them," I said.

"Exactly."

"How can I help?"

"One member of the gang is reading the marks, and signaling the information to the others," Valentine said. "That's how marked card scams work. We need to figure out who the reader is, arrest him, and make him talk. That's our best chance of nailing the gang."

It was common when the police were stymied in a case to bring in a fresh pair of eyes to examine the evidence. I didn't know anything about gambling or cheating, but I was good at picking slime-bags out of a crowd.

"I'd be happy to give it a try," I said.

Standing in front of the wall-sized monitor, I tried to pick out the reader.

Cheating at blackjack wasn't hard. Each player at the table received two cards, as did the dealer. The object was to get close to twenty-one, without going over. The dealer went last, and had the advantage of receiving one card facedown, the other face up. If the cheaters could learn the value of the dealer's facedown card, they would know if the dealer was weak or strong, and play accordingly.

At first, I saw nothing out of the ordinary. The gang was drinking and smoking and having a swell time. So was the crowd standing around them. It was like one big party, and had Valentine not tipped me to the scam, I would have been clueless.

After twenty minutes of watching, something strange happened.

The dealer flipped over his facedown card, revealing an eight. His other card was a three, making his total eleven. The dealer dealt himself another card. It was a ten, giving him twenty-one, a winning hand. As the dealer raked in the losing bets, the seven men at the table frowned disapprovingly.

"Somebody screwed up," I said.

Valentine put down the can of diet soda he was drinking. He shouldered up next to me, and stared at the monitor.

"You think so?" he asked.

"Yeah. I want to see this again."

Valentine crossed the room, and two-finger typed a command into the keyboard that was wired to the monitor. The film was rewound. Again I watched the dealer pull twenty-one, and the cheaters' reaction.

"See their faces?" I said. "That wasn't supposed to happen."

"You're right," Valentine said. "So who's the reader?"

"I'm not sure. Can we watch it in slow motion?"

"Sure."

Valentine typed another command into the keyboard. This time, the clip ran in slow motion. Behind the cheaters I noticed a tall, menacing-looking Hispanic wearing a glittering array of gold jewelry. As the dealer raked in the losing bets, the Hispanic brought his hands up to his eye as if to replace a fallen contact lens.

"The tall Hispanic standing behind the players is your

reader," I said. "His contact lens fell out, which caused him to screw up."

Valentine picked up a house telephone and called downstairs to the floor. "Put an RF tracking device on Table Sixteen."

Hanging up, he smiled at me and resumed drinking his soda.

"What are you doing?" I asked.

"The Hispanic is standing too far behind the table to be using signals," Valentine explained. "I'm guessing he's got an electronic transmitter in his pocket that he's using to signal the others. Cheaters call these transmitters thumpers. A radio frequency tracking device should pick up the signal, and we'll have our proof."

"Are thumpers illegal inside a casino?"

"They sure are."

A few minutes later the house phone rang and Valentine took the call.

"So they *are* using a thumper," he said. "Go ahead and arrest them, but be careful. One of these guys slit our dealer's throat."

Valentine dropped the phone into the receiver. He looked tired but satisfied. All his hard work had paid off, and now he was going to get his reward. He called the other men over, and explained that the bust was about to go down.

I continued to watch the lanky Hispanic on the monitor. He had a menacing quality that the other members of the gang didn't have. Then I spotted something that I hadn't seen before. Beneath the Hispanic's right eye was a small tattoo. I edged up to the monitor for a better look. It was a tear drop. Criminals often had tear drops tattooed beneath their eyes after they murdered someone. In a loud voice I said, "The Hispanic is your killer. Tell your guys on the floor to be careful when they arrest him. He's probably carrying a weapon."

Valentine grabbed the house phone and relayed the information to the men downstairs. "Put the heavy on these guys," he said.

"That's a new one," I said.

"Just watch," he said.

Sixty seconds later, an army of security guards appeared on the monitor, and swooped down on the table where the cheaters were sitting. Working in tandem, the guards upended the table, and wrestled the gang and the Hispanic to the floor. It was lightning fast, with the cheaters never knowing what hit them.

The Hispanic was handcuffed and frisked. From his pockets the guards removed the thumper, along with a thick wad of cash. Strapped to his leg was a stiletto, which was held up to the camera for us to see.

"You were right," Valentine said. "Sure you've never done this before?"

"Beginner's luck," I said.

A bottle of champagne was broken out, opened, and poured. I had not had champagne since my wedding, and forced a glass down.

"So what can I do for you?" Valentine asked.

"Help me find a missing girl," I said.

CHAPTER 15

I GAVE VALENTINE the details of Sara Long's visit to the Hard Rock. He was frowning by the time I finished filling him in.

"I've got some bad news for you," Valentine said. "We may not have this guy on any of our surveillance tapes."

"But I thought the surveillance cameras were on twenty-four/seven," I said.

"They are, but they don't catch everyone."

My knowledge of how casino surveillance worked was limited to what I'd seen on TV and at the movies, where bad guys inside casinos always seemed to get caught on film. I shook my head, not understanding.

"The Hard Rock's casino is the size of three football fields," Valentine explained. "At any given time, the eye-in-the-sky cameras are watching half the floor, leaving the other half unwatched. That means that one hundred percent of the time, fifty percent of the casino isn't being watched. A bad guy can come in, pull a scam, and walk out, and the cameras may never spot him."

"So your systems aren't foolproof."

"If they were, I'd be out of a job. Now let me ask you

a question. This young woman who was abducted, was she pretty?"

"Very pretty."

"That's in our favor. Most of the technicians working surveillance are men, and they usually film the pretty girls that come in. It's against the rules, but they do it anyway."

"So there may be a tape of Sara."

"Yes. And hopefully, a tape of your suspect. Let's go find a tech."

I followed Valentine across the surveillance control room to where a tech sat staring at a computer screen while eating his lunch. The tech had wild, unkempt hair, and two-day stubble sprouting from his chin. His work station was littered with fast-food wrappers and Post-it Notes stuck to every available space. He glanced at Buster, who had not made a sound since entering the room, and tossed him a french fry.

"What kind of dog is that?" the tech asked.

"Australian Shepherd," I replied.

"He's cool. I want one."

"Joey Riddle, this is Jack Carpenter," Valentine said. "He's an ex-cop."

Riddle looked me up and down.

"You could have fooled me," Riddle said.

"I need a favor," Valentine said. "A pretty college girl was on the casino floor two nights ago, and I want to see if one of the hot-blooded males on duty filmed her."

"What time was she here?" Riddle asked.

"Around eleven p.m.," I replied.

"Did she gamble?"

"No. She was with two of her friends. They just people-watched."

"Then they probably hung around the Tower of Power Center Bar," Riddle said. "It's a real popular spot with the ladies."

"We'd like to see the film from the Tower of Power two nights ago," Valentine said.

"Your wish is my command."

Riddle's bony fingers danced across his computer's keyboard. A surveillance film of the Center Bar appeared on his computer screen. The bar was circular, and situated in the middle of the bustling casino floor. Stamped in the corner of the film was the date and time the film had been taken. It was from two nights ago at 11:00 p.m.

My eyes scanned the bar. Sara Long, Amber Woodward, and Holly Masterson were sitting together, sipping Cokes. I pointed at Sara.

"That's her," I said.

"Beau-ti-ful," Riddle declared.

"Do you see the stalker?" Valentine asked.

I edged closer to the screen. The strange little man who called himself Mouse was not in the picture.

"No," I said.

"Maybe he'll show up later on," Valentine said.

We watched Sara, Amber, and Holly mingle at the bar, then take a stroll through the casino, stopping to watch the different games or when someone hit a jackpot on a slot machine. The three young women were all pretty, and the camera never left them. It didn't help my cause, because I couldn't see if anyone was following them.

"Damn," I said. "I can't see who's around her."

"Joey, can you check the database to see if we have

any other surveillance footage of these girls?" Valentine asked.

"Sure thing," Riddle said.

Freezing the images on the screen, Riddle typed a command into the computer while tossing pieces of bread from his unfinished sandwich to my dog.

"Our system stores all the films taken inside the casino over a thirty-day period," Riddle explained. "I just fed the images of these ladies into the hard drive, and asked the system to find identical images that might be stored in its memory banks."

A new film appeared on his computer screen. On it, Sara and her friends were standing at the Hard Rock's entrance, and Amber was wagging her finger in the face of a small man wearing khaki shorts, a faded T-shirt, and a baseball cap. It was Mouse.

"That's the stalker," I said.

I placed my face a few inches from the screen and lip-read. Amber was telling Mouse to leave them the hell alone. Mouse held his arms out innocently while shaking his head like he didn't understand. Finally he shrugged and walked out the door.

"Want me to see if there are any more films of this guy?" Riddle asked.

"Yes," I said.

Riddle checked the system, and came up empty.

"That's the only film of him inside the casino," Riddle said.

My spirits sagged. The film proved nothing that I didn't already know. It wasn't anything I could take to the police to prove my case. Feeling defeated, I looked over my shoulder at Valentine to see if he had any ideas.

"What about films of this guy outside the casino?" Valentine asked.

"There's an idea," Riddle said.

Riddle typed another command into the keyboard. The bread from his sandwich was gone, and he was now feeding Buster pieces of meat. The dog sat at stiff attention by Riddle's desk, avoiding eye contact with me.

"The casino is required to film the grounds in case we get sued for a slip and fall," Valentine said. "It's a pain in the ass, but the insurance companies won't cover us if we don't. I'm guessing this guy had a vehicle, which might have been picked up by one of the cameras on the side of the building. Maybe we can get his license plate."

"That would be great," I said.

"Here we go," Riddle said.

A film appeared on the computer screen showing the Hard Rock's enormous parking lot. Mouse appeared, walking toward the back of the lot.

"There he is," I said.

Mouse's vehicle was parked in the last row. It was the same stolen maroon Ford minivan he'd been driving when he'd abducted Sara.

"Shit," I said.

"What's wrong?" Valentine asked.

"The vehicle he's driving was stolen. He and his partner already dumped it."

"So getting the license plate won't do you any good."

"No."

My eyes were starting to hurt from staring at the screen, and I wearily rubbed them. There was no greater frustration than chasing down a lead, only to find that it was a dead end. I clicked my fingers, and Buster reluctantly left his spot beside Riddle's chair.

"Thanks for your help," I said.

"Sorry it didn't pan out," Valentine said. "I'll show you out."

I followed Valentine across the surveillance control room. Riddle stared at his computer, oblivious to my leaving. He pointed an accusing finger at the screen.

"Whoa! Take a look at this."

I hurried back to his desk. The film of Mouse in the parking lot was still playing. Mouse stood by the minivan along with two poorly dressed men holding knives. Mouse handed his wallet to them, then slipped off his watch and one of his rings.

"It's a stick-up," Riddle said. "These two guys have robbed patrons before."

"You know them?" I asked.

"They're a couple of crackheads. They hide in the bushes at night, and rob people leaving the casino. We've tried to catch them, but never had any luck."

I watched Mouse hand over his jewelry. One of the crackheads pointed at the minivan. Mouse unlocked the rear door and stepped back.

Both crackheads stuck their heads into the back of the minivan. As if being sucked by a giant vacuum, they were pulled inside. As they struggled helplessly, their weapons and loot fell to the ground. One lost a shoe. Although the tape had no audio, I could almost hear their screams.

"What was *that*?" Riddle asked.

"Your crackhead thieves just got the tables turned on them," I said.

"I saw that. But what was *that thing* inside the minivan?"

I wanted to tell him, only I'd grown tired of telling a story that no one believed. On the screen, I saw Mouse close the minivan door, and retrieve his belongings from the ground. He got behind the wheel and drove away.

"I need a copy of this, as well as the surveillance tape inside the casino," I said.

"Right now?"

"Please."

Riddle burned two copies of each film and handed me the CDs. I slipped them into my pocket.

"Tell me what was in the back of the minivan," Riddle said. "If you don't, I'm going to have nightmares about that thing."

"It was a bad guy with a bad attitude."

"But he looked like a monster."

"He is a monster."

Valentine was waiting on the other side of the room. As I followed him out, I glanced over my shoulder. Riddle had rewound the film taken in the casino parking lot, and was watching it again. The look on his face told me that he believed me.

CHAPTER 16

VALENTINE WALKED me to the casino's entrance. We shook hands, and he handed me his business card. It said *Grift Sense* and had a phone number.

"Call me if you need me," Valentine said.

I pocketed his card. "I will."

Valentine reached down and petted the top of Buster's head.

"I like your pup. Is he much trouble?"

"Him? Never."

I walked outside. The afternoon sunshine was blinding, and there was no breeze. The sunshine felt good on my skin, and I headed toward the back of the parking lot with the heat rising through my sandals.

I was sweating by the time I found the spot where Mouse had been mugged. It was in the very rear of the lot, near a stand of bushes. I searched the ground for anything that might have been dropped.

Buster hit the bushes with his nose to the ground. He reappeared with a sneaker in his mouth. I made him drop the sneaker into my hand, and he took several excited steps back, hoping I'd throw it.

"Good boy."

I examined the sneaker. It was made by Reebok and was missing its laces. It was old, but not dirty. It looked like something a homeless person might wear, and I found myself wondering if it had belonged to one of the crackhead robbers.

I walked to my Legend holding the shoe at arm's length. It stunk to high heaven, and I unlocked the passenger door, and threw it on the floor. I made Buster get into the passenger side, which he happily did.

The neighborhoods around the Hard Rock were upper middle class. I drove down their narrow streets with my windows down. Buster was good at picking up scents, and I was hoping he'd pick up the shoe's scent in one of the neighborhoods. Mouse wasn't stupid, and I had a feeling he'd gotten rid of the crackheads quickly.

I entered a subdivision called Shady Oaks. Not a single oak tree in the entire place. A large number of "For Sale" signs were planted on front lawns. Nearly half the houses looked empty.

Passing a street called Whisper Lane, Buster got animated. He stuck his head out the window and began pawing his seat. I looked around to see if there was another dog in the area, but didn't see any.

"What is it, boy? You smell something?"

Buster's head was firmly stuck out his window. Backing up, I turned down Whisper Lane. A dog's sense of smell was a thousand times more sensitive than a human's, and my dog let out a mournful whine.

I braked at a two-story Spanish-style home with a "For Sale" sign on the lawn. The house was under construction, and looked half-finished. I leashed Buster and got out of the car. He pulled me up the path.

Buster hit the front door with his nose, and it swung open. I didn't like entering strange houses uninvited, even unfinished ones.

"Hello? Is anyone home?"

My voice echoed across the high-ceilinged foyer. The sweet smell of sawdust hung in the air, mingling with spackle and drying paint. I found it surprising that the house was under construction considering the number of "For Sale" signs I'd seen, but after all, this was south Florida. No matter what state the economy was in, they just kept building.

Buster led me down a hallway to the back of the house. He was straining at his leash and pulling my arm. He had locked onto a scent and was not stopping until he'd found its origin.

The hallway led to a family room, which in turn led to a screened-in lanai. The slider to the lanai was pulled open. I went up to it and stopped. Then I stared.

The lanai contained a swimming pool shaped like a lima bean. The water in the pool was a sickening blood red. Floating in the water were two men, both bloated and very dead. One was missing a sneaker on his left foot.

Buster looked up at me, his tail wagging.

"Good boy," I said quietly.

I had seen the dead more times than was healthy. Something about these two wasn't right. After a pause, I realized what it was. Their killer had twisted their heads so they were floating facedown in the water, while their torsos were floating face up.

Protocol would have dictated that I call one of the several detectives that I knew in Homicide, but I wanted

Burrell to see the crime scene first, and hear what I had to say. I called her from my car. Fifteen minutes later, she pulled up in her red Mustang with the racing stripes down the sides. It was the kind of car I would have owned if I could afford it. I told her about the dead floaters, and we headed inside.

"Please leave Buster outside," she said.

"But he found them," I replied.

"Leave him outside anyway. I don't want him contaminating the crime scene."

"He's not going to piss on anything."

"Just do it."

I tied Buster to a tree, then led Burrell inside to the floating corpses. She picked up on the unnatural position of their heads quicker than I had, and turned her eyes away.

"Jesus Christ. Who are they?"

"A couple of druggies. They were mugging people in the parking lot of the Hard Rock, and picked the wrong victim."

"How did you happen to find them here?"

I told her about my trip to the Hard Rock, and what I'd learned from viewing the casino's surveillance tapes. When I was done, I removed the two CDs Riddle had burned for me from my pocket.

"The first CD contains a casino surveillance film of a guy named Mouse who was stalking Sara Long," I said. "The second CD shows Mouse getting mugged by these two guys behind the casino, and what happened to them. Mouse is driving the same minivan that was used to abduct Sara Long. He and his partner are responsible for Sara Long's abduction, and for killing these guys."

Burrell stared at the CDs and shook her head.

"You don't want them?" I asked.

"I'll just throw them in the file."

Disgusted, I slipped the CDs back into my pocket.

"I'm sorry, Jack, but more evidence has surfaced linking Tyrone Biggs to the abduction," Burrell said. "I was in the process of charging Biggs when you called me."

"What evidence?"

"Biggs secretly made sex tapes of himself and Sara when they were dating. They're pretty steamy. In one, he ties Sara facedown to a bed and has sex with her multiple times. The tapes were found hidden in the trunk of his car."

"What does that prove beside they were into kink?"

"He was blackmailing her with them."

"Why? He's going to be rich once he's in the NBA."

"He didn't want money. He wanted Sara back. Biggs told us so after we confronted him with the tapes. He's in love with Sara, and wanted to be her boyfriend again."

"That doesn't prove Biggs abducted her."

"Yes, it does. It was his motive. We have our case, and we're moving forward with it."

"You're making a mistake."

"I don't work for you anymore, Jack. Don't lecture me."

Burrell and I did not argue well, and our arguments often ended with one of us getting our feelings bruised. She took out her cell phone and called for backup, then called EMS. Folding her phone, she gave me a harsh look.

"I'm going to play devil's advocate," she said. "Let's pretend you're right, and the goons that killed these two guys are Sara Long's abductors. Tell me what their motive is. Are they kidnappers?"

"No," I said.

"Serial killers?"

I shook my head.

"Then what are they?"

"Serial abductors."

"You still think this is linked to that cold case from eighteen years ago that you never solved?"

"Yes, I do."

"All right, let's pretend that these guys are serial abductors. What's their motive? Why did they abduct that college student from her apartment when you were a rookie? And why did they abduct Sara Long?"

"I don't know. But I'm going to find out."

"Look all you want, Jack. No one's stopping you."

"You're still going to arrest Tyrone Biggs?"

"Damn straight. Then I'm going to grill him, and find out where he put Sara Long. Biggs killed Sara, and I want to know where he hid her body."

Outside I heard the wail of sirens. As a rule, police cruisers only came quickly when another cop was making the call. Burrell walked out of the lanai, and stopped at the entrance to the hallway.

"Without any real evidence that someone else abducted Sara Long, you've got nothing, Jack," Burrell said.

I gazed at the bloated corpses floating in the pool. I'd just given Burrell all the evidence she needed, only she'd chosen not to look at it. I was done with the police.

CHAPTER 17

I SAT ON A CHAIR in the empty room, and gave my statement to a Homicide detective, who wrote it down on a notepad. Then he videotaped me. Later, he would compare my answers for any inconsistencies or things I might have left out. The process lasted forty-five minutes, and was draining.

When the detective was done, Burrell entered the room with Buster on a leash. She handed the leash to me, and we walked outside.

"I took him for a walk and gave him some water," she said, trying to make nice.

"Thank you, Detective," I said.

"Are you still mad at me?"

"Whatever gave you that idea."

I put Buster into my car and climbed behind the wheel. Burrell rapped the driver's window with her knuckles. I lowered the window and she knelt down so our faces were a few feet apart.

"I hate when you pout," she said.

Her conscience was eating at her. I jammed the key into the ignition and turned on the engine. I left the engine running and looked at her.

"What do you want me to do?" she yelled at me. "Disobey the mayor, and get my ass fired? I don't want to end up . . ."

She didn't want to end up like me. I couldn't blame her, but that didn't mean I was going to back off.

"Go ahead and charge Biggs," I said. "He's pond scum and deserves the humiliation. When you talk to the press, tell them he's the main suspect *at this time*. Then have a meeting with the chief, and tell him that you have doubts about Biggs, and you want to continue to pursue other leads. The chief will understand and give you his blessing. By doing that, you've covered your ass."

Burrell dipped her chin and shut her eyes. I thought I saw her lips move. The detective who'd interviewed me came to the front door of the house, and called to her.

"All right, Jack. I'll do it." She banged twice on the hood of my car and went inside.

I got on 595 and headed east. I had lived with Naomi Dunn's abduction for so long, it had eaten an invisible hole in me. I could only imagine what Sara Long's disappearance was going to do to my psyche if I didn't find her.

Soon I was driving south on I-95, my destination the FBI's Miami field office in North Miami Beach. The office handled criminal activity stretching from Vero Beach to Key West, as well as Central America and Mexico, and was a hotbed of activity, with over seven hundred special agents and support personnel housed in a single facility.

One of those agents was Special Agent Ken Linderman. Linderman ran the Child Abduction Rapid Deployment

Unit, and was responsible for investigating nonparental abductions of kids in Florida. As a rule, the FBI didn't work with private investigators, and Linderman was no exception. But he did work with me. We had a history, and Linderman never failed to take my phone calls, or see me if I asked for an appointment.

The afternoon skies were darkening as I drove up to the guard booth. A man in uniform came out, and glanced suspiciously at me and Buster.

"What can I do for you?" the guard asked.

I handed him my driver's license. "My name's Jack Carpenter. I'm here to see Special Agent Linderman. He runs the CARD unit."

"Hold on."

The guard called into the building. I popped my trunk in anticipation of being searched. The guard came out and did a quick inspection.

"Have a nice day," he said.

I did my usual hunt for a parking place. Finding one with shade, I rolled down my windows. Buster curled up on the passenger seat and went to sleep.

Soon I was sitting in Linderman's office. The office had a nice ocean view, only Linderman chose to sit at his desk with his back to the window. Nearing fifty, he was thin and compact, his gun-metal gray hair cropped short like a Marine's, his eyes as hard as stones. Before coming to Miami, he'd run the FBI's Behavioral Sciences Division, where he'd profiled the nation's worst serial killers and mass murderers. Then, five years ago, his daughter Danielle had vanished while jogging at the University of Miami. He'd been looking for her ever since, and had taken the CARD job to continue his search.

We'd met a year ago. We didn't have much in common except a shared passion for our work. In that regard, we were like brothers. I'd helped Linderman chase down many leads. We had traipsed through mosquito-infested swamps together, and searched abandoned scrap yards. I had seen him break down when we'd found a bone in a shallow hole, only to later discover that it belonged to a dead animal. I've heard it said that a person who loses a child dies every day. If that was true, then I'd seen Linderman die many times.

"I need your help," I told Linderman.

He hit his intercom, and told his secretary to hold his calls.

"I'm listening," Linderman said.

"Eighteen years ago I got called to an apartment complex where a coed named Naomi Dunn was being assaulted. I got knocked down by the attacker, and he left with Dunn slung over his shoulder. The case was never solved.

"Last night, a Florida State female basketball player named Sara Long was abducted from her motel. It was the same guy who abducted Naomi Dunn. I tried to stop him, and he put me in the hospital."

"Did you get a good look at him?"

"The abductor was this huge guy, and incredibly strong. I spent today running down leads and looking at evidence. This guy has a partner, and I've decided that they're a pair of serial abductors who specialize in abducting athletic young women. I need the FBI to help me find them."

Linderman's eyes narrowed. His daughter's high school graduation photograph sat on the windowsill directly behind him. Danielle Linderman was tall, blond, and athletic, just like the two victims.

"Could this pair have abducted my daughter?" he asked.

His voice was flat and hard. I detected no outer emotion on his face, but I knew it was there, buried deep within him like a smoldering flame. I didn't want to fill him with false hope, but for all I knew it could be true.

"Yes," I said.

His eyelids fluttered almost imperceptibly.

"I've spoken with the police several times," I continued. "Unfortunately, they're stuck on another suspect. Sara Long's boyfriend is going to be charged with her abduction."

His jaw tightened. "You obviously came here with a plan of action. What is it?"

"I'd like you to do two things for me. The cops have located the stolen minivan used in the abduction. The abductors wiped it clean of fingerprints, but there's a chance they left behind some trace of DNA. I was hoping the FBI would inspect the minivan to see if I'm right."

"That's not a bad idea. Where's the minivan now?"

I gave him the address where vehicles were impounded by the Broward cops.

"What's the second thing?" Linderman asked.

"The police have checkpoints at all major highways and roads. I'm certain the abductors are lying low, waiting to move Sara. Once they turn on the TV and hear that Sara's boyfriend is being charged, they'll know that the checkpoints have been lifted, and will try to move her."

"What do you want me to do?"

"I want the FBI to turn on their cameras."

"I don't know what you're talking about."

"Your cameras. I want you to turn them on and look for these guys."

"I still don't know what you're talking about."

I put my elbows on Linderman's desk, and gave him my best no-nonsense look. "A few weeks after 9/11, I spotted crews in Broward installing surveillance cameras at the major intersections and tollbooths. I'm a nosy guy, so I took down the license numbers on their trucks, and checked them out. Guess what I found?"

"What?"

"They were all FBI."

Linderman shifted uncomfortably in his chair.

"It didn't take me long to figure out what was up. Thirteen of the 9/11 hijackers lived in south Florida, so the FBI decided to install street cameras to hunt future terrorists. You probably don't keep the cameras on all the time. Too expensive to operate and to monitor effectively. But you do turn them on when a suspected terrorist slips into town. Am I right?"

A thin smile crossed Linderman's face. Then it was gone. That was as much as he gave you.

"You've very observant, Jack. Yes, there are surveillance cameras at every major intersection and tollbooth, and a few other places you might not imagine. It's a secret, so I'm not supposed to talk about it."

"Can I ask how they work?"

"The cameras are connected to a computer in this building that has a sophisticated facial recognition program built into its hard drive. We can burn a photograph of a suspected terrorist into the program and ask the computer to tell us when a person who resembles that photo passes in front of one of our surveillance cameras."

"How well does it work?"

"We've nabbed several bad guys trying to slip in through Port Everglades just last month."

"If I gave you a film of one of Sara Long's abductors, could you take his photo off the film and put it onto your program?"

"It all depends upon the quality of the film."

"It's a surveillance tape from a casino."

"That should be fine. We've used casino footage before."

From my pocket I removed the two CDs I'd gotten at the Hard Rock, and handed them to him.

"Here you go," I said.

Linderman slipped the first CD into his computer, turning the screen so it was visible to both of us. The tape of Mouse talking to the girls appeared.

"Any idea who this guy is?" Linderman asked.

"He calls himself Mouse. That's all I know about him."

"What's on the second CD?"

"Another tape of Mouse. This time he's outside the casino."

"I'll send both CDs downstairs, and have a tech burn Mouse's photograph into our facial recognition program. It would be helpful if we had some idea of the vehicle he's driving."

"He'll be driving something big. Like a van, or a small truck."

"Why not a car? They could drill airholes in the trunk, and hide Sara there. That's how most serial abductors move a victim."

"His partner would have a hard time fitting into a regular car. He's about six-ten and three hundred pounds."

"You weren't kidding when you said he was huge."

"He's also a killer."

Linderman punched a button on his desk. His secretary appeared, and he handed over the CDs and explained what he wanted done with them. She left, and he got on his laptop, and began typing.

"I'm going to send an e-mail to the other CARD teams around the country, and see if these guys might have struck before," he said. "Give me the details again."

I repeated my story to Linderman, and he wrote down every word. When he was done, he read back what he'd written, and asked me if I was satisfied.

"Yes," I said.

Linderman punched a key on his computer and sent the e-mail.

"Now let's hope someone has seen this pair before," he said.

I leaned back in my chair and felt the air escape from my lungs. It was the first time that I'd told someone my story, and hadn't had my sanity questioned.

I was getting somewhere.

CHAPTER 18

I PURCHASED two bitter cups of coffee from a vending machine down the hall from Linderman's office. Linderman was busy on his laptop when I returned, and I came around his desk and placed a cup on his blotter.

"Cream, no sugar," I said.

"You remembered," he said.

I took the opportunity to glance at his computer screen. While I'd been gone, he'd sent e-mails to the National Crime Information Center, the Justice Department, the Florida Department of Law Enforcement, the U.S. Marshal's Service, and the National Center for Missing and Exploited Children, alerting them to our pair of serial abductors. He was casting a wide net, and leaving no stone unturned.

"Any word from the CARD teams?" I asked.

He checked his e-mail inbox. "Not yet. You're going to have to be patient. It might be a few days before some of them get back to me."

"Can't you goad them along?"

"This is the FBI, Jack. I can't goad anyone. Why don't you have a seat?"

Sitting still was not one of my strong points. Nor was

being patient. I went to the window. Darkness had set, and a carpet of twinkling lights stretched clear to the Atlantic. Although I could not see the ocean, I could feel its presence, and it calmed me.

Through my mind flashed everything that had happened that day. The sexy image of Sara Long in a bathing suit on the news stood out. By showing Sara half-dressed, the media would make people think she had somehow been complicit in her assault. No victim deserved that.

In the window's reflection Linderman rose from his desk.

"You're driving me up the wall," the FBI agent said.

"I can sit in the hall if you want."

"You'll be poking your head in every thirty seconds, asking to look at my e-mail."

"What are you suggesting?"

"I'll call you when I learn something, okay?"

Linderman was throwing me out of his office. I could have been angry, only there was a flame in his eyes that hadn't been there before. I'd seen that same flame when we'd hunted together for his daughter. It was the undying passion of someone who refused to quit. He was not going to let me down.

At the door, I asked, "Can I call you later to see how things are going?"

"Of course. And Jack? I'll make sure the street cameras are turned on."

I took the elevator downstairs and signed out at the reception area. Outside the temperature had dropped, the heat no longer rising off the macadam like a sauna.

I found Buster sitting behind the wheel, an impatient look on his face.

Leaving the FBI Building, I drove on 167th Street west, then headed north on I-95 into Broward in rush-hour madness. Maniac drivers raced illegally down the highway's shoulders while a posse of highway patrol cars pulled them over.

I checked the time. Jessie's basketball game had already started. I'd wanted to be in the stands for the opening tip-off, and found myself settling for halftime. I powered up my cell phone to see if she had called.

I had a lone message. I called my voice mail and heard Sonny's familiar voice.

"Hey, Jack. The excrement just hit the air-conditioning. Call me, man."

I dialed the Sunset and Sonny picked up. His voice was drowned out by the dreadful singing of the Seven Dwarfs in the background. The same seven drunks had frequented the Sunset since I'd lived there. I called them the Seven Dwarfs because it was rare to see any of them standing upright.

"Hold on," Sonny said.

Sonny screamed at the Dwarfs. The singing stopped. Sonny came back on.

"Do you miss me?" I asked.

Sonny laughed into the phone. It wasn't a pleasant sound.

"What's wrong?"

"Ralph came by and saw the damage Buster did to your room," Sonny said. "He figures there's about three thousand bucks in damages to the walls and furniture."

"Come on, that stuff was old."

"You know how Ralph likes to inflate things. He

wanted to call the police and press charges, seeing how you never gave him a deposit when you took the place."

"Oops."

"I talked him out of it, thank you very much. We went downstairs to the bar, and I got him liquored up. I thought Ralph was going to forget about it, but then this asshole attorney named Frank Yonker came in. He had a subpoena for you."

"Let me guess what happened next. Ralph and Frank Yonker got to talking, and discovered that they both had a shared interest in tracking me down. Yonker offered his services, and Ralph accepted."

"Very good."

"Did Ralph file a complaint with the police?"

"He sure did. Yonker now has two subpoenas with your name on them."

My exit was up ahead. I flipped on my indicator and drifted into the right lane. Cars around me blared their disapproval, refusing to slow down.

"You on I-Ninety-five?" Sonny asked.

"How did you guess?"

"I'm a mind-reader. I tend bar for laughs."

"Look, I want to ask you a favor."

"What's that?"

"Is Ralph gone?"

"Yeah. I took him to the airport an hour ago. What's the favor?"

"Can I sleep in my room tonight? I haven't had time to find a place to stay, and I'm low on funds. Just for a couple of days until I find a new place."

A long moment passed. Sonny had a comment for just

about everything, and finally I pulled the phone away from my face, and looked at the screen.

The line was dead.

I pulled into the Bank Atlantic Center and killed several minutes looking for a parking place. Buster was not happy at my leaving, and crawled into my lap. I scratched his ears until I saw his tiny tail wag, then got out.

I approached the Center's main entrance. A small mob of people congregated by the doors, chatting away while puffing on cigarettes. I called to them to find out what the score was.

"Florida State is down by six at the half," a woman called back.

"How are they playing?" I asked.

"They're holding their own," the woman said.

I went inside. It was only natural that the Lady Seminoles would play poorly, considering the circumstances. Hearing that they were toughing it out made me proud of them.

I spotted one of the other player's dads. He was a podiatrist named Robin Schwartz, and his daughter was the team's star center. Schwartz carried a flimsy cardboard tray holding several cups of beer.

"Need some help?" I asked.

"Hey Jack, we were starting to worry about you," Schwartz said.

I took three of the cups out of the tray, and held them between my fingers.

"Sounds like the game is close," I said.

"The girls are playing great," Schwartz said. "Your daughter is the top scorer."

"Yay," I said.

We headed toward the arena's entrance. The sound of angry male voices carried from the other side of the lobby. People were hurrying away from the voices, which sounded ready to escalate into a fight.

"What's the problem?" I asked.

"Karl Long is being interviewed by one of the TV stations," Schwartz replied.

"What's he yelling about?"

"The TV stations heard about Sara's sex tapes. A reporter tried to ask him some questions in the stands. I thought Long was going to take the guy's head off."

I stood on my toes, and spotted Long talking to a TV newsman named Chip Wells. Chip was one of the reasons I was no longer a cop. He had done a series of unflattering pieces after I'd beaten up a suspect, calling me "a stain on the conscience of the community." It hadn't mattered that the suspect had murdered eight women, and would have killed more had I not stopped him. I'd stepped over the line, and Wells had made me pay for it. I handed Schwartz the beers.

"I need to talk to Karl," I said.

"Be careful," Schwartz said.

I sifted my way through the crowd. Long was shaking his fist in Chip Wells's face, and looked ready to punch his lights out. Wells was the picture of calm, and kept politely nodding his head.

Something didn't feel right. Maybe it was the smug look on Wells's face that bothered me. Or maybe it was Wells's cameraman, a smarmy guy with a limp ponytail. The cameraman had his camera down by his side, and appeared not to be filming. Only the red light on the camera was blinking. I hurried toward him.

"Excuse me," I said.

The cameraman looked my way. "What's up?"

"Got a light?"

"Don't smoke."

I pretended to trip and fell forward. The cameraman let out a startled yelp, and we went down together in a heap. His camera banged on the floor. I grabbed it, and stood up. "Sorry about that," I said.

The cameraman got up, and dusted himself off.

"Give me my camera," he said.

I feinted giving the camera back, then opened up the back, and pulled out the film.

"You can't do that," the cameraman said angrily.

I shredded the film in front of his disbelieving eyes. Then I looked at Long. He was staring at Chip Wells, and the murderous look in his eyes told me that he understood what had happened.

"You son-of-a-bitch," Long swore.

"Now wait just a minute," Wells said.

Long smacked Chip Wells in the head. It was a glancing blow, but I sensed that he was going to unleash all his rage on the newsman if I didn't stop him. I grabbed Long by the arms, and steered him toward the men's room.

"Let go of me," Long said angrily.

"We need to talk," I said.

"I'm going to rip that shit stain's head off."

"Come on. It's about Sara."

Long snapped out of his rage and looked me in the eye.

"You know something?" Long asked.

"Yes, but I don't want them hearing it."

The anger left his body almost instantly.

"Of course," Long said.

During the drive over, it had occurred to me that Long needed to hear the things that I knew about Sara's abduction. He was a rich man with powerful connections, and that power might prove useful down the road. I didn't like the guy, but that wasn't going to stop me from using him any way I could.

We stood in front of the sinks, and Long crossed his arms.

"Tell me what you know," he said.

I glanced beneath the stalls to make sure they were empty. I tended to be overly cautious, and I turned on the water in the sink before I spoke.

"Despite what the police are saying, Tyrone Biggs did not abduct your daughter last night."

Karl's mouth dropped open. "Are you sure about this?"

"Absolutely. The real culprits are a pair of serial abductors. They've been following Sara around the state, and chose to strike last night. I was able to obtain a film of one of them from the Hard Rock Casino. The film is now in the hands of the FBI. They're going to use it to try and catch them before they leave the area with your daughter."

"Is Sara . . . alive?" he asked.

"I think so."

"What proof do you have?"

"These two men stole your daughter because she fits a profile. Abductors who do that rarely kill their victims."

"What kind of profile?"

"Tall, blond, and athletic."

"What do they want with her?"

"I honestly don't know."

"You've dealt with men like this before?"

"Yes. Many times."

Long suddenly stopped speaking. It was like he'd run into a wall, and the pain had just hit him. He covered his face with his hands and let out a muffled cry. I ripped a paper towel from the dispenser and handed it to him. Long dried his eyes and tossed the towel into the trash.

"That's the best news you could have told me," he said. "After I lit into you earlier, I would have thought you would have given up looking for Sara."

"I never give up," I said.

"I realize that now. I'm sorry about what I said. Really."

"You had to let your anger out. I was the closest target."

"You're not angry at me?"

I shook my head. Long gave me a good-natured whack on the arm. Despair brings out the true character in just about everyone. Beneath the arrogance was a loving father, and I knew that I'd made an ally.

"What can I do to help?" he asked.

"The FBI will call me if they learn anything," I said. "I may need to contact you, and ask you to pull some strings. Rescues are never easy."

"Of course."

Long gave me his business card. His private cell number was printed on it. As he handed the card to me, Long asked for one of mine.

"I must have lost the one you gave me," he said.

I gave Long another card, and he tucked it into his billfold.

"Let's go watch the rest of the game," I said.

CHAPTER 19

WE SAT in the stands with the rest of the fathers and rooted for our daughters' team. I don't know if cheering yourself hoarse ever accomplished anything, but it felt good, and let me forget about my problems for a while.

With two minutes left in the game, the Lady Seminoles went on a scoring blitz, and I stomped my feet and yelled at the top of my lungs until the final buzzer went off. The team had won a game no one thought they would win, and they assembled in the center of the floor, hugging one another and shedding tears.

I filed out of the stands with everyone else. By the time I'd reached the lobby, I'd lost Long. I'd wanted to talk to him more, and remind him that the things I'd told him were in confidence, and not to be repeated. The last thing anyone needed was for a reporter like Chip Wells to hear that the FBI was conducting an investigation far different from the one the police were conducting.

I rescued Buster from my car, and took him for a walk. He needed some quality time, and I let him pee on anything that wasn't moving.

Back in my car, I called Jessie. During the game she'd made eye contact with me from the floor, and I'd seen an expression of grief that told me how much she was hurting. Getting voice mail, I left a message. She called right back.

"Hey, Daddy," she said.

"Great game," I said.

"Thanks. It was a tough one."

"Those are the ones that count the most."

"Did you make any progress looking for Sara? I saw Karl Long sitting next to you in the stands. He almost looked happy."

My daughter had inherited my instincts for reading people. She'd once told me that she was thinking of a career in law enforcement, and I'd tried to talk her out of it. Two cops in the family was one too many.

"We've got some promising leads," I said.

"Tyrone didn't abduct Sara, did he?"

Whatever I told Jessie was going to be passed among her teammates, and from there, the information could go just about anywhere. I wanted to tell Jessie what I'd learned, but in the end, it might only end up hurting Sara's chances.

"That's not what the police think," I said.

"I guess you don't want to talk about it, huh?"

"I'm sorry, but I can't."

"I understand. The bus is leaving for the motel. I need to go."

"When do you head back to Tallahassee?"

"First thing in the morning."

"Have a safe trip. Call me when you get there."

"I will. By the way, did you call Mom? You said you would."

"Not yet. But I will."

"Daddy, you promised."

I heard a click on the line that indicated I had an incoming call.

"I need to run. Love you," I said.

"I love you, too, Daddy."

Jessie hung up. I punched the call button on the phone.

"Carpenter here."

"This is Karl Long. Where are you?"

Long's voice had a mean edge, and did not sound like the man I'd just sat with at the game. He definitely had a Jekyll and Hyde personality.

"I'm still in the parking lot," I said.

"So am I. Flash your brights so I can see you. We need to talk."

Long made the words sound like an order. He was the general and I was the lowly foot soldier. But I wanted to hear what was on his mind, and I hit my brights until an expensive Italian sports car pulled up alongside me. In south Florida, you were judged by what you drove, and Karl's wheels said that he was at the top of the food chain. I made Buster get in the backseat, and Long climbed in.

"What's with the mutt?" Long asked. "I don't like dogs."

"Feel free to get out of the car."

Long clenched his jaw and stared through the windshield.

"You don't mince words, do you?" he asked.

"Why should I?" I replied.

The parking lot had emptied out, the halogen lights beginning to dim. Long let a long moment pass, then spoke without making eye contact with me.

"I just got off the phone with the head of the goddamn detective agency I hired to find Sara," he said. "I asked him for a progress report, and he fed me a line of bullshit about the police arresting Tyrone Biggs, and that it was only a matter of time before Biggs confessed, and told them where he'd put Sara. I played along, and made him think I believed him. Then, I asked him if he'd talked to the FBI. Do you know what he said?"

I shook my head.

"He said 'What for? This is out of their jurisdiction.' That's when I realized that all the guy was doing was feeding me the police reports on my daughter's case. He's done nothing, absolutely nothing."

"There's a reason they call them dicks," I said.

Long turned in his seat. "I fired the son-of-a-bitch."

"That's a good start."

"I want to hire you. You know more about what's going on than anyone else. Say yes, and the job's yours."

I had already committed myself to finding Sara. I had to find out what had happened to her, and also what had happened to Naomi Dunn. In a way, the job was already mine. Long was offering to pay me for it.

"I'm game," I said.

Long visibly relaxed. He was the kind of man that needed to move the needle. He removed a folded piece of paper from his shirt pocket, and passed it to me. I was not proud, and held the check up to the faint light coming through my window. It was a personal check made out to me for the sum of $50,000.

"You can't be serious," I said.

"Karl Long is always serious," he said. "That's the amount I advanced to the detective agency, and you deserve the same. If you find Sara, I'll double it. She's the only family I have. She's worth everything to me."

I folded the check and slipped it into my shirt pocket. My wife had a favorite expression: Everything happens for a reason. I shook Long's hand, sealing the deal.

"I want regular updates on your progress," he said. "Even if the news is bad, I want you to call me."

"You'll be the first to know. You have my word."

The car fell silent. I sensed that Long wanted to continue the conversation, only there wasn't much left to say. He glanced into the backseat at Buster.

"What kind of dog is that?"

"He's an Australian Shepherd, but he's got a nose like a bloodhound," I said.

"Is the breed really from Australia?"

"Northern California. They were originally bred for herding sheep and cattle. He's a champ at finding things, especially people."

"So he's your partner."

"I guess you could call him that."

Long bravely stuck his hand beneath my dog's snout, and to my surprise, got his fingers licked in return. "Sara's mother and I divorced when Sara was two," he said. "I didn't see Sara much when she was growing up, too busy building shopping centers and strip malls. When Sara was fourteen, my ex-wife got killed in a car wreck, and I suddenly became a parent. I struggle with it."

"We all do," I said.

"My situation is different. You have a good relationship with your daughter. I could tell by the way she looked at you during the game. I don't have a good relationship with Sara. She hates me, thinks I'm an egotistical blowhard. I started coming to her games hoping to break the ice, but it hasn't worked. The only time we speak is when she needs money for schoolbooks or to pay the rent on her apartment. I want to change that. I'm *committed* to changing that. I just need a second chance. Please find her for me, Jack."

Making promises to clients was a curse in my line of work, but I was going to make an exception for Long. Maybe it was the blunt honesty in his words. That counted for something in my book.

"I'll do everything I can," I said.

"Thank you."

I watched Long peel across the lot in his fancy sports car, ignoring the lane markings and stop signs. I took the check out of my pocket, and stared at the sum, just to be sure it was real. Whoever had said that money didn't buy happiness had never been broke. Buster poked his head between the seats, his cold nose pressed against my arm.

"We're eating steak tonight," I told him.

PART 2

BUYER'S REMORSE

CHAPTER 20

I BOUGHT two filet mignon dinners from the takeout at Outback, and I ate in my car with Buster. Then I drove to a nearby Holiday Inn, and rented a room with a king-size bed, an in-room coffeemaker, and seventy-two channels of cable TV. Buster seemed to know that there had been a seismic shift in my world, and would not stop wagging his tail.

I awoke with the first rays of sunlight and took my dog for a walk. The sky was an aching blue without a single cloud, the air warm and moist. Back at the motel, I peeled off my clothes, and took a swim in the motel pool in my underwear, the chilly, overchlorinated water snapping me awake and clearing my head.

The motel offered a free continental breakfast, and I grabbed a couple of warm rolls and a newspaper before hopping on 595 and heading east along with a few thousand other commuters. My destination was the First Atlantic Bank on Sheridan Street, where I'd done my banking for most of my adult life. It was just past eight when I pulled into their parking lot, found a shaded spot, and spread the paper across my lap.

At 8:30 the first employees began to trickle in. At 8:45

it was upper management's turn. At 8:58 the bank manager arrived, a short, thick, disagreeable guy with an architecturally complex comb over. His name was Ed Nagle.

"Stay," I told Buster.

I followed Nagle into the icy building. I'd heard it said that Florida could solve half its problems by outlawing air-conditioning. The idea certainly appealed to me.

Nagle's office was a corner space with plenty of light. I found him at his desk, erasing voice mails. I rapped on his door, and he looked up with a start.

"Top of the morning," I said.

Nagle scrunched his face, trying to place me.

"I'm sorry, but do I know you?" he asked.

"Jack Carpenter," I said.

"I remember you. You're the detective who got thrown off the force. What can I do for you this morning?"

Nagle's words stung like a hornet. I entered without being invited and plopped down in the chair directly across from his desk. The expression on Nagle's face told me I wasn't a pretty sight. Unshaven, wearing two-day clothes, hair uncombed. The beach bum look.

"I have a business proposition for you," I said.

Nagle drummed his fingers on his desk. I removed Karl Long's check from my shirt and laid it on his blotter, smoothing the crease as I did. Nagle stared down at the piece of paper like I'd dropped a turd.

"Is this a joke?" he asked.

"Not at all," I replied.

"Karl Long is a client of this bank. I know his signature."

"Then you should be able to identify the one on this check as being his."

Nagle picked up the check with both hands and studied the signature. The expression on his face changed from hostile to pleasant in a snap of the fingers.

"Well, this is definitely Mr. Long's signature," he said, passing the check back to me. "May I ask why Mr. Long gave you this?"

"He hired me to find his missing daughter."

"I heard about his daughter's disappearance on the news. Such a tragedy."

"Yes, it is."

"So, what can I do for you?"

I looked Nagle squarely in the eye, and watched him squirm uncomfortably. Twelve months ago, I'd sat in this same room with Nagle, and begged him not to foreclose on my house. Nagle's response had been to cut me off at the knees.

"I want to buy my house back," I said.

Nagle's face became a frown. It was not the reaction I was expecting, considering the dismal state of the housing market.

"Did you already sell it?"

Nagle shook his head sadly as if to say *I wish*.

"Then what's the problem?"

"The bank entrusted your home to a real estate agent, who was negligent in the care of your property," the bank manager said. "Your home was vandalized several months ago and the agent did nothing about it. The agent also turned off the air-conditioning to save money. I'm afraid there's been considerable damage."

I'd woken up on a high, and felt myself crashing back to earth. Everyone had dreams: Mine was to buy back my old house, stand on the front lawn and snap photos with my cell phone, then e-mail them to my wife and my daughter with a one-word message: *Surprise!*

Nagle rose from his chair. "Take a look at the house, and decide what you want to do. I'll call the new agent handling the listing, and have her meet you there."

Nagle was dismissing me, just like he had a year ago. I wanted to slug him, only I didn't need the aggravation that would cause. I emptied the candy dish on his desk and went outside to my car. Buster crawled into my lap as I fired up the car.

"Different day, same shit," I told him.

My old neighborhood was south of the city nestled between a public park and an elementary school playground. Twenty-six houses on a dead-end street. The name of each owner painted on the mailbox. Bikes in the driveways and plenty of dogs. Home sweet home.

The agent was there when I arrived. A young Hispanic woman with big hair, full red lips, and a pair of hips that could have stopped traffic. Real estate was a tough sell these days, but she had all the right equipment.

"Well, Mr. Carpenter, there's a lot of work that needs to be done," she said.

"How bad a shape is the house in?" I asked.

"It's a catastrophe. Why don't you let me show you some of our other homes? They're much more attractive than this one."

She headed down the sidewalk toward her car. The dull realization hit me that Nagle hadn't told her that I was the previous owner. Son-of-a-bitch.

"I'm just interested in this house," I said.

She shot me a look that said I was crazy. I held my ground, and saw her remove a key ring from her purse, and toss it to me.

"Suit yourself," she said.

"You're not coming in?"

"No. Toss the keys under the mat when you're done."

She left without saying good-bye.

I unlocked the front door with a sense of mounting dread. A wave of warm, sticky air swept over me. I entered without turning on the lights.

I padded silently through my house. Memories floated through the air without any regard to time. In the living room, my mother, father, and older sister sat on a couch with wineglasses in their hands. In the bedroom, Rose lay on our bed, her swollen stomach carrying our soon-to-be-born daughter. In the foyer, Jessie stood in her first prom dress, her face flushed with excitement. More than once, I choked up.

After all the memories had played themselves out, I flipped on the lights. Vandals had spray-painted the walls and torn out the light sockets, leaving gaping holes that made the place look like a war zone. Light fixtures were smashed, toilets cracked, the carpet torn to bits. But what concerned me most were the walls. Mold had settled into the plaster and was wet to the touch. It smelled like a rotting corpse.

I went to the garage. I'd spent many hours there repairing stuff on my worktable or tooling around with my car. Thankfully, it looked the same as before. My old furniture was lined up on the far wall, covered in plastic sheeting. I'd left it behind because I didn't have the money to store it. That was how bad things had been.

I noticed that the sheeting was torn. I pulled it away, and had another setback. The vandals who'd destroyed my house had also ruined my furniture. Not a single piece looked salvageable.

Opening the garage door, I dragged the furniture down to the curb. I could taste my anger now. It was like a spoonful of acid swirling around in my mouth.

My cell phone rang. Caller ID said LINDERMAN. I took a deep breath.

"Hey," I said.

"How far are you from Hollywood Beach?" Linderman asked.

"About ten minutes."

"I need you to go there right now."

"What's going on?"

"I e-mailed the Dade and Broward police, and asked them to report any sightings of guys who were unusually big. This morning, an elderly woman reported seeing a giant taking a piss on Hollywood Beach. The Hollywood police sent a bicycle cop to investigate. So far, they haven't heard back from him."

"Where on the beach was the sighting?"

"Near the parking garage south of the Hollywood Beach Hotel."

The area was not far from where I lived. It was a hangout for vagrants, the covered levels a perfect place to camp out for the night. I pulled out my car keys.

"I'm leaving right now," I said.

"Good. I'm heading there myself."

I ended the call and hurried toward my car. A black Cadillac Eldorado was coming down the street toward me. The Eldorado braked at the curb, and the driver's door flew open. Frank Yonker leapt out, appropriately dressed in a sharkskin suit and bloodred tie. Yonker had a pasty white face and crooked eyebrows. Clutched in his hand were the subpoenas he wanted to serve me.

"Just the man I was looking for," Yonker declared.

"How did you find me?" I asked.

"This was your last known address, so I took a shot."

"Business must be bad for you to take up process serving."

"On the contrary, business is great. I just happen to dislike you, so I'm getting pleasure out of this."

"What did I do to piss you off?" I asked.

"You think you're above the law."

"It's better than being below it."

"Aren't we funny."

Yonker came forward, waving the subpoenas. I didn't have time for this, and let out a shrill whistle. Buster, who'd been watching the action from the car, scampered out the open driver's window, barking ferociously.

"Get that beast away from me," Yonker cried.

"Go for the throat!" I yelled.

Yonker stumbled backward and tripped over the curb. The subpoenas fell from his hand. The gods must have been smiling down on me because a stiff wind lifted the papers into the air and carried them across the street into a vacant lot. Grabbing Buster by the collar, I dragged him to my car.

"Have a nice day, Counselor," I said.

CHAPTER 21

I DROVE SOUTH to Hollywood Boulevard, and headed east toward the ocean.

Back in the 1920s, Hollywood had fancied itself the moviemaking capital of the east, and had been filled with sound lots and production companies. Brutal summers and giant mosquitoes had driven the moviemakers away, leaving palm tree-lined streets and scores of Art Deco homes.

I crossed the Hollywood Bridge, the historic Hollywood Beach Hotel directly in my path. Exiting the bridge, I drove a hundred yards on A1A, and turned down a side street where the elevated parking garage was located. The garage was four stories high and self-service. A perfect place to hide out for a few hours, or even a day.

I parked on the street and got out with Buster. A policeman's bicycle was parked by the garage's first floor. As my dog sniffed its tires, I looked for its owner. The first floor of the garage was filled with cars, yet quiet. I guessed their owners were on the beach getting turned radioactive by the sun.

"Help me."

The voice came from somewhere inside the garage. Buster's hackles rose.

"Please, somebody help me."

I wanted to go in, but I knew better. It could be a trap. Taking out my cell phone, I called Linderman's cell, and heard him answer on the first ring.

"I'm at the parking garage in Hollywood," I said. "Where are you?"

"I'm still stuck in traffic. Did you find anything?" the FBI agent asked.

"There might be a policeman down, but I can't be sure. I need you to call the Hollywood police and ask them the name of the bicycle cop they sent over to investigate the old lady's complaint."

"Hold on."

I heard the *click-click* sound of Linderman putting me on hold. I'd worked with the Hollywood bicycle cops on occasion, and found them an athletic, fun-loving group of guys. Most of the calls they handled were drunks disturbing the peace, and rarely anything serious. I found myself fearing for the poor officer who'd taken the call.

Linderman returned to the line. "His name is Officer Marc Georgian."

"Thanks. I'll call you right back."

I folded the phone and slipped it into my left pocket while drawing my Colt from my right. I stepped into the first floor of the garage with Buster glued to my leg. A sharp breeze was coming off the ocean and tiny particles of sand tore into my skin.

"Officer Georgian!" I called out.

"Yes," the voice replied weakly.

"My name's Jack Carpenter, and I'm an ex-cop. Are you hurt?"

"*Yes.*"

"Can you tell me where you are?"

"*Between two cars.*"

"I can't see you. Can you signal to me where you are?"

"*I can't move.*"

"Before I come in there, I need to ask you a question. What's your first name?"

"*Marc.*"

"All right. I'm sending my dog ahead of me. His name is Buster."

"*Okay.*"

I nudged Buster with my knee. "Go find the policeman."

Nose to the ground, Buster cautiously entered the garage, and did a serpentine route around the cars, then suddenly darted between a Malibu and a station wagon. I followed him with my Colt clutched in front of my body. The sound of the ocean was magnified inside the garage, and the sound of crashing waves echoed around me.

I entered the space between the Malibu and the station wagon. Officer Georgian lay face up on the pavement, a tanned, muscular guy dressed in the familiar blue shorts and bright white shirt of the Hollywood bicycle cops. His face was battered, his eyes swollen and blackened. I knelt beside him.

"Who did this?" I asked.

"*I don't know. He jumped me from behind.*"

Georgian was bleeding from the nose and mouth and his voice was weak. Placing my Colt on the ground, I pulled out my cell phone, and started to dial 911.

"*No cell service inside the garage,*" Georgian whispered.

Picking up my Colt, I stood up.

"I'll be right back."

Georgian blinked, saying nothing. He was going into shock, and would die if I didn't act fast. Buster was lying beside him with a concerned look on his face. I told my dog to stay, then ran out of the garage, and made the call from the sidewalk. An automated operator answered, and put me on hold.

A shadow appeared above my head, blocking out the sun. I looked straight up. A vending machine was falling from the second floor of the garage, the words *Everything Goes Better With Coke!* rushing down at me. I dove into the grass.

The machine hit the spot where I'd been standing with an enormous crash, then toppled over. Brown liquid poured out of the cracked front glass like blood. I stared at the spot where I'd just been standing, seeing my after-image lying broken and dying on the pavement. I'd been spared again.

Tires screeched inside the garage, snapping me back to reality. A vehicle was racing down from one of the upper levels. Sara's abductors were making their escape.

My call went through. I tried to give the operator the address. My voice was trembling, and I heard the operator tell me to take a deep breath, and calm down. She was trying to be nice, but it had the opposite effect. I couldn't have calmed down if my life had depended on it. Folding my phone, I ran back into the garage.

On the first floor, a few cars away from where Officer Georgian lay, I positioned myself in front of the exit, and went into a crouch, holding my gun in both hands. The concrete was vibrating, the roar of the getaway vehicle's engine drawing closer. In a matter of seconds it would be on top of me.

I debated my plan of action. I could shoot out a tire as the vehicle came into range, only there was a chance the driver—who I assumed was Mouse—would lose control and crash. That would be a disaster, for Sara Long would certainly be hurt.

Or I could shoot, miss the tire, and *hit* Sara. Another disaster.

I lowered the gun.

Shit.

The sound of squealing brakes ripped through the garage. The vehicle had reached ground level, its muffler roaring. It came around the corner, a multicolored Volkswagen van with giant peace symbols painted on the sides. Mouse was behind the wheel, and I had to give him credit. It was the last kind of vehicle I would have expected him to use to transport Sara Long.

I jumped behind a parked car, ready to catch the license plate. Hollywood employed a hefty police force, and I decided to call the van's license in, and let the Hollywood cops do the rest.

To my horror, Buster darted out from between the cars, and started trotting toward me, his tail wagging furiously. I'd forgotten all about him.

"No, boy, no!" I shouted.

Buster ignored my pleas, and kept coming forward. The day I'd gotten Buster from the pound, he was going to be given the needle. Somehow, I think he knew this; a more loyal animal I was never going to find.

I jumped out from behind the car. Buster let out a joyful bark. My eyes shifted to the van. There was more than enough room for Mouse to have driven around Buster, and avoid hitting him. It said something about the man that he bore down on my dog instead.

CHAPTER 22

THE HIPPIE VAN'S front bumper was twenty feet from sending Buster to doggie heaven. I was too far away to save him. All I could do was watch.

Then I had a thought; maybe Buster could save himself.

I clapped my hands and yelled his name like we were playing a game of fetch. We did that every night on the deserted stretch of beach outside the Sunset; it was Buster's favorite thing to do.

His upper lip curled up in a doggie smile, Buster's back legs accelerated just as the van was about to take him out. I extended my arms and kept yelling encouragement. I was going to end up getting killed if I wasn't careful. Yet it felt like the right thing to do. Then Buster did something I'd never seen him do before: He jumped off the ground, and flew through the air like a Frisbee dog on Animal Planet, his pink tongue hanging out of his mouth. I caught him in midflight, his body knocking the air out of mine. The van was right behind him. I dove between a pair of cars, my dog in my arms.

"Good boy," I said.

Buster licked my face. Mouse angrily blared his horn as he flew past.

I rushed into the aisle with my dog still cradled in my arms. Mouse had driven through the exit and was burning down A1A toward the city of Hallandale. Sara Long was in the back of that van, and it tore at me to think I'd gotten this close, and hadn't saved her. I pulled out my cell phone and punched in 911.

"This is nine-one-one," an operator said. "What is the nature and location of your emergency?"

The operator's voice sounded familiar. Back when I was a cop, I'd made it a point to know all the operators, and to send them small gifts on their birthdays.

"This is Jack Carpenter. Who is this?"

"Well, hello Jack. This is Edie Burgess. It's been a while. What's wrong?"

Edie had been with the department over twenty years, and there wasn't much she hadn't seen. I gave her the *Reader's Digest* version of everything that had happened.

"My, haven't we been busy," she said.

Hollywood was God's waiting room, and there were always ambulances on call. EMS showed up a few minutes later, and a pair of medics attended to Officer Georgian before loading him into an ambulance. I stood nearby with Buster still in my arms.

One of the medics asked me if I'd seen Georgian's assailant. I started to tell him that a sociopathic giant was responsible, then realized the medic might want to take me away for a psychiatric evaluation. Instead, I shook my head like I didn't know.

Georgian was loaded into the ambulance. His eyes

were shut, and I said a silent prayer for him. I'd been hospitalized several times as a cop, and more than once I'd seen a dark, ethereal figure hovering over me while in an emergency room. It was the kind of experience that forever changed a person. I knew that it had changed me.

I lowered Buster to the ground and went to the curb. Fluid still trickled out of the soda machine. I wrenched the door open, and removed an unexploded can of Coke. As I sucked it down, a siren broke the stillness, and a police cruiser raced across Hollywood Bridge and down the exit ramp. Trailing the cruiser was a black Toyota 4Runner with tinted windows and Virginia license plates. Linderman.

The cavalry had arrived.

Linderman pulled up to the curb and jumped out of his vehicle. His face was flushed, his eyes betraying a tinge of desperation. Traffic in south Florida could turn the sanest people into lunatics, and he looked ready to rip the head off a live chicken.

"What happened?"

"They got away. I called the vehicle make into the Hollywood police. They're running them down right now," I said.

"How long ago was this?"

"Five minutes."

I was trying to sound optimistic. The Hollywood cops were as good as anyone at running down a stolen car, but Mouse and his partner were proving far more elusive than I would have guessed.

A pair of uniforms had gotten out of the cruiser and were coming toward me. I was in luck. They were both cops I knew.

"I need to talk to these guys," I said.

"Be my guest."

I gave the uniforms a blow-by-blow account of what had transpired while Linderman searched the garage for clues. While one of the uniforms scribbled down my story in his notepad, his partner examined the broken soda machine lying on the sidewalk.

"Someone *threw* this at you?" the uniform asked incredulously.

"That's right," I said. "He was on one of the elevated levels of the garage, and tossed it down."

"What do you think this thing weighs?"

"I don't know. Maybe four hundred pounds," I said.

"Was this the same guy who beat up Officer Georgian?" the uniform asked.

"Yes. He's a crazed giant, and unbelievably strong."

The uniforms exchanged funny looks that told me my sanity was once again being questioned. They took a statement from me, and asked for a phone number in case they wanted to follow up with more questions. Then they left.

The sun had broken out from behind the clouds, and the pavement was baking. I ducked into the shade and waited for Linderman to come out.

I stared at Linderman's car. The FBI agent had been living in Miami for over a year, but still hadn't bothered to change his plates. Although he'd never said so, I'd assumed that once he found out what had happened to Danielle, he planned to move back north.

Linderman came out of the garage. The frantic look had left his face and his brow was gleaming with sweat. His jacket and tie had to be killing him, only I knew from past experience that he wasn't going to take them off.

"Take a look at this," he said. "I found it on the second floor."

From his hand dangled a white paper bag with the McDonald's logo printed on the side. He tossed the bag to me. Opening it, I found myself staring at an assortment of greasy fast-food wrappers and crumbled paper napkins. One of the napkins caught my eye. It was smudged with pink lipstick. Kneeling, I dumped the bag's contents onto the ground, and began sorting through them. I was certain that Linderman had already done this. Now, he was waiting to see if I drew the same conclusions.

The bag contained ten fast-food wrappers. Nine of the wrappers were for Big Macs, the wrappers stained with the secret sauce that made Big Macs so tasty. The other wrapper was for a fish sandwich. There was also a french-fry container with a few loose fries stuck to the bottom. And a receipt containing the time the food had been bought, and the amount paid. I was staring at the remains of last night's dinner.

My eyes kept drifting to the napkin with the lipstick stain. Picking it up, I saw tiny bits of food stuck next to the lipstick. I sniffed them.

"Smells like fish," I said to Linderman.

"That was what I thought," Linderman said. "Do you think she's talking to them?"

That was what I *wanted* to think. Only I needed verification before I jumped to any more conclusions. Removing Karl Long's business card from my pocket, I called his private number on my cell phone.

My call went through and rang several times. Then I

heard a man's voice that was unmistakably Long's. Harsh and loud and no pretense at being friendly.

"Who is this?" Long demanded.

"Jack Carpenter."

"I'm on the other line. Let me call you right back."

"Hang up the other fucking line. This is about Sara."

Long gasped. Maybe no one had talked to him like that in a while. Or maybe he wasn't expecting me to be getting back to him so soon. I didn't know and didn't much care.

"Hold on." Long went away, then came back. "I'm here. What did you find?"

"Let me ask the questions," I said. "I need to know what Sara likes to eat."

"How can this be important?" Long asked.

I looked at the lipstick-smudged napkin still in my hand. Please let this be Sara's lipstick, I thought. *Please*.

"Answer the goddamn question," I shot back.

"All right. Sara's been a vegetarian since she was in high school. She hasn't eaten red meat or chicken for years. She's into healthy organic food, sometimes drives me crazy she's so picky. Does that help?"

I found myself smiling. "Does she eat fish?"

"Yes, it's one of her favorite things."

I had been in a McDonald's recently, and visualized the menu that hung over the checkout. There were many different sandwiches and burgers. The chance that Mouse had bought Sara a fish sandwich on a whim was slight. More than likely, he'd asked Sara what she liked, and Sara had told him that she wanted a fish sandwich.

"Are you still there?" Long asked nervously. "Please tell me what this means. I have to know."

Normally, I didn't share information with clients during investigations. It was a mistake to raise people's expectations or give them false hope. But I'd brought Long into the process, and didn't see how I could shut him out without giving him a heart attack.

"One of Sara's abductors bought food last night at a McDonald's, and got her a fish sandwich," I said. "They couldn't have known that Sara liked fish without Sara telling them."

"And why is that important?"

"Two reasons. The first, which is the most important, is that her captors aren't experiencing buyer's remorse. That sometimes happens during abductions."

"Buyer's remorse? What the hell is that?"

"The goods aren't what you're expecting, so you get rid of them."

"Sweet Jesus," Long whispered.

"The second reason is that Sara's abductors could have just bought her a burger, and shoved it down her throat. That's what the majority of abductors do. They don't care about what their victims like, and just feed them whatever they happen to be eating. Sara's abductors are different. They asked her what she wanted to eat. That means Sara is talking to them, and has established a line of communication."

"That's good, isn't it?"

"It depends upon what the line of communication is," I said. "If a victim is constantly whining and complaining, then no, it's not good. In this case, I think Sara has established a positive line of communication, and gotten on her captors' good side."

The napkin was still in my hand. One of Sara's captors had used it to wipe Sara's mouth after she'd finished eating her fish sandwich. It was as compassionate a gesture as I could envision between a victim and her kidnapper.

"Now I need to go," I said. "Thanks for your help."

"Wait!" Long said. "I have something to tell you."

I glanced at Linderman. The FBI agent had his cell phone out and was talking to someone. The frown on his face was so deep it almost looked permanent.

"Go ahead," I said.

"I was just talking with the guy who runs my company," Long said. "I've instructed him to put all of my people at your disposal. That includes my two bodyguards and my driver and my helicopter pilot. They're yours, if you need them."

"You have a chopper?"

"Yes. Call me anytime you want to use it."

Linderman had finished his call and was shaking his head in disgust. To Long I said, "That was smart thinking. I'm sorry I cursed you earlier."

"I'm used to it," Long said.

We exchanged good-byes, and I put my phone away. To Linderman, I said, "What's going on?"

"The Hollywood police just found the van burning in a deserted lot in Hallandale," Linderman said.

"Any sign of Sara or her captors?"

"Not a trace."

CHAPTER 23

HALLANDALE was part of Broward County, only it felt more like Miami, the soulless apartment and condo buildings crammed together, the sprawl of concrete so pervasive that you could drive for blocks without seeing a blade of grass or a tree.

I followed Linderman west on Hallandale Beach Boulevard, then south on South Federal Highway to a deserted strip mall inside Bluesten Park. Hallandale was a town of retirees, and the traffic moved in slow motion.

The strip mall had seen better days, the shops lifeless and empty. Linderman drove around the building, and parked beside a Dumpster overflowing with garbage. Parking beside him, I stared at a line of police cruisers. Everywhere I looked, uniformed cops were traipsing around, poking their noses where they didn't belong. Police departments in south Florida were revolving doors, and most cops didn't know the first thing about preserving a crime scene. I leashed Buster and got out.

A large dirt lot sat behind the strip center. The lot was flat and dusty and filled with tire rims and torn bags of garbage. It backed up onto a large warehouse whose walls were painted white and without graffiti. Only in a retirement area did you see that.

The van sat in the lot's center, a plume of gray smoke still billowing from its hood. The gas tank had ignited, causing the van's roof to melt down and disappear. The smell of gasoline and burnt upholstery hung in the air like a toxic bouquet.

Linderman stood beside me, his badge pinned to his lapel. Although he'd never expressed it in words, he had a low tolerance for the local cops.

"Do you think there are any clues these guys haven't trampled on?" he asked.

A baby-faced cop stood a dozen yards away from us. As we watched, he picked up an empty soda can with his bare hand, and dropped it into an evidence bag.

"Probably not," I said.

Linderman shook his head, clearly disgusted.

"Sara's abductors didn't pick this place randomly," I said. "They'd been here before, and knew that it was deserted. I'm guessing they had another escape vehicle parked nearby, in case of an emergency. They came here, burned the van they were driving to destroy any clues, then transported Sara to the other vehicle, and bolted."

"That was smart."

"Yes, it was. I originally thought these guys were both nutcases, but now I'm not so sure. The big guy is definitely off his rocker, but I think his partner is cagey, and might be calling the shots."

"One is the brains, the other the brawn."

I pointed at the burned-out van. "That's another important clue."

"How so?"

"Sara's abductors used a stolen minivan as their first

getaway vehicle," I said. "The Fort Lauderdale cops found it in a parking garage across the street from the Broward Library. The van had been wiped clean."

Linderman gave me a puzzled look. He was one of the few law enforcement agents I knew who didn't get offended when he was in the dark.

"Why is that important?" he asked.

"They wiped the painter's van down because they didn't want their fingerprints getting lifted," I said. "They would have wiped this van down as well, only there wasn't enough time, so they burned it instead. But the end result was the same: Their fingerprints were destroyed."

"So one of these guys has a criminal record and doesn't want his fingerprints being found," Linderman said. "Which one do you think it is?"

"It's Mouse. The Broward cops checked the police databases for the big guy, and he didn't turn up. If we can identify Mouse, we'll have a much better chance of finding Sara. If we can't, we're in for the long haul."

Linderman shot me a look that said he understood. Catching criminals was a numbers game. We'd had our chance to catch Mouse and his partner, and they'd slipped through our fingers. Our odds were getting worse by the minute.

Buster pulled at his leash. I looked down at him, and saw that his hackles stood straight up. He had locked onto a scent.

"I'm going to let Buster sniff around and see what he can find," I said.

"And I'll talk to the Keystone Kops," Linderman said.

I walked toward the smoldering van. One of the cops working the scene stopped me, and asked me what the hell I was doing. I pointed at Linderman, who was talking to the officer in charge on the other side of the lot.

"I'm working with the FBI," I explained.

The cop let me pass. I walked up to the van, stopping when I was ten feet away. Buster had his nose glued to the ground, and had not stopped pulling. He was seventy pounds of pure muscle and strong enough to make my arm ache. From my pocket, I removed the paper napkin with Sara Long's lipstick, and put it up to my dog's snout.

"Find the girl," I told him.

Buster sniffed the napkin. He resumed sniffing the ground, and crossed in front of me, pulling to my left. I shortened his leash, and let him drag me clear across the lot, stopping at the boundary to the warehouse. I glanced over my shoulder. We had walked in a perfectly straight line from the van. My experience told me that when hurried, people took the shortest route possible. Buster had found the escape route.

"Good boy."

I let Buster move ahead. There was pavement here, most of it broken. My dog went fifty feet, then came to an abrupt halt. We were beside the warehouse, the shade a welcome relief from the burning sun.

I stared at the ground. My eyes locked on a pair of tire tracks and a fresh cigarette butt. Mouse had been smoking a cigarette the night of Sara's abduction. This was where their second vehicle had been parked.

The tire tracks were muddy and looked fresh. As a detective, I'd used an online company called TirePrint to identify tire tracks that I'd discovered at crime scenes. I would e-mail the company the tire track and wheel base measurements of a vehicle I wanted to identify, and they would input the information into a database, and determine the make and year of the vehicle. The simple procedure rarely took more than a few minutes.

I felt my spirits soar. I was going to find the vehicle Mouse and the giant were using, and I was going to alert every law enforcement agency in the state to be on the lookout. I scratched behind my dog's ears.

"You make me look so good," I told him.

Then, I cupped my hand over my mouth.

"Over here," I called out.

Linderman was the first to reach me. The FBI agent inspected the tracks, then went to his SUV, and returned with an evidence collection kit. Using a tape measure, he measured the tire tracks and jotted down the numbers onto a notepad. He also snapped a photo of the tracks with a small digital camera. The cigarette butt was placed in a plastic evidence bag, onto which he scribbled the date, time, and location. Then he took out his cell phone.

"Calling TirePrint?" I asked.

"Yes. Let's hope they can tell us what these guys are driving."

Linderman's call went through. I heard my own cell phone ring, and stepped away to answer it. Caller ID said it was JESSIE.

"Hey, honey," I said.

"Hi, Daddy. I'm sorry to be bothering you, but I need your help."

"What's wrong? Where are you?"

"I'm on the team bus heading back to Tallahassee. It's an eight-hour drive, so I decided to catch up on my homework, only I realized that I didn't have the schoolbooks I loaned Sara Long. I've got an exam next week, and I really need them."

It was rare that my daughter called me with her problems, but there was something in her voice that I didn't like.

"Did Sara bring the books on the trip?" I asked.

"Yes. Sara had them the other night. I figured the Broward police were holding them as evidence, so I called the detective in charge of the investigation, and asked her if I could have them back."

"Detective Burrell?"

"Yes. She was very nice, and went to the evidence locker to find my books for me. So here's the weird part. They weren't there. Detective Burrell found a copy of the police report that listed everything in Sara's motel room, and my schoolbooks weren't listed."

"So the books weren't in Sara's room when the police got there."

"No. I figured maybe they fell under the bed, so I called the motel, and asked the manager if one of the cleaning people found them. No luck there either."

There was a simple solution to Jessie's problem, which was to go to the campus bookstore, and buy another copy of her missing books. Only there was something else going on here that I was missing. I said, "Tell me what you're thinking, honey."

"This is going to sound crazy . . ."

"Say it anyway."

"I think the people who kidnapped Sara made it a point to take my books."

"Why do you think that?"

"Because Sara's other schoolbooks were left behind in

the motel room. Detective Burrell told me so. They were in the evidence locker."

I felt myself stiffen. Jessie had stumbled upon something. I said, "Well, that certainly sounds strange. The books you loaned Sara . . . what were they?"

"My nursing books. *Manual of Medical-Surgical Nursing Care* and *Taber's Medical Dictionary.* Sara sometimes borrows them from me when we travel. They're a real pain to lug around."

"Are they big?"

"Yeah, they're both doorstops."

I spent a moment processing what Jessie had just told me. Sara's abductors had purposely removed two nursing books from Sara's motel room during her abduction. They were big books, and had been taken for a reason. I found myself thinking back to Naomi Dunn, who'd also been a college student. Dunn's books had been scattered around her apartment, and I didn't remember the police taking an inventory of them.

The police file of Dunn's case was in the trunk of my car with the rest of my belongings. I decided it was time to take a look at it.

"I need to go," I told my daughter. "Thank you for calling, and telling me this."

"I hope it means something," Jessie said.

"It does. You did good, honey."

I went to my Legend and popped the trunk. The cardboard box containing all my earthly possessions stared up at me. It should have given me pause, but it didn't. Life was too short. I pulled out Dunn's file and slammed the trunk shut.

I got into my car for some privacy. The interior was as hot as an oven. I looked at the thermometer on the dash. The interior was 96 degrees, and I was parked in the shade.

I started up the engine. Soon cold air was blowing through the vents. Buster climbed onto the passenger seat and promptly fell asleep. I opened Dunn's file on my lap and sifted through the pages. A list of Dunn's classes at Broward Community College had been included as evidence, along with the names of her classmates who'd been interviewed by the police.

The list had been typed on a typewriter, the block letters badly faded. Dunn had been taking four classes at BCC. One was in contemporary American literature, the other three medicine-related. Her major was listed at the bottom of the page.

Nursing.

Thank you, Jessie.

I flipped to the evidence log. Forty-eight items had been removed from Dunn's apartment and cataloged by the police, including her clothes, toiletries, jewelry, a tennis racket, several pieces of expensive camera equipment, and a stack of novels written by Ayn Rand, Norman Mailer, and Saul Bellow. It was heavy reading, and no doubt part of her American literature class. Yet her nursing books, which was her major, were nowhere to be found.

I combed through the report. If I remembered correctly, the police had searched Dunn's car, an old Mazda that she parked outside her apartment. Perhaps her nursing books had been found inside the trunk.

The car's items were buried in the back of the file. The police had found five items in the trunk. Two beach blankets, a tube of suntan lotion, a straw hat, and a portable radio. Dunn's nursing books weren't there either.

I slapped the file shut and cursed. I'd been looking at Dunn's file for eighteen years, yet somehow I'd failed to see the discrepancy. Dunn's abductors had taken her nursing books, just like they'd taken Sara's nursing books.

I'm sorry, Naomi.

Linderman materialized beside my car. He'd undone the knot in his tie, and giant drops of sweat dotted his brow. The look on his face was anything but happy.

I lowered my window. "What's up?"

"Good news, and bad news," Linderman said.

"Why don't you climb in? It's nice and cool."

"Don't mind if I do."

I made Buster get into the back, and Linderman took his place. I let him enjoy the cool air for a few moments, then said, "What's the good news?"

"TirePrint just made the vehicle. Sara's abductors are driving a 2006 Jeep Cherokee with Goodrich tires. I called the Miami and Broward cops to see if any Jeep Cherokees have been stolen in the past week, and none have been reported."

"Do you think it's their car?"

"Yes. I'm guessing they kept it parked here, and used stolen vehicles to move around town. I've alerted the police and Highway Patrol to be on the lookout for the vehicle, not that I think they're going to find it."

"Is that the bad news?"

"Yes. Jeep Cherokees are one of the most popular makes on the road. There are literally thousands of them. Since we don't know the color of the Cherokee they're driving, our chances of spotting them are slim."

I stared at the file lying in my lap, my mind racing.

"I think I know how to find these guys," I said.

Linderman's head snapped, and he stared at me.

"Then what the hell are we sitting here for?"

CHAPTER 24

I NEEDED a computer. Since my office in Dania was closer than Linderman's office in North Miami Beach, we'd caravan there. Linderman opened the door and started to get out of my car. I stopped him.

"I've figured out what these guys' motivation is." I tapped the file. "The evidence is right here."

Linderman pulled his leg back in and shut the door. He was sweating profusely, even though the car's temperature was comfortable.

"Go ahead," the FBI agent said.

"They're abducting nursing students."

His face clouded. He shifted his gaze and stared out the windshield.

"My daughter was a nursing student," he said quietly.

"I remember you telling me that."

Linderman looked back at me. The pain had disappeared from his face. I'd seen this happen before. One minute he was a grieving parent, the next an unflappable FBI agent. I didn't know how he did it. I know I couldn't.

"Time's a-wasting," Linderman said. "Let's go."

I drove to my office with Linderman riding my bumper. I ran my business above a restaurant called Tugboat Louie's in Dania. Louie's boasted a good-time bar, dockside dining, and a busy marina. Not many respectable businesses would operate out of a place where drunkenness and all-night partying were considered appropriate behavior, but I wasn't one of them. Louie's owner, my friend Kumar, didn't charge me rent, and that made the place perfect in my book.

The Rolling Stones' "Can't You Hear Me Knocking?" was blaring out of Louie's outdoor loudspeakers as Linderman and I entered the building. Kumar sat on a stool by the front door, wearing his traditional white Egyptian cotton shirt and oversized black bow tie. Next to him was a blackboard with the day's lunch specials. Cheeseburger, grouper sandwich, conch fritters, Key lime pie. I'd been frequenting Louie's for years, and the specials never changed. Seeing me, Kumar exclaimed "Hello, Jack! Hello, Buster! Hello, Jack's friend!" He clapped his hands. "There is always excitement when you're around, Jack. How about some lunch? I can heartily recommend the cheeseburgers. They are *very* good!"

"Sure. I'll take a cheeseburger, medium rare," I said.

"Well done," Linderman said.

"And Buster?" Kumar asked.

"He would like the usual," I said.

Kumar hopped off his stool. "Coming right up, gentlemen."

I entered the restaurant and walked behind the noisy bar. Unhooking the chain in front of a narrow stairwell, I climbed the stairs to my office, Linderman behind me.

The second floor contained two offices: mine and Kumar's. My office was long and narrow, and contained a desk, an ancient PC, two folding chairs, a rusted file cabinet picked up at a yard sale, and a wall containing the photographs of a dozen missing children I looked for but never found. Sitting at my desk, I booted up my computer and opened my e-mail.

Typing with two fingers, I composed a letter that I planned to send to every law enforcement agency in the state, asking them to search their databases for young women who'd gone missing in the past eighteen years who were nursing students.

Linderman stood behind my chair as I typed, staring at the computer. In the screen's reflection I saw him shake his head.

"Something wrong?" I asked.

"How many police departments are there in Florida? Sixty-six?" he asked.

"Sixty-seven," I said.

"How many of them are going to drop whatever they're doing to help you? Based upon my experience, they'll pass the request down the line, and it will end up in the hands of a secretary, who may or may not look through the files."

"Do you want to write it?"

"I won't get any better response. The FBI isn't liked by most cops."

Our food came. Two cheeseburgers swimming in french fries, and a bowl of ground beef for Buster. Linderman pulled up one of the folding chairs, and we ate our lunches.

I couldn't taste the food. Sometimes that happened to me when I was on a search. My appetite disappeared and nothing tasted particularly good. I had lost weight since leaving the force, and didn't want to lose any more.

I forced the food down, then got up from my chair and went to the window. Parting the blind with my finger, I stared down at Louie's dock and watched a teenage girl wait on a table of drunk guys with sunburns and loud shirts. The waitress didn't look like she was more than sixteen years old. Staring at her gave me a thought.

"I'll talk the Broward cops into helping us," I said. "They can get the cops in the other counties to respond to my request."

Linderman put his burger down. "And how would the Broward PD do that?"

"Fort Lauderdale is a magnet for teenage runaways. I can't name a county that hasn't had to send a cop down here and retrieve a kid who's run away from home. The Broward cops always treat the visiting cops nice, and make sure the kids get home safe."

I returned to my computer and redid my letter. I addressed it to Candy Burrell, marked the e-mail urgent, and hit Send. There were several stray french fries left on my plate. I started tossing them to Buster when my phone rang.

"Carpenter here."

"Burrell here," Candy said. "I just picked up your e-mail on my BlackBerry."

"I need your help."

"Back at ya, pal. I'm sort of up to my eyeballs right now."

"What's going on?"

"A thirteen-year-old girl named Suzie Knockman

didn't come home from school yesterday, and no one knows where she is. One of her classmates said she was having problems at home. Suzie has a large extended family—two sets of grandparents, an uncle and his wife, two older male cousins, and her parents. We interviewed the family and got all sorts of conflicting information. When we tried to reinterview them, they lawyered up, which is really weird. This girl's in trouble, Jack."

"How can you be so sure?"

"There was a photograph of Suzie in the house. She was all dolled up and looked like she was going on twenty-one."

"Girls do that sometimes," I said.

"The photo was taken last year. Looking at it gave me the creeps. Take my word for it, the kid's in trouble."

Burrell had to make her own priorities. Right now, Suzie Knockman was at the top of her list and nothing I was going to say would change that.

"Who's the lawyer they're using?" I asked.

"Some white-haired creep out of Miami."

"Leonard Snook?"

"That's right. Do you know him?"

I tossed my paper plate into the trash. Leonard Snook was on speed dial for every drug dealer and murderer in town. For Suzie's family to have hired Snook meant something really bad was going down. Burrell was a hundred percent right in her assumption that the girl was in trouble.

"Snook is your key," I said. "He should lead you right to Suzie."

"And how is he going to do that?"

I hesitated. I had a priority list as well, and Sara Long was at the top of my list.

"I'll show you, but you have to do me a favor."

"You want me to respond to your e-mail?"

"Yes."

"You want the detectives in my unit to call every police department in the state?"

"You got it," I said.

"When do you need this done?"

"The moment after I find Suzie Knockman."

"This sounds like extortion, Jack."

I frowned into the phone. Burrell was tired, her voice on edge. Unfortunately, so was I. "How is that extortion? I'm putting your case first, and I won't even charge you for my time. All I'm asking you to do in return is to assign the unit to work on my case when we're done. There's no skin off your nose for doing it that way. No one's going to complain because your phone bills went up for one day."

"Jesus, Jack. Don't be so angry."

"Do we have a deal or not?"

A long moment passed. I didn't like to resort to these tactics, but there was nothing else I could do. This was my last lead toward finding Sara Long. If I didn't pursue it, Sara was as good as gone.

Burrell started to speak, and I heard a catch in her voice. Something told me that I'd burned another bridge with the Broward County Police Department.

"All right, Mr. Carpenter. You have a deal," Burrell said.

I started to say thanks, but she hung up on me.

CHAPTER 25

LINDERMAN AND I parted ways in Louie's parking lot. Linderman was heading back to his office, where he planned to spend the afternoon contacting other CARD teams around the country, while I helped my old unit find a missing thirteen-year-old girl.

"I'll call you if I turn up anything," Linderman said.

"I'll do the same," I said.

Linderman nodded and stared at the ground. In a flat voice he said, "I looked through the Naomi Dunn file while we were eating lunch. Is it my imagination, or were the police trying to hide something during that investigation?"

His words caught me off guard, and for a moment I didn't speak.

"I don't know what you mean," I said.

"You saw a huge guy with mental problems kidnap a college student from her apartment. Yet the police swore that there was no record of this guy. I find that hard to believe. In fact, I don't believe it."

It was my turn to stare at the ground. It was the one aspect of the Dunn case that had always baffled me. The giant hadn't just stepped off a spaceship, and neither had his partner. They were both bad guys, and bad guys always left trails.

"I wish I knew the answer," I said.

Linderman pressed me. "You must have a suspicion."

"I called every mental hospital in the country," I said. "There was no record of the giant. As far as they were concerned, he didn't exist."

"Did any of them try to stonewall you?"

I shook my head.

"Did any of the mental hospitals stand out?"

"One did," I said. "There was a mental institution in Broward called Daybreak that had been shut down after a TV news show exposed the horrible practices going on there. In the beginning, I focused on them almost exclusively."

"Why?"

"Daybreak had a ward for the criminally insane, and I wondered if the giant had been institutionalized there. I spoke to Daybreak's managing director and several doctors who'd worked there. Nobody remembered a crazed giant. I also checked with several Broward cops who helped move Daybreak's patients when the facility was closed. They had no memory of the giant either."

"Did you ever visit the place?"

"No. The place had already been closed when I started my investigation."

"So all of the information you got about Daybreak was secondhand."

"It was all I had to work with."

"What about records?"

"I looked high and low for their records, but could never locate them."

Linderman's expression had turned cold. Most law

enforcement agents did not deal well with bad news or hitting dead ends. He was no exception.

I waved as he drove off, but he did not wave back.

I got back into my car, and headed west into the far reaches of Broward County.

Suzie Knockman's family lived in Plantation, a monied area of horse farms, high real estate taxes, and private schools. The Knockman address was one of the better zip codes in town. Which made their decision to hire defense attorney Leonard Snook all the more damning.

Everyone was entitled to hire an attorney; it was written in the Constitution. Only it didn't make sense to hire an attorney when you hadn't been charged with a crime. Yet that was exactly what the Knockmans had done.

I had seen Snook represent families of missing kids before, and I knew how he worked. His playbook went like this:

First, Snook would make the Knockmans circle the wagons and stop talking with the police. Snook would become the conduit for any communication between the family and the cops. All information would flow through him.

Then, Snook would not allow any family member to be given a polygraph test by the police, and would cite the unreliability of polygraphs in a court of law if questioned by the media.

Finally, Snook would hold a circuslike press conference. Standing with members of the grieving family, he would publicly question the police's handling of the case, and point out leads the police had not followed up on. He would paint the police as idiots and bunglers, and divert attention away from the family.

That was Snook's deal. I did not know of a single instance where he had helped the police find a missing child. But he had kept quite a few highly suspicious family members out of jail.

I drove down the Knockmans' street. By south Florida standards, it was fairly wide, with generous sidewalks and plenty of trees. Many of the houses were two-story mansions surrounded by paddocks with three-board fencing and horse barns in the back of the property, the majority painted fire-engine red. Parked in the driveways were spotlessly clean Mercedeses and Beemers. The area reeked of money.

I drove past the Knockman address. Four police cruisers and several colorful TV news vans were parked in front of the house, a palatial white Colonial with navy blue shutters. A mob of reporters filled the lawn, jockeying for space while they gave their reports.

I parked on the next block behind a black Lincoln town car with a Hispanic chauffeur wearing a uniform. Loud music was blaring out of the car's stereo of an unidentifiable origin. I got out with my dog and approached the vehicle.

"Are you Leonard's driver?" I asked.

Snook's chauffeur tilted back his hat and shot me a wary look.

"Who's asking?" the chauffeur said.

I handed him my business card. He didn't look too bright, and I said, "Leonard has hired me to help find the kid. He said the police are really screwing up the case."

"Ain't that the truth?" the chauffeur said.

"Where's Leonard?"

"He's already at the house, doing his stuff."

"So tell me something. Which member of the family called Leonard?"

"I don't know. Why?"

"I was just wondering who was going to pay me, that's all."

"My cell phone's vibrating. Hold on a second." The chauffeur pulled out his cell phone and stared at the Caller ID. "There's Mr. Snook. Want me to ask him?"

The last time I'd seen Snook, he'd been tied to a chair and had soiled his pants while watching a client murder two innocent people. I'd called him a coward, and left him tied to the chair. Hearing my name was not going to bring back any fond memories.

"Don't worry about it," I said.

"Suit yourself, man."

I started walking toward the Knockman house, Buster close behind.

Snook stood on the front lawn with a group of people I assumed were the Knockman family, looking resplendent in his thousand-dollar suit and silk necktie. He was small, maybe five-six and a hundred fifty pounds, and had snow white hair and a goatee, which was also snow white.

"The Broward County Sheriff's Department has done nothing but harass the Knockman family from the moment this investigation began," Snook stated into the bouquet of reporter's microphones. "There is not a single shred of evidence linking the Knockman family to this tragedy, yet the police are expending most of their energy here, instead of out in the surrounding neighborhood, looking for poor Suzie."

Poor Suzie. It had to be a new low, even for Snook. I skirted around the house, and walked to the back of the property. A chestnut quarter horse galloped past me in a nearby paddock, then started bucking, the wild energy a sight to behold.

"Jack."

I turned to see Burrell standing at the back door of the house. Looking tired and pissed off at the same time. I held up two fingers.

"I come in peace."

"Get in here."

Burrell ushered me into the kitchen, a gleaming, high-ceilinged room that contained matching pairs of every expensive appliance and cooking utensil made.

"Nice place," I said.

Burrell stood directly in front of me with her arms crossed. Her face was red, and there was anger written all over it. I'd crossed a line that I shouldn't have crossed.

"You shouldn't have spoken to me like that," she said.

"I know. I was wrong. It was the way I was raised."

"Are you trying to be funny?"

I shook my head. My father was the most stubborn man I'd ever known, and I was my father's son.

"I'll make it up to you," I promised.

"I'm going to hold you to that," Burrell said. "Let's go."

I followed her through the house. The downstairs was deceptively large. I peeked into the rooms at antique furniture too old to have been made in Florida. The joint reeked of old money, and I wondered whose side of the family it had come from.

We came to a winding staircase and Burrell halted. The living room was off to her right, and through a picture window I saw Snook out on the front lawn, basking in the TV camera's bright lights.

"Come on, Jack, hurry," Burrell said.

"What's the rush?" I asked.

"If Snook sees you inside the house, he'll start screaming his head off. He'll want to know why the police are letting a civilian work the case."

"Who's running this investigation? You or him?"

Burrell acted offended. "What kind of question is that?"

I went to the front door and locked it.

"Screw Snook," I said.

Suzie Knockman's bedroom was on the second floor at the end of the hallway. As was customary with missing children investigations, it had been classified as a crime scene and yellow police tape crisscrossed the door. Burrell pulled the tape down.

"It's all yours," she said.

I handed Burrell Buster's leash, and entered the bedroom. It was lavishly decorated, with a four-poster bed, a closet filled with expensive clothes, and a wooden toy chest overflowing with beautiful dolls and teddy bears. It was too much, even for a rich kid. Someone was indulging Suzie.

A framed photograph sat on the dresser. Suzie was slender and dark-skinned and had multiple earrings in both ears. She was extremely attractive, only she wasn't smiling in the photo. I looked at Burrell, who'd remained in the hallway with my dog.

"Give me a timeline," I said.

"Suzie left school yesterday afternoon at three-thirty, but never came home. She normally walks home with a group of friends, but they didn't see her. Her mother says she tried Suzie's cell phone, but it wasn't turned on."

"What was Suzie carrying?"

"Her books and her purse."

"Does she have credit cards?"

"Yes, and a debit card that she used to withdraw two hundred dollars last night."

"Where does the family money come from?"

"Her mother. She's loaded."

Kids did not run away from happy homes. They were either pushed out or forced out. I had to figure out why Suzie had run. Once I did, I would have a better idea how to find her.

I walked around the bedroom and stopped at the toy chest. A Winnie the Pooh teddy bear caught my eye. There was something dark and slender sticking between Winnie's legs. I started to reach for it, then stopped.

"Is it okay if I touch this?"

"Go ahead."

I removed the object from the toy chest. It was a baseball bat, only smaller, the kind used by kids in Little League.

"Did you see this?" I asked.

"Yes," Burrell said. "I mentioned it to the girl's father. He said that Suzie was a tomboy, and liked to play softball with the boys on the street."

The reason struck me as lame. I hit the bat against the palm of my hand.

"Where's her glove?" I asked.

"Beats me."

I kept hitting the bat against my palm and walked around the room. I had a bad feeling in my gut, and needed one more piece of evidence to confirm that feeling.

I stopped at the door. It was being held open by a doorstop. Thirteen-year-old girls didn't use doorstops, and I kicked the doorstop away, and pulled the door back. My eyes fell upon the deadbolt directly above the doorknob. The wood around it was badly chipped. Suzie had installed it herself.

I quickly checked the other bedrooms on the second floor. There were four, all occupied by adults. None had deadbolts on their doors. I returned to Suzie's room.

"Someone's been trying to molest Suzie Knockman," I said.

CHAPTER 26

"GIVE ME that thing before you hurt yourself," Burrell said.

I handed Burrell the baseball bat I'd found in Suzie's toy chest. Holding up my hand, I extended all of my fingers.

"We have five suspects," I said.

"Five? I only count four," Burrell said. "Suzie's father, her uncle, and two male cousins, who are sixteen and eighteen years of age. Who am I leaving out?"

"The grandfather."

"Oh, come on. He's eighty-five years old."

"Viva Viagra."

"That's sick, Jack."

"You can't rule him out."

"He uses a walker."

"And he has a penis."

"That's *really* sick."

"Is it any sicker than her father, or uncle, or a cousin coming on to her?"

"All right. We have *five* suspects in the house, one of whom is trying to molest Suzie, if the deadbolt on the door and baseball bat mean what you think they do. So which one of them is it?"

"I'm leaning toward the father. The line about his daughter being a tomboy is lame. But I need to look around the bedrooms before I start accusing anyone."

Burrell glanced at her watch and shook her head. "Snook isn't going to stand on the front lawn forever. If he comes inside and sees you, there will be hell to pay."

"So stall him."

"How can I do that? I can't control the length of his press conference."

"There are a dozen reporters questioning Snook. How many do you know?"

"Five or six. Why?"

"Which of the reporters do you know best?"

"Deborah Bodden with Fox News. She covers the crime beat."

Bodden had been a reporter for as long as I'd been finding kids, and I'd never had a bad experience with her. I said, "Call Bodden on your cell phone, and ask her to keep questioning Snook. Promise to give her an exclusive when you bust the case open."

"That's not ethical, Jack. I could get in trouble."

"If you don't want to do it, I'll call her."

Burrell shot me a cold stare. When it came to finding missing kids, ethics were situational. I was willing to do whatever was necessary to find a child and get him or her home safely. Sometimes that meant skirting the law or breaking it. It was one of the reasons I wasn't a cop anymore.

Burrell took out her cell phone. "You don't back down, do you?"

"Never," I said.

I left her standing in Suzie's bedroom, and started my search.

Suzie's parents' bedroom was at the opposite end of the hall. Buster had joined me, and put his paw against the door.

"Let's find out what Dad's been up to," I said.

I pushed the door open with my foot and stood in the doorway. The bedroom was the width of the house and looked like it had been decorated by Laura Ashley. A private bathroom was off to my left. The door was open, and I spied glistening marble countertops and a bathtub fit for a Roman emperor.

I went to the window beside the bed, and looked down at the lawn. Snook was still talking up a storm, and I saw Fox reporter Deborah Bodden ask him a question, and stick a mike in his face. Snook was not the kind of guy to walk away from free publicity, and he answered Bodden while dramatically waving his arms.

"Beautiful," I said.

I went around the bedroom pulling open drawers. I didn't know exactly what I was looking for. Just another piece of evidence that said Dad was a creep.

The drawers turned up nothing. Nor did I find anything inside the walk-in closet—which was bigger than my old apartment—or beneath the bed. I was beginning to doubt myself when I came to a dresser and felt the hair rise on my arms.

A framed wedding photo sat on the dresser. It had been taken on the dock of the Rusty Pelican restaurant in Key Biscayne, the restaurant's colorful sign visible in the background. Mom wore a floor-length wedding dress, Dad a tux and red bow tie. They were holding champagne flutes, their arms interlocked as they drank from the other's glass. Both stared lovingly into each other's eyes.

Suddenly the situation became clearer. I did another search of the bedroom. The closet was divided into His and Hers, and I focused on Dad's side. Two dozen expensive suits hung from the racks, and I searched the pockets. In one jacket, I found an envelope inside the inner pocket, and pulled it out. It was filled with photos of Suzie lying asleep on a bed in her underwear clutching a teddy bear. The photos could have been touching, only they were focused on Suzie's breasts and her crotch.

I grabbed the wedding photo off the dresser and snapped my fingers for my dog. Buster emerged from the closet with a smelly running shoe in his mouth.

"Drop it," I told him.

I headed down the hallway to Suzie's bedroom with my dog hugging my leg. Burrell was inside the room, taking photos of the deadbolt on the door.

"Who interviewed Dad?" I asked.

Burrell lowered her camera. "I did. Why? What did you find?"

I showed her the photos of Suzie I'd found in the closet. Then I showed her the wedding photo, and pointed at the sign. "The Rusty Pelican burned down ten years ago. It took the owners several years to rebuild the place. It didn't open again until six years ago. I know this because Rose and I celebrate our anniversary there every year. The sign in this photograph was installed after the restaurant was rebuilt."

"Which means that this photo was taken within the past six years," Burrell said.

"That's right. I'm guessing this guy isn't Suzie's actual father."

"He never told me that."

"What's his name, anyway?"

"Richard Knockman."

Burrell's face went blank, but I felt her rage bubbling below the surface, the deception making her want to explode. Men who carried on sexual relationships with underage girls came in a variety of forms. Some were teachers, some were coaches, and some even pretended to be men of faith. Each of these men had one thing in common: They used their positions of authority to get close to their victims, who were young and vulnerable. They were predators.

Richard Knockman was a special breed of predator. He had married Suzie's mother to get at Suzie. Suzie was the prize. More than likely, he had dated other women with young daughters, and settled on Suzie's mother because she desperately wanted a man in her life. That was how it usually worked.

Richard Knockman had worked on Suzie slowly, lavishing her with gifts and attention and whatever she'd desired. He'd made her feel like a princess, and worked his way into her heart. Then one night, Richard had paid an unexpected visit to his stepdaughter's bedroom. Suzie had awoken to find him rubbing her back, or even lying next to her. He made physical contact with her to see how she reacted. When she didn't scream or try to scratch his eyeballs out, he told her how special she was. Then he left, with a promise to return.

Only the next time Richard Knockman had visited Suzie's bedroom, he was in for a surprise. The door had a deadbolt. When Richard knocked and asked to be let in, Suzie told him he couldn't enter. Maybe she even told him that she had a baseball bat. That was how little girls dealt with men like Richard Knockman.

But Richard didn't stop. He kept coming on to Suzie

when no one was around. She tried to stop his advances, only it got worse. So she ran away.

"I want to talk to Suzie's mother in private," I said.

Burrell had taken the wedding photo out of my hand, and was still studying it.

"Do you think the mother knows what's going on?" she asked.

"I won't know until I talk to her."

Burrell placed the wedding photo on the dresser next to Suzie's photo. It was ironic to look at them sitting side by side, knowing what we knew.

"All right. You can talk to the mother," Burrell said.

I walked outside to the barn with Buster. There were six stalls, one of which contained a chestnut pony that a brass sign identified as *Suzie's Girl*. I grabbed some carrots out of the feed room, and fed them to the pony until Suzie's mother came outside.

"I'm Rebecca Knockman," the woman introduced herself.

She was a petite woman with red hair and a pale Irish complexion. As she attempted to pet *Suzie's Girl*, the pony retreated into the stall. Rebecca Knockman withdrew her hand, which I noticed was trembling.

"She's never done that to me before," Rebecca Knockman said.

"How long have you had her?"

"A little over a year. Richard bought her for our daughter."

My grandfather had raised horses, and I knew something about them. A horse's sense of smell was their primary source of protection, and I wondered if *Suzie's*

Girl had picked up on Rebecca Knockman's fear, and decided to back away.

"Did Detective Burrell tell you what I do for a living?" I asked.

Rebecca Knockman crossed her arms and gave me a distrustful stare. "No, she didn't."

"I help the police find missing kids. When Detective Burrell told me your family had hired Leonard Snook, I knew that I wouldn't have a problem finding your daughter."

"Why is that?"

"Because Leonard Snook represents criminals. Innocent people don't hire him, but bad people do. Once I find out which member of your family hired Snook, I'd know what was going on. Make sense?"

She swallowed hard. "Yes."

"Your husband hired Snook, didn't he?"

Rebecca Knockman's eyes turned into slits. She didn't answer my question.

"Let me tell you what I think, Mrs. Knockman. I think you know where Suzie is hiding. I also think your daughter told you what your husband has been up to. Deep down, you're hoping to somehow fix this mess, and keep your family intact."

Rebecca Knockman lowered her gaze to the concrete floor and hugged herself. I felt bad for her, but not as bad as I felt for her daughter.

"Only you can't," I went on. "Your husband is a bad man. If the police haul him in, and he gets the opportunity to give his story first, he'll drag you and Suzie down with him. He'll say it was *your* idea for him to sleep with Suzie, and that you're into kinky sex, or some other kind of nonsense. He'll make you into the villain."

"Richard would never do that," she said, still looking at the floor. "He didn't have sex with Suzie."

"But he tried," I said emphatically. "Your husband is a sexual predator. Once he's been exposed, he'll do everything in his power to protect himself. That's why he hired Leonard Snook. For damage control. I've dealt with hundreds of men just like your husband. I know exactly what they're capable of."

Rebecca Knockman shivered from an imaginary chill. She had come to that terrifying brink called reality, and it was ripping her apart.

"Tell me what you want," she whispered.

"Go inside and tell Detective Burrell the truth, no matter how painful that might be. Lay it all out. You have to protect yourself and Suzie before it's too late."

"But I love my husband."

"I'm sorry, Mrs. Knockman. I really am. Do it for Suzie."

Rebecca Knockman said something under her breath that I didn't understand. She went to *Suzie's Girl*'s stall door, and made a clucking sound with her tongue. The pony refused to come to her, and remained in the corner of the stall. Rebecca Knockman brought her hand to her mouth.

She walked away without another word.

CHAPTER 27

I FED THE PONY carrots while the situation played itself out inside the house. I would have given anything to be a fly on the wall, and see Leonard Snook's reaction as Rebecca Knockman turned the tables on her husband. If Snook was smart, he'd run like hell.

I heard a crash that sounded like glass being broken, followed by a yell that shattered the still air. Buster dashed out of the barn with me holding his leash.

"Is everything all right in there?" I called out.

I halted at the back stoop, and made my dog do the same. There was no response. Sexual predators were dangerous when cornered, and have been known to attack the police when threatened with arrest. I didn't want Burrell to get hurt, but at the same time, I wasn't going to stick my nose where it didn't belong. Burrell was already angry with me, and there was no point in making it worse.

"Hey! What's going on?" I called out.

Still nothing. Buster was straining at his leash. The back door slammed open, and Snook staggered outside. His thousand-dollar suit was ripped at the shoulder, and his mouth was spitting blood. Snook took a few uncertain steps, and promptly fell down the stairs.

I might have broken his fall, but stepped back instead. Snook hit the ground, and my dog lunged at him. I loosened the leash just enough to scare Snook half to death.

"Get that beast away from me!" the defense attorney bellowed.

"He's really a nice dog, once you get to know him."

"Away!"

I reined Buster in. Snook was a real mess. His upper front tooth was busted, and there was a purple swelling above his upper lip.

"Who gave you the knuckle sandwich?" I asked.

Snook started to reply, but then he realized who he was speaking to.

"Carpenter! You son-of-a-bitch!"

"It's been great catching up."

Hurrying past him, I entered the house. A cyclone had swept through the kitchen, with pots and pans and broken dishes scattered across the floor. Men who molested kids tended to be cowards, and I envisioned Richard Knockman throwing the items at everyone in the room, and running for his life.

I ran down the hallway to the front of the house, and found Burrell consoling Rebecca Knockman in the living room.

"I'm sorry things turned out this way, Mrs. Knockman," Burrell said.

"He *hit* me with a sauce pan," Rebecca Knockman said under her breath.

"I know. You need to call your daughter, and tell her to come home."

"How could Richard do this?"

"Mrs. Knockman, listen to me. You have to call Suzie. It's important that we get her home right away. Please."

Rebecca Knockman pulled out her cell phone.

"Of course," she said.

The front door was wide open. Outside I found Snook's chauffeur sitting on the lawn.

"Is my boss okay?" the chauffeur asked.

"He's just dandy," I said. "Where's Richard Knockman?"

"Mr. Knockman came outside waving his arms, and told me that Mr. Snook had a heart attack," the chauffeur said. "I got out of the car, and Mr. Knockman jumped behind the wheel, and took off."

I went back inside. "Richard Knockman's stolen a car," I said.

"He won't get far," Burrell said. "I posted patrol cars at both ends of the block."

Back when I'd run Missing Persons, I'd always had a cruiser parked a block away from a crime scene, just in case. Burrell had done me one better, and used two cruisers. Back outside, I cornered the chauffeur, who'd thrown his hat on the ground in disgust.

"Which way did he go?" I asked.

The chauffeur pointed west, and that was the way Buster and I headed.

I don't know why I ran down the street. It wasn't my case, and I was probably never going to see Rebecca Knockman again.

I'd arrested many men like Richard Knockman, and I knew the damage they were capable of causing. Not just to their victims, but also to every living soul around them. They were human cancers, not fit to be loose in society.

The block was long and the air was hot. Soon I was drenched in sweat. On the next block a cruiser was parked on the grass, its bubble light flashing. I picked up speed, and soon was staring Richard Knockman in the face. He was tall and rather thin, and wore his hair stylishly long. He'd driven Snook's town car off the road, and into a cluster of royal palm trees on someone's front yard. The hood was crushed, and the engine was spewing black smoke. The car was a goner.

A pair of uniforms had handcuffed Richard Knockman's hands behind his back and were reading him his rights. His face was covered in bright red cuts and he looked dazed. It was impolite to stare, but I did anyway.

"Jack Carpenter," I said to the uniforms. "I'm working with Detective Burrell."

One of the uniforms called Burrell on his walkie-talkie and confirmed my identity. The uniform handed me the walkie-talkie.

"Detective Burrell would like to speak with you," the uniform said.

"Your boys got him," I said into the walkie-talkie.

"Great," Burrell said. "Keep your eye out for Suzie Knockman. She's holed up in an abandoned house in the neighborhood. Her mother called her, and she's walking home."

"Will do." I handed the walkie-talkie back to the uniform. "Detective Burrell said that it would be okay for me to shoot your suspect."

"Want me to take the cuffs off?" the uniform asked.

"That's probably a good idea."

Richard Knockman's head snapped so hard that I thought he had broken his neck. The uniforms held their stomachs and laughed.

Buster saw her first; the wisp of a girl standing across the street, hidden in the shadows. I crossed to get a better look at her, and saw her back away.

"You must be Suzie Knockman," I said. "My name is Jack. I'm working with the police."

Suzie eyed me suspiciously. She wore the uniform of girls her age: pink shorts, a colorful T-shirt, tanned arms and legs. She carried a backpack loaded with stuff and a pillow popping out of the top. I guessed she'd planned to stay away from home for a while.

"Is my stepfather going to jail?" she asked.

I glanced over my shoulder. Richard Knockman was being put into the back of a cruiser, the uniform holding his head down. I turned back to her.

"Yes. He's going to jail."

"They won't let him out on bail, will they?"

I shook my head. If I'd left any legacy as a detective, it was that every judge in the county had gotten an education about child molesters, and never let them post bail.

"He's going away for a long time," I said.

"Good. What's your name again?" Suzie asked.

"It's Jack."

A cell phone appeared in Suzie's hand. She said her mother's name and the phone dialed itself. She lifted the phone to her face.

"Hey, Mom. It's me. Some surfer dude named Jack wants to escort me back to the house. He says he's working with the police. He's got this neat-looking dog."

I hid a smile. I'd been called a lot of names recently—most of them unpleasant—and Suzie's description of me and Buster told me there was still hope. Suzie said good-bye to her mother and flipped the phone shut.

"Mom says you're okay. Let's go."

We started toward her house. Her movements were slow, and I sensed that she was afraid to go back to that house. I wanted to tell her that her life was about to get a lot better, but I knew that these words would have to come from her mother, or someone else she trusted. Several times she glanced yearningly at Buster.

"Do you like dogs?" I asked.

"Yeah, but my stepfather Richard wouldn't let me get one. I think he was afraid I'd keep it in my room."

We stopped at the corner, and Suzie leaned down to pet Buster. That was when I saw the tears pouring down her face. It made my heart ache to think that Richard Knockman had been controlling her life like this, and I handed her the leash.

"Why don't you walk him?" I said.

"Cool," she said, managing a half smile.

CHAPTER 28

REBECCA KNOCKMAN was standing on the sidewalk in front of her house with Burrell. Suzie ran to her mother, and they embraced. Looking for missing kids didn't always have happy endings, and I probably should have been celebrating, only I was in no mood for that. Sara Long was still being held captive by a couple of sociopaths, and I needed to rescue her. Burrell came down the sidewalk toward me.

"I need to take Suzie and her mother to headquarters and get statements from them," Burrell said. "Follow me, and I'll get the unit started on your request."

"Sounds good," I said.

I pulled my keys out of my pocket. My heart was pounding the way it did when I was working a case, my radar on full alert. I was ready to slay the dragon. Burrell placed her hand on my arm.

"Hold on a second," she said.

I gazed into her eyes. Their expression was one of concern.

"I don't want us to be at odds, Jack," she said.

"Nothing wrong with an argument between friends," I said.

"It was more than that."

I looked deeply into Burrell's slate-blue eyes. I had *hurt* her. She was one of the best friends I had, and there was no excuse for that.

"I'm sorry," I said.

Burrell crossed her arms in front of her chest and waited me out. I didn't know what else to do, so I gave her a hug. She didn't seem to mind that I was covered in sweat, and hugged me right back.

"That's more like it," she said.

I followed Burrell to police headquarters on Andrews Avenue. She got me a visitor's pass at the front desk and took me upstairs to the War Room, which was used as a strategy center during emergencies like wildfires and hurricanes.

"I need to get the Knockmans squared away," Burrell said. "Stay here, and I'll send over the other detectives from Missing Persons so you can get started."

Burrell left before I could thank her. I went to the window and looked out on the vast parking lot. It occurred to me that I hadn't told Burrell what I was searching for. Nor had I mentioned that I had proof that Sara Long and Naomi Dunn's abductions were linked. Burrell needed to know these things, and soon. Otherwise, our friendship would take another major hit.

A noise turned my head. My old unit had silently entered the War Room and lined up behind me. Their names were Tom Manning, Jillian Webster, Rich Dugger, Shane James, and Roy Wadding. I had trained each one of them to find missing people, and it made me proud to know they were still at it.

"You're back," Manning said.

"Just for a little while," I replied. "I don't know how much Burrell told you. I need for you to make phone calls to police departments around the state."

"What are we looking for?" Webster asked.

"Missing young women who were nursing students," I said.

"Over what period of time?" Manning asked.

"The past eighteen years. So far, we have two victims, both of whom were tall and athletic. I'm guessing this will hold true for the others."

"How do you know there are more victims?" Webster asked.

I hesitated. Experience came from practice, and practice made perfect. Mouse and the giant had done this many times before—that was why I was having such a hard time catching them. There were more victims, and they were hiding in musty police files across Florida.

"Trust me," I said. "There are more."

The War Room was outfitted with sixteen phone lines, and my old unit was soon talking to their brothers-in-arms around the state. They didn't need me looking over their shoulders while they worked, and I crossed the room and stood at the windows.

I stared at the mind-boggling sprawl, the cookie-cutter developments and cloned shopping centers stretching as far as my eyes could see. Growing up, two hundred thousand people had lived in the county; now it was almost two million. The past was gone, and I could not look at what had replaced it without feeling regret.

"I've got a hit," Manning called out ten minutes later. I went to Manning's desk. The detective sat with his necktie undone and a phone pressed to his ear. He cupped his hand over the mouthpiece before speaking.

"I'm talking to a detective in Alachua County," Manning said. "Guy's going to retire in two weeks, so he pulled out a stack of cold case files to give to the guy replacing him. He was reading them the other day, and found a case from twelve years ago where a college girl disappeared. She'd been in the nursing program at the University of Florida in Alachua."

My hands gripped the back of Manning's chair. "Can you get this guy to e-mail you the file?"

"He doesn't know how to operate a scanner, so he's going to fax the report to me."

I went to where the fax machine sat and made sure there was paper in the tray. Sixty seconds later I grabbed the sheets as they were printed. The typeface was faint, and I held them up to the light as I read. The missing girl's name was Cindee Hartman, and she'd been twenty when she'd vanished. Cindee hailed from Orlando, was tall and comely, and played on the women's field hockey team. Cindee's apartment had been ransacked during her abduction, the furniture all but destroyed. The abduction had taken place over a holiday weekend, and there had been no witnesses. The report referenced the fact that Cindee's complex was where Danny "The Gainesville Ripper" Rolling had butchered three students in 1990. Although the complex's security had been updated since the killings, Cindee's abductor had still managed to avoid detection.

My hands started to tremble. Two similar abductions could be written off as a coincidence, but not three. Cindee Hartman had proven my case.

"Find what you were looking for?" Manning called out from across the room.

"Yeah," I said.

I ran down the police station stairs and outside to my car. Buster danced on the upholstery as I hopped in and grabbed the Naomi Dunn file from where I'd stuck it between the seats. I got out of the car and shut the door, and he howled disapprovingly. Buster didn't like to be left alone, and was letting me know it in no uncertain terms.

His barking grew louder. I saw people pop their heads out of their cars and from windows inside the building. Buster was going to stir the whole place up if I didn't do something. I opened the driver's door, and my dog happily scrambled out.

I locked my car up, and dragged Buster inside by the collar. The desk sergeant was yakking on the phone, and I got onto an empty elevator without being spotted.

Next stop was the War Room. I made Buster lie down in the corner, where he promptly fell asleep. Then I got to work.

In the room's center was an oval table covered with empty coffee cups. Sweeping them into the trash, I pulled a photograph of Naomi Dunn from her file and placed it on the table. To the right of Dunn's photo, I placed a photo of Cindee Hartman from her file, and to the right of that, the photo of Sara Long I'd been carrying around. Then I found a yellow legal pad, and ripped away three sheets.

I placed one sheet beneath each of the photos. Using a black Magic Marker, I wrote down the date of each woman's abduction, and beneath that, the things that linked them—age, athleticism, and the fact that they were all nursing students.

I stepped back to stare at the information. One thing immediately jumped out at me. Cindee Hartman had been abducted four years after Naomi Dunn. Then there was a sixteen-year jump to Sara Long's abduction. That was a long time. Serial abductors were similar to serial killers in that they tended to abduct in cycles. I didn't see a cycle here, and kept studying the women's photographs.

A hand touched my arm. I was too absorbed to turn around. Webster shouldered up beside me. Webster had worked Vice before joining Missing Persons, and had seen her share of ugly. The expression on her face was particularly grim.

"Something wrong?" I said.

"We just found two more victims," Webster said.

CHAPTER 29

THE VICTIMS' NAMES were Victoria Seppi and Karen Kingman.

Seppi was from Chatham, a small town thirty miles due west of Daytona Beach. She had been studying nursing at a Daytona community college when she'd gone missing from her dorm room in the fall of 1999. Tall and athletic, Seppi had swum competitively in high school and played water polo at the YWCA. She was so similar to the other victims it was unnerving.

Because Seppi had been living in Daytona at the time of her disappearance, the Volusia County Sheriff's Office had handled the investigation. At first, the cops had focused on Seppi's boyfriend, a biker with a string of arrests for selling speed on Daytona Beach. When the biker had come up with an airtight alibi, the case had gone cold, and the investigation had been put on the back burner, where it had remained until now.

I found myself shaking my head as I read the Seppi report. Back when I'd run Missing Persons, I'd made it my business to be familiar with every "open" missing person case in Florida, but I had never heard of Victoria Seppi. That was because the Volusia County Sheriff's

Office hadn't classified her as missing, but had simply left the case open. I didn't know what their thinking was, and probably never would.

I went to the next report. Karen Kingman had been a nursing student at Pensacola Junior College when she disappeared in the summer of '04. A native of the nearby town of Brent, Kingman had played tennis in high school and gone to the state championships in singles twice. The photo in her report showed an athletic young woman with dimples in her cheeks, shoulder-length blond hair, and a radiant smile.

Kingman's abduction had occurred over the Fourth of July weekend, when her apartment complex was nearly empty. While there had been no witnesses, the evidence at the scene had indicated that Kingman had not gone quietly. Her blood had been found throughout her apartment, along with several torn pieces of clothing that had been identified as hers.

Pensacola is in Escambia County, and the local sheriff's department had handled the investigation. They had launched a massive search that had included the police from neighboring Alabama and Mississippi. The Florida Department of Law Enforcement and the FBI had also gotten involved. Hundreds of law enforcement officers and volunteers had looked high and low for the missing girl, and found nothing.

I had followed the Kingman case closely at the time. What I remembered most was how little information the Escambia police had given to the media. Withholding information was common with active investigations, but not when cases went cold. I would have to call the Escambia police, and ask them if they would now be willing to share the information they had.

I spread the photos already lying on the table, and placed Victoria Seppi's photo between Naomi Dunn and Cindee Hartman's. Then, I inserted Karen Kingman's photo between Hartman's and Sara Long's.

"I need a map of Florida," I said.

Webster found a road map of Florida. I placed it on the table next to the five victims' photos. Using a red Magic Marker, I circled the five cities where the victims had disappeared, and below the circles, wrote the dates of each disappearance. Then I took a step back.

"There's been one abduction every four to five years," Webster said. "What do you think they're doing with them?"

It was obvious to me what was going on here: These young women were fulfilling a need, with each one replacing the last. Sara Long was the latest victim, and would later be replaced by another college student studying nursing.

"They're keeping them until they stop being useful," I said.

"God," Webster muttered under her breath.

I continued to stare at the map. Something important was right in front of me, but I couldn't put my finger on it.

My eyes settled on Naomi Dunn's photograph. She was smiling in it. I had looked at that photograph so many times I felt as if I knew her.

Then I saw what I'd been missing. Naomi was *first*.

My hand slapped the table in anger. I had missed clues before, but never one this obvious.

"What's wrong?" Webster asked.

I pointed at the circle on the map I'd drawn to signify Dunn's abduction.

"Serial abductors are like serial killers," I said. "They start out timid and weak, and grow strong. Their first abduction is always committed near where they live."

"A safe zone."

"That's right. Fort Lauderdale was these guys' safe zone. They were living here when they abducted Naomi Dunn."

I took the stairs to Burrell's office with my footsteps ringing in my ears. Her door was wide open, and I stuck my head in.

"Are you busy?" I asked.

Burrell sat at her desk facing her computer, her face illuminated by the faint images on the screen.

"I'm watching Howdy Doody," Burrell replied.

Howdy Doody was cop speak for hardcore porn. It was not the kind of stuff that I expected Burrell to watch, and I came around her desk. Playing on her computer was a grainy video of a heterosexual couple having sex, the woman bouncing atop a man on a bed. The woman had bleached blond hair and enormous breasts that defied gravity. Her partner was a huge guy, his upper torso covered in garish tattoos.

"Who are they?" I asked.

"The guy is Tyrone Biggs, Sara Long's boyfriend," Burrell replied. "The bimbo is named Sky. She's an exotic dancer at a strip club called Showstoppers. Sky tried to sell this video to the TV stations. The stations thought it was too sleazy, and turned it down, so Sky sold it to a tabloid news show. Deborah Bodden at Fox sent it to me as a favor."

"Why is this tape important?"

"Take a look at what's playing in the background."

I brought my face up to the computer screen. A boxy TV sat on a dresser behind the bed. A women's basketball game was playing on it.

"It's the Lady Seminole's game from two nights ago," Burrell explained. "Sky had sex with Biggs while he watched his girlfriend play basketball. The tape lasts for about an hour, and proves that Biggs didn't abduct Sara Long."

Burrell shut off her computer. The screen went blank, and for a long moment she did not speak. I put my hand on her chair, and stared at her profile.

"You okay?" I asked.

"No, I'm not okay," Burrell said. "I sent the mayor this tape, and now he's claiming he never told me to arrest Biggs. Chief Moody has shut himself in his office, and won't talk to me. They're playing politics with a poor girl's life."

"That's how they've lasted so long."

Burrell laughed without smiling. It was a dead sound. Her eyes, which were normally dancing, were equally dead. She'd been running Missing Persons for six months, and she was already being thrown under the bus. It was the nature of the beast, and there were times when I wondered how I'd lasted as long as I had.

"Come with me," I said. "I want to show you something."

We went upstairs to the War Room. The photos of the five victims lay on the table with the map of Florida beside them. Burrell studied the photos and map with a look of disbelief on her face. I gave her a moment to absorb everything before speaking.

"Sara Long was taken from her motel room by a pair

of serial abductors," I said. "These are the rest of their victims."

Burrell glanced into the faces of the other five detectives from Missing Persons, who stood silently on the other side of the table. "You in agreement on this?" she asked.

The other detectives nodded in unison. Burrell turned to me.

"Should I call the mayor?" she asked.

"Fuck the mayor," I said.

The other detectives burst into laughter. Burrell was in no mood for games, and shot them a murderous look. The sound quickly died.

"So what exactly are you suggesting I do?" Burrell asked.

"Call Deborah Bodden at Fox News, and tell her what you've found," I said. "Tell her that a pair of serial abductors have been abducting young women in Florida for the past eighteen years, and the detectives in your unit uncovered them."

The other detectives broke into smiles. They were going to be heroes when this was all over. Burrell wasn't sold, and continued to press me.

"What about Sky's sex tape?" she said.

"What about it?"

"The tape proves that we arrested the wrong guy. I'm still screwed."

"You're spinning it wrong."

"What do you mean?"

"If Sky had handed over the tape to the police two days ago, you *never* would have arrested Tyrone Biggs. Right?"

Burrell considered what I was saying, then nodded.

"Sky withheld evidence that crippled your investigation," I went on. "Because of her, you made a false arrest. Let Biggs go, and throw Sky in the county lockup."

"You're saying I should make Sky the bad guy."

"Sky *is* the bad guy. She deserves whatever she gets."

"That doesn't seem right somehow."

"You want to take the fall, be my guest."

Burrell gave me a funny look. I could tell that she didn't like what I was saying. Burrell was one of those cops who wanted to do her job well, *and* for people to like her. I had never had that problem.

Burrell shook her head. "I don't know, Jack."

"Just do it. You'll thank me later."

"You think so?"

"Yes, Candy, I do."

Burrell started to reply, then looked down at her side. Buster stood by her leg, wanting to be petted. Burrell scratched the top of his head.

"What do you think, boy?" she asked my dog.

Buster wagged his tail enthusiastically. It brought a smile to Burrell's face, and I realized that it had been awhile since I'd seen her do that.

"I guess it's worth a shot," Burrell said.

CHAPTER 30

BURRELL QUICKLY took charge. The first thing she did was to make me write down everything I knew about the five abductions on a legal pad. I was carrying a lot of information in my head, and the details ended up covering several pages.

Burrell then read everything back to me. Several times she stopped to question something I'd written or to clarify a point. It was an exhausting process, but there was no other way to bring her up to speed.

A half hour later, we were done. Burrell rose from her chair at the table in the War Room, and so did I.

"One last thing," Burrell said. "You said the FBI determined that the abductors are driving a late-model Jeep Cherokee based on the tire tracks you picked up. Can I give that information to the media?"

"You mean without pissing off the FBI?" I said.

"Yes. They don't always share with us."

I probably should have called Linderman and gotten his permission, only I'd found the tracks, and could have just as easily made the vehicle without his help.

"Go ahead," I said.

Burrell called Deborah Bodden at Fox on her cell.

While she was on the phone, I went to the copy machine, and made copies of the missing women's files, along with a copy of my own notes. I handed the originals back to Burrell as she hung up.

"A Fox News team is on their way over," Burrell said.

"That was fast."

"I told Bodden I was giving her an exclusive."

"Anything else I can do?"

"I hate to ask you this Jack, but you need to leave before they get here."

The request did not offend me. My work for the police was strictly under the table. The last thing Burrell needed was for me to be seen by the media.

"Good luck," I said.

Buster and I took the stairs to the first floor. I stuck my head into the reception area to make sure no reporters were there. The reception area was deserted, and I stole outside and jogged across the parking lot to my car. The sun hung directly overhead, the midday heat like an oven. A brightly painted Fox News van entered the lot and drove directly past me. I kept my head down and my hand in front of my face.

Reaching my Legend, I glanced over my shoulder. The Fox van had braked next to the front entrance. Deborah Bodden and her cameraman hopped out and ran into the building, their bodies a blur.

I jumped into my car and fired up the engine. Back when I was a cop, TV news reporters had taped their interviews and edited them before putting them on air. But times had changed. Most TV reporters now broadcast their interviews live in order not to be scooped by iReporters, who sent out their stories instantly on the

Internet. I was guessing that Bodden would broadcast her interview with Burrell live.

I burned rubber leaving the lot, and drove down Andrews Avenue looking for a bar with a TV.

Broward County had so many bars that people called it Fort Liquordale. The bar I picked was called The Pour House, and was located within a dingy shopping center filled with empty storefronts. The place had no windows, just a small sign with its name.

I bellied up to the bar and ordered a soda. A giant-screen TV showed a mixed martial arts bout while the jukebox played Bob Seger's "Against the Wind." A crew of aging, pot-bellied bikers sat at a corner table, drowning themselves in beer.

The bartender was a small, hardened woman with fresh stitches on her chin. I saw her eyeing Buster.

"You got bad eyes?" she asked.

She thought Buster was a Seeing Eye dog. "Yeah," I lied.

"I don't have no problems with dogs. Two bucks for the soda."

I slapped a five-dollar bill on the bar and told her to keep the change. She stuffed the tip down the front of her blouse.

"It's safer than putting it in a bank," she explained.

She put my drink down in front of me. I asked her if she would change the TV to FOX. She agreed, and surfed the channels and found FOX. The words *Special News Report* were running across the bottom on the screen. I took out my cell phone and called Linderman at work. He picked up right away.

"Turn your TV to FOX," I said.

"What's going on?" Linderman asked.

"The Broward cops are about to blow this case wide open. It's coming on the TV right now."

"I'm turning on the set in my office," he said.

I ended the call. The interview had started, and a life-size Candy Burrell appeared on the giant screen. Her hair was tied into a bun, and she wore a dark shade of lipstick. One of the bikers gave a wolf whistle.

Deborah Bodden stood beside Burrell and began to ask questions. The TV's volume was muted, and the text ran across the bottom of the screen. I had been interviewed enough times to know when a reporter was on my side. It showed up in how the questions were posed, and whether the reporter interrupted you. Bodden liked Burrell, and was making her look good.

The interview lasted five and a half minutes. That was an eternity in TV time. Moments after it ended, Linderman called me back.

"What did you think?" I asked.

"Why didn't you call me with this information, instead of going to the police?"

Linderman's voice was strained. He sounded angry.

"The Broward cops helped me find these new victims," I explained. "It was their information to begin with. Is something wrong?"

"I want you to tell me why my daughter Danielle wasn't included with the other victims," he said. "I told you that she was taking nursing classes at the University of Miami when she disappeared five years ago. Why was she left out?"

Linderman had raised his voice and was yelling at me. I was no longer speaking with an FBI agent, but with the distraught parent of a missing child. I didn't want to upset him any further, and chose my words carefully.

"There are five victims that we know about," I said. "Each of them was abducted from their apartments. There was a reason for that. The giant is big and he's slow. By going to his victims' apartments, he's able to trap and subdue them. That's his M.O., and he's used it every time he's abducted a young woman.

"Your daughter's abduction was different. Danielle went for a run in the woods near her dormitory, and was never seen again. She was a good athlete, and could have run away from her abductor, if she'd realized she was a target. But she didn't. My guess is, she was tricked by her abductor and then subdued, which is how those type of abductions usually happen. Based upon that information, I decided not to include her in the group."

My explanation was met with stony silence. One of the bikers fell off his chair in a drunken haze, and his buddies began ridiculing him. Their noise couldn't have come at a worse time, and I cupped my hand over my cell phone.

After a few moments, Linderman spoke to me.

"Are you ruling Danielle out completely?" he asked.

I was good at what I did, but I wasn't infallible. What if the giant had gone to Danielle's dorm room, found her gone, and had tracked her down in the woods and abducted her? There was a possibility that this had happened, and I had no right to tell Linderman otherwise. He had lost a child, and people who lost children needed to believe that one day they'd see those children again, or at the very worse, find out what had happened to them. All of my experience did not give me the right to extinguish that hope.

"No, I'm not," I said. "Your daughter was athletic, and she was studying nursing. She's still a *possible* victim. I just didn't feel comfortable including her in the group of known victims. I'm sure you've done that with investigations before."

Linderman exhaled deeply into the phone.

"Yeah, a few times," he said, calming down.

"Then you understand what I did," I said. "I'm not giving up on finding your daughter."

"I know you're not. I'm sorry. I just lost my cool."

"You don't have to apologize."

"Thanks, Jack."

I heard a click on the line. Someone was trying to call me. I told Linderman I'd call him right back, and took the incoming call. It was Burrell.

"You were a star," I said.

"Where are you? What's that noise in the background?" Burrell asked.

"Just some drunks. I went to a bar to watch you."

"Well, get in your car," she said. "I think we may have found your abductors."

CHAPTER 31

BUSTER JUMPED into my car and I drove to the address Burrell had given me.

Ten minutes earlier, a 911 call had come from the Happy Days motel in east Davie. According to the caller, a customer had tried to leave without paying his rent, and the motel's owner had confronted him in the parking lot. A fistfight had ensued, with the owner getting his nose busted and some teeth loosened. The customer had gotten away.

As 911 calls went, no big deal. People skipped out on their motel bills all the time. What made the call notable were two things. It had come two minutes after Burrell's interview on FOX had aired. And the customer in question had been driving a Jeep Cherokee.

By exceeding the speed limit and running several red lights, I made it to the Happy Days in five minutes flat. Had I been able to make my car fly, I would have willed it to do so as well.

I pulled into the Happy Days' lot with tires squealing. A police cruiser was parked in front of the manager's office. A man with a bloodied face leaned against the cruiser, giving a statement to a beefy uniformed cop with a bored look on his face.

I parked and got out with my dog. The uniform shot me a look that said not to interfere. I approached him anyway.

"I'm Jack Carpenter," I said. "Detective Burrell sent me."

"Who?" the uniform asked.

"Candace Burrell. She runs Missing Persons. With your permission, I'd like to case the place."

The uniform scratched his chin. It was a known fact that the local police did not look for high IQs when fielding new hires. Occasionally, someone smart slipped through the cracks, but the majority of the officers were like the big lug standing before me.

"Well, okay. Just don't touch anything," the uniform said.

"I won't," I replied.

I did a quick tour of the grounds. The motel was an L-shaped building with a sagging roof line and window AC units. It was painted tropical pink, the color washed out by the sun. Twelve units faced the street, each with a car parked in front.

Something didn't feel right. Normally when the cops were called to a disturbance at a motel, people came out of their units to see what was going on. Not here.

I walked around to the back of the motel. A dozen more units faced a retention pond. Each of these units had a car parked in front as well. I banged loudly on several doors, but no one answered.

Then it hit me what was going on. The Happy Days was a hooker hangout, or what cops called a hot-bed joint. It was against the law for motels to rent by the hour, but that hadn't stopped the practice. There were streetwalkers in every one of these rooms, and they weren't coming out unless the doors got knocked down.

One room did not have a vehicle parked in front. It was at the very end of the building, and its door was ajar. I rapped on the door frame.

"Anybody home?"

I pushed open the door with my toe. The interior was darkened, and I found the light switch on the wall, and flooded the interior. The room had a king-size bed and some junky pieces of furniture. I stared at the pieces of white rope tied to the bed frame that had been used to hold Sara Long captive.

My breath caught in my throat as I entered.

I quickly inspected the room. The TV was turned onto FOX, the volume a whisper. On the floor in front of the TV was an open box of Animal Crackers. I glanced inside the box without touching it. It was filled with crumbs.

The closet and under the bed revealed nothing. The garbage can by the door was more helpful. It contained take-out bags from Burger King and McDonald's. I dumped the bags' contents on the floor and unfolded the wrappers. Mouse and the giant seemed to exist on a diet of greasy hamburgers and french fries, while Sara continued to eat fish sandwiches.

I checked the bags for sales receipts. I was guessing that Mouse had purchased the meals from drive-throughs. Many fast-food restaurants employed call centers to process their drive-through orders, and these centers used hidden cameras to snap photos of the driver placing the order, along with the driver's license plate number. If I was lucky, a receipt would lead me to the license for Mouse's vehicle.

The bags did not contain any receipts. I cursed under my breath.

I inspected the bathroom last. It was the size of a phone booth, and just as inviting. The walls were peeling paint, and the shower stall looked like a science experiment gone bad.

Buster brushed past my leg, and stuck his head into the garbage pail beneath the sink. I pulled his head out of the pail, and found two items. The first was a cotton swab covered in blood, the second a plastic syringe with the needle still attached. The blood was fresh, and had not congealed. Every piece of information was helpful in an investigation, and this was no exception. Either Sara was being drugged, or one of her abductors was an IV drug user. Or they both were, and shared the same needle.

I brought the pail into the bedroom, placed it on the floor, and sat on the edge of the bed. I called Burrell on my cell phone, and heard her pick up.

"Where are you?" I asked.

"Stuck in my office," Burrell replied. "The switchboard has gotten fifty phone calls from drivers on their cells who've spotted suspicious Jeep Cherokees. I've got half the cruisers in the county tracking them down."

"Tell the cruisers to concentrate on the Davie area," I said.

"Why? What did you find?"

"They were at the Happy Days motel, and took off. I'm sitting in their room. They left the ropes they used to tie Sara to the bed."

"Do you know which way they went?"

"No."

"How about the color of the Jeep Cherokee, or any distinguishing features, like a missing hubcap or a dent."

"I'll go ask the motel manager. You need to send a CSI team over here and have them check out the room they were staying in. They left lots of evidence behind."

"Will do. Call me back once you know something."

I hurried from the motel room. Outside, I nearly collided with an overweight Hispanic woman pushing a cleaning cart. She was heading for the room I'd just left. My wife was Mexican, and I knew enough Spanish to carry on a conversation.

"You can't go in there," I said in Spanish.

"Gotta clean up the room," she replied in broken English.

"Leave it alone."

"We got to rent it out again. Boss's orders."

She started to enter the room. I pulled a business card from my wallet, and shoved it into her face. Then I drew my Colt, and showed it to her in a nonthreatening way.

"I'm with the police," I lied. "Stay out of the room."

"Okay, okay," she said.

She left. She would probably return once I was gone. I went into the room, and snatched up the garbage pails and the box of Animal Crackers. Walking to the front of the building, I found the slow-witted uniform sitting in his cruiser, filling out a report.

"Where's the motel manager?" I asked.

"In his office. He decided not to file a complaint."

"Did he tell you anything?"

"He suddenly got amnesia."

"You need to put the heat on this guy. A woman's life is in danger."

The uniform continued writing his report. I'd planned to give him the evidence so he could turn it over to the CSI team when they arrived, but he impressed me as someone who might just toss the stuff away.

"Do you mind if I go talk to the manager?" I asked.

"Be my guest."

I put everything I'd found into my Legend along with Buster. Then I entered the motel manager's office. The room was small and stifling hot. I rang the bell hard.

The manager appeared from the back with a Scotch in his hand. He wore his hair slicked back like a mobster, and sported a pencil-thin mustache. His face was busted up, with a little purple pig below his left eye.

"I need to ask you some questions about what happened," I said.

"I already told you—I didn't see nothing," the manager declared.

"You called in the make of the car they were driving, a Jeep Cherokee. Did you bother to write down the license plate?"

"Nah."

"What color was it? You must remember that."

The manager took a swig of his drink and wiped his mouth on his sleeve. "Look, it's over. I don't want any more trouble."

"Listen to me. Those guys were holding a young woman hostage in their room."

"It's a sick world."

No longer being a cop had its advantages. For one

thing, I didn't have to respect people's rights, especially when those people had just crawled out from beneath a rock. Reaching across the counter, I grabbed the manager's shirt and lifted him into the air. His teeth chattered in his skull as I shook him.

"You're hurting me," the manager cried.

"I'm just trying to jog your memory."

"I remember now!"

I dropped him on the counter without letting go of his shirt. His drink hit the floor. "Start talking," I said.

"I think it was black. Or maybe navy blue," the manager said.

"Make up your mind."

"Okay. It was navy blue with tinted windows. Hadn't been washed in a while. The rear bumper was dented, and someone had keyed the driver's door."

"Which way did they go after they left your motel?"

"Right."

"You mean west?"

"Yeah, they headed west. I ran into the street after them. I wanted my money, you know? The driver was heading toward 595."

I released his shirt and patted him on the head.

"See how easy that was?" I said.

I went outside. The uniform was long gone. I called Burrell and got voice mail. I left a message and asked her to call me back. After a few minutes had passed, I started calling the other detectives in Missing Persons whose numbers were in my address book.

On my last try, Detective Rich Dugger picked up. I had hired and trained Dugger. With his school-boy face and calm demeanor, he could extract more information out of a witness than any cop I'd ever worked with.

"Hey, Jack, what's shaking?" Dugger asked.

"I need to speak to Burrell. Any idea where she is?"

"She's racing down the shoulder of I-95. I'm in a car behind her."

"What's going on?"

"There's a Jeep Cherokee in the median, and the driver is refusing to get out. Two highway patrol cars have the vehicle surrounded, and traffic is backed up in both directions. We think it's Sara Long's abductors."

It was not uncommon for vehicles to pull into the median on I-95 when they had mechanical problems. "What's the color of the Jeep in the median?" I asked.

"I'm driving on the shoulder, and can't see the car yet," Dugger said.

"The manager at the Sunny Days motel made the get-away vehicle. Sara's abductors are driving a navy blue Jeep Cherokee with a dented rear bumper and a scratched driver's door."

"Shit! Now the traffic's stopped dead."

"Can I make a suggestion? Climb onto the hood of your car, and try to see the Jeep that's stuck in the median."

"That's not a bad idea. I'll call you right back."

The line went dead. I let Buster out of the car, and watched him chase his shadow. Finally my cell phone rang. It was Dugger calling me back.

"The Jeep in the median is blood red. It's not them," Dugger said.

"You need to turn around and get everyone back here. Sara's abductors are heading west on 595."

"I can't. The highway patrol officers are pointing

their guns at this guy. We've got to deal with this. Later."

Again the line went dead. Sara's abductors were in Broward, and I couldn't get a cop to help me find them. I kicked my front tire in anger, then jumped into my car.

CHAPTER 32

EVEN WITH the windows down, the interior of my car was broiling hot. I put on the air, then punched in Karl Long's number. His secretary stuck me on hold.

"Pick up your damn phone," I said angrily.

My heart was pounding in my ears. Mouse and the giant were on the run. They'd been waiting for two days to move Sara Long out of Broward County, and now they had no choice. If they didn't immediately get out, they were going to get caught.

Desperation time.

I knew how to catch them. The motel manager had said they'd driven west. That meant they were either heading for the swampy Everglades, or would drift north through Palm Beach County. My guess was that they'd pick the Everglades. The back roads were desolate, and they wouldn't have to drive fast, or risk getting stuck in traffic.

Finally, Long picked up the line.

"I'm sorry, Jack," Long said.

"Your daughter's abductors are making a run for it."

"For the love of Christ. Do you know where they are?"

"I've got a general idea. Is your private helicopter still available?"

"It's on the helipad behind my office. My pilot is here as well. Tell me where you are, and I'll have him pick you up."

I was still parked in the Sunny Days lot. The motel's address was printed on the manager's door. I read it to Long.

"I'm staring at the map of Broward hanging behind my desk," Long said. "I own a ten-acre parcel of land three miles west from where you are, on the same road. Go there, and my pilot will pick you up in ten minutes."

"Make it five minutes," I said.

"I don't know if he can move that fast."

"Then kick him in the ass. This may be our last chance to find Sara."

I dropped the phone in my lap and burned rubber leaving the motel lot.

Karl Long had to be one of the richest men in south Florida. The number of office buildings and pieces of undeveloped land that bore his name were endless. I parked in front of the parcel where I was going to meet his pilot, and leashed Buster.

The land was surrounded by a white three-board fence. I hoisted Buster over the fence, then climbed over myself. My dog quickly found a stick in the grass and offered it to me. He wanted to play. I was in no mood for games, and I pulled the stick from his mouth, and tossed it onto the other side of the fence.

"No," I told him.

Dead center in the property was a billboard with Karl Long's name printed on it. As Buster and I headed toward it, a chopper roared overhead.

I glanced at my watch. Four and a half minutes.

The chopper landed fifty yards from where I stood. It was a metallic blue and had the initials KL painted in gold on the wings and on the tail. Through the tinted windshield I spotted two individuals, one of whom waved to me. My jaw tightened.

"For the love of Christ," I said.

The passenger door banged open. Long jumped out, wearing combat fatigues and a leather holster with a sidearm. A red bandanna was tied around his forehead that made him look like a mini-Rambo. Had he not given me fifty thousand bucks to find his daughter, I would have laughed in his face. Instead, I scowled at him.

"What are you doing here?" I yelled as he came toward me.

"I'm going with you to rescue Sara," Long replied.

"Bad idea, Karl."

"You don't want me along?"

"No. You'll only be in the way."

Long grabbed my arm and squeezed the biceps so hard it made me wince. The desperation in his face was all too real. I didn't back down.

"Stay here," I said.

"I can't do that," he yelled back at me.

"I'll give you my car keys. You can drive back to your office. I'll call you once I know something."

"No! I'm coming with you."

I would have stood there and argued with him, only Sara's life hung in the balance. I picked up Buster and put him into the backseat of the chopper, then climbed in myself. Long climbed into the front seat, and told the pilot to take off.

People thought flying in helicopters was glamorous. My guess was none of them had ever been inside a chopper. The engine noise was deafening, the vibrations scary, and if you didn't focus on the ground as you rose into the air, you threw up.

I buckled myself into the backseat, grabbed my dog, and braced myself for the ride. Long introduced me to the third man in the chopper, a silver-haired, retired air force chopper pilot named Steve Morris.

"Which way do you want to go?" Morris asked.

I pointed at I-595, which was off to our right.

"Follow the interstate toward the Everglades," I shouted.

"What are we looking for?" Morris said.

"A navy Jeep Cherokee with a dented rear bumper and tinted windows."

"Got it."

Morris lifted the chopper into the air, steered us over I-595, and headed due west. The legal flying limit for choppers was a thousand feet. It felt like we were flying much lower, and I was able to tell the makes of the cars speeding down the highway. None matched the getaway vehicle.

Within minutes we reached the exit for U.S. 27, the last exit before the tollbooth for Alligator Alley. Traffic had thinned, and I asked Morris to lift the chopper into the air as high as the law would allow. He complied, and we hovered in the cloudless sky.

"Do you have binoculars?" I shouted.

"Sure do," Long replied.

Long removed a pair of binoculars from a bag lying at his feet and passed them to me. Holding them up to my face, I looked down Alligator Alley. The Alley was ninety miles of four-lane highway that dissected the lower half of the state. It was ruler-straight and had no housing developments or strip centers on either side of it. If Mouse had gone this way, all we had to do was follow the Alley, and we would eventually spot him.

I lowered the binoculars into my lap. I didn't think Mouse had gone this way. The Alley was bordered by swamps on either side, and contained only a handful of exits. It was a bad road to use as an escape route.

I looked down at State Road 27 directly beneath us. Twenty-seven ran due north, and had plenty of cut-offs. Mouse would feel safer on 27, and I envisioned him taking it north until he reached 441, where he could then easily get lost. I tapped the pilot's shoulder.

"Let's take Twenty-seven," I yelled in his ear.

Morris gave me a thumbs-up. The chopper turned, and we roared north.

Broward is one of the most populous counties in America; when you head west into the swamps the population drops to nothing and vast farms spring up. If Mouse had driven this way, we would find him soon enough.

I glanced at the pilot's instruments and found the speedometer. We were pushing a hundred twenty miles per hour, or a mile every thirty seconds. Long turned around in his seat and addressed me through cupped hands.

"How can you be sure they went this way?"

I stared down at the highway. "I'm not," I yelled.

"But what if—"

"Shut up, and watch the road."

Long didn't like that. People hired me to do a job, and that didn't include explaining my actions. I grabbed him by the shoulders and spun him around.

"Look at the road!"

"You're a real prick!" Long said angrily.

"Who cares?" I replied.

The chopper suddenly slowed. Morris waved to me, then pointed straight down. He had spotted something and wanted to take a closer look. I gave him the thumbs-up, and he took us down. It felt like the floor had dropped out from beneath our feet, and Buster buried his head in my lap and shut his eyes.

I continued looking down at the highway. A crew of tree cutters were trimming back the overhang on 27, and had traffic stopped in both directions. If Mouse had run into this during his escape, it would have slowed him down considerably. I hadn't had much to cheer about lately, but this turn of events lifted my spirits. Maybe I'd finally caught a lucky break.

We flew another five minutes, each of us focused on the backed-up line of vehicles below. Long had stopped speaking to me. I supposed I could have apologized, but I didn't look very good on my knees.

Another minute passed. Off to my left, I spotted something strange. A compound of white, deserted buildings sat in an overgrown field, the buildings surrounded by a chain-link fence topped by razor wire. It looked like an abandoned prison, yet I knew of no prison in this part of the county.

"I want to take a look at that," I yelled to Morris.

The chopper dipped, making me feel weightless. Morris brought us down directly over the compound's entrance. I stared at the shell of a guard house. At one time, the abandoned place had been some type of institution.

A single road made of crushed seashells led into the compound. I spotted a fresh pair of tire tracks in the shells, their indentations several inches deep. Someone had recently been here, and I told Morris to see where the tracks led.

Morris followed the road into the compound. It was an enormous facility, and I counted six towering buildings, each painted an institutional white. The buildings' windows had been knocked out, as had the doors, giving them a ghostly feel. On one building, rusted bars covered the windows on every floor. Not a prison, I thought, but a mental institution.

The tracks stopped in a courtyard, then made a complete circle, and went back out. It could have been teenagers, or some curious tourists looking for a photo opportunity. Or it could have been Mouse and the giant, looking for a place to hide.

Long turned around in his seat. "Why are we stopping?"

"I think they came here," I said.

"You're nuts. This is a ghost town."

It *was* a ghost town, its memories long since displaced. But sometimes people returned to places that filled their souls with darkness. Mouse and his partner had been in Broward eighteen years ago, and something told me that this was where they'd lived.

"Let's go!" Long told the pilot.

The chopper left the compound. Flying over the entrance, I spotted a rotting wood sign lying on the ground beside the front gate. The name of the institution was painted on the sign in bold letters, and it screamed up at me like a horrible voice from my past.

Daybreak.

PART 3

DAYBREAK

CHAPTER 33

THE AIR escaped from my lungs, and I felt light-headed. An old joke came to mind. A Buddhist walks up to a hot-dog stand and says, "Make me one with everything."

I had become one with everything about this case. I knew exactly what was going on and who these guys were. All from staring at a rotting wooden sign lying in an overgrown field.

The infamous Daybreak Mental Health Center had once stood in this field. Up until the 1980s, this was where the county's mentally disturbed citizens had been put, usually against their will. It had been a state-funded snake pit of abuse, neglect, and wasted lives, with more people dying here each year than in all of the state's jails combined. It had gotten so bad that the governor had shut the place down.

I had focused on Daybreak when I'd first started looking for Naomi Dunn. Because it was closed, I had relied on phone interviews and had spoken to different people associated with the facility, including the center's director, the doctor who ran the ward for the criminally insane, and two Broward County cops who worked there.

I closed my eyes and plumbed my memory. My conversations with the director, the doctor, and the two cops quickly came back to me. Each had sworn to me that they had no knowledge of a disturbed giant as a Daybreak patient. Their denials had almost been identical, like they were reading off a script. I should have seen through the ruse, but hadn't. They had lied. And men lied when they had something to hide.

I opened my eyes. We had stopped and were hovering in the air, the pilot waiting for instructions. I glanced at Long. He was still livid with me, his face bright red.

"This is it," I shouted.

"How can you know that?" Long asked.

"It's an old mental institution. Sara's abductors were inmates here."

Long acted stunned. The idea seemed to upset him more than if I'd said his daughter's abductors were convicted murderers.

"We need to look around down there, and see if the Cherokee is stashed somewhere," I said.

The pilot looked to Long for approval.

"Do what he says," Long told him.

We circled the grounds. Daybreak was surrounded by a chain-link fence with several gaping holes in it. Each time we passed over one of these holes, I looked for tire tracks leading out. I had hunted for mentally disturbed people before. They were difficult to track down, their behavior unpredictable at best. But they shared one thing in common. When they were being chased, they would often hide instead of running. In the past two days, Mouse and his partner had hidden all over Broward County, and I sensed they were doing the same thing right now.

"Look! Down there!" the pilot said.

I strained my eyes to see what Morris was pointing at. Just north of Daybreak was an orange grove with a brown dirt road running through its center. There were fresh tire tracks in the road, and I felt my heart start to race.

"Follow that road," I said.

Morris brought the chopper directly over the road, then headed down it. It was hard to judge distances from the air. After what felt like two or three miles, we came to a clearing with a cracker house that had a corrugated metal roof covered with mold. The structure appeared to be part of a farm, the surrounding yard filled with rusting tractors and farm equipment. The brown dirt road ran past the cracker house and all the way down to 27, its length over a mile long. The tire tracks appeared to stop at the house.

"We need to go down," I shouted.

Morris landed the chopper in a pasture two hundred yards from the cracker house. The grass was knee-high, and my foot sank in a pile of ancient cow dung as I jumped from the cockpit. Buster strained at his leash, the enticing smells too much to bear.

Long climbed out and headed straight for the ramshackle structure. The strap on his holster was unbuckled, his fingers gripping the handle of his gun. If he wasn't careful, he was going to shoot himself in the leg.

"What are you doing?" I asked.

"I'm going to storm the house and rescue my daughter," Long said.

"That's a good way to get Sara hurt."

"Do you have another plan in mind?"

"We need to find their vehicle, and make sure those tire tracks are theirs," I said. "For all we know, they might belong to someone else."

Long backed down. "All right. We'll do it your way."

I made Long get behind me, and approached the house. The windows were covered in plywood, and a yellow "No Trespassing" sign was stuck on the front door. I tested the knob, and found it locked.

I circled the house while checking the boards on the windows. They were nailed down tight. The house had not been lived in for years, and I turned my attention to the grounds. There was farm equipment scattered around, including rusted combines and ground busters. The age of the equipment confirmed that the place had been abandoned. Buster continued to strain his leash. A part of me wanted to let him go to see what he could find. But I knew the woods were filled with gators, wild boars, and panthers. If Buster ran across one of these animals, he'd be ripped apart, and my company would lose half of its employees.

"This is a goddamn waste of time," Long said a few minutes later.

"You can leave if you want to," I said.

We were standing by the dirt road next to the house. I spent a moment studying the tire tracks I'd seen from the air. They were fresh, and about a half inch deep in the soft earth. The tracks left the road, and I followed them around the house with my eyes peeled to the ground.

Behind the house was a shaded backyard. There was no grass, the ground as hard as a rock. The tracks disappeared, and I got on my knees, and placed my cheek next to the ground. My grandfather had taught me how to track, and my eyes picked up the faint disruption in the earth. It was the outline of a car's tires going straight into the forest. I stood up and dusted myself off.

"What did you find?" Long asked.

I brought my fingers to my lips and shushed him. Long grew infuriated.

"Are they in there?" he asked.

I pulled out my cell phone. Long was my client, and I had an obligation to tell him what I knew. But my greater obligation was to make sure no harm came to Sara. I needed backup, and I called Burrell's number.

"Who are you calling?" Long asked.

"The police."

"But they might get away! We have to save Sara!"

Long had watched too many TV cop shows. In those shows, the heroes saved the day during the last few minutes of the program, and shot the bad guys while rescuing the victim. In real life, the police showed up and displayed a massive show of force that convinced the bad guys to throw down their weapons and give up. That was the script I was going to follow.

Long drew his gun from its holster. It was a Glock 19, and it looked like it had come right out of the box.

"Put that away before you hurt yourself," I said.

"Like hell I will."

Long ran into the forest brandishing his gun. He was going to get us killed if I didn't do something. Dropping my phone into my pocket, I started to run after him. I had not taken five steps when I heard a gunshot, followed by Long's ghastly scream.

CHAPTER 34

"KARL, you all right?" I called out.

"Help me!" Long screamed.

I instinctively drew my Colt. Someone had taken Karl's gun away from him. That was usually what happened when people who didn't know how to handle firearms decided to play John Wayne.

I cautiously entered the forest. Buster was glued to my side, his hackles sticking straight up. The forest was thick with oak and punk trees, the ground peppered with tiny flecks of light. Dozens of birds chattered overhead, and I heard the unmistakable rustle of a squirrel running across a pile of leaves.

It took a moment for my eyes to adjust. When they did, I saw Long hanging upside down thirty feet from where I stood. He had walked into some kind of animal trap, and been jerked into the air. Blood ran freely down his leg, and there was a nasty bullet hole in his shoe. The stupid son-of-a-bitch had shot himself in the foot.

"I'm trapped," Long gasped.

Long was lucky to be hanging upside down, since it restricted the amount of blood he was losing. I started toward him, then froze.

To Long's right was a clearing filled with tree stumps. In the middle of the clearing stood Mouse and the giant with their shirts off. The navy Jeep Cherokee was parked behind them, and had a camouflage tarp covering its roof.

The giant was swinging a tree limb in his hands like a Louisville Slugger, and was preparing to bash Long's skull in. He had a perfectly round, childlike face, the skin soft and without lines. Living on the beach, I'd seen plenty of muscle heads, and none had held a candle to this guy. He had muscles *on* his muscles.

Buster went low to the ground, and emitted a menacing growl. The giant checked his swing and glared at my dog.

"Bad dog," the giant said.

Buster sprang forward and let out a vicious bark. The giant jumped back in fear and dropped the limb to the ground.

"Bad dog," he said again.

The giant talked like a little kid. It occurred to me that he wasn't the one I should be focusing on. His partner was the problem.

I shifted my attention to Mouse. He was small and emaciated. His sunken chest was covered in crude ink tattoos that told me he'd done time in the federal pen. He was holding the Glock, and was aiming it directly behind him at the front seat of the Jeep.

"Drop your gun, or I'll kill the girl," Mouse said.

I looked inside the Jeep. Sara Long sat in the passenger seat. She was tied up, and had duct tape over her mouth. Her beautiful face was distorted with fear. Her terrified eyes locked onto mine.

I cursed myself. I should never have let Long come

along for the ride. In all my years hunting down missing kids, I'd never let a parent do that. I'd let the money Long had given me cloud my judgment, and now I was paying for it.

I took a step back without lowering my Colt.

"Drop your gun right now, or she's history," Mouse said.

I saw the giant pick up the limb from the ground, and rest it on his shoulder. He was going to smack Karl right in the back of the head with it.

"Not happening," I said.

I aimed at a tattoo directly above Mouse's heart. Fear flashed across his eyes.

"You want to cut a deal?" Mouse asked.

"What kind of deal?"

"Back up with your fucking dog, and we'll leave and not kill the girl or her daddy."

"Nobody will die?"

"That's right. You have my word."

I trusted Mouse about as far as I could kick him. If I backed up out of the forest with Buster, the giant was going to bash Karl.

"Make your friend get in the car first," I said.

Mouse flashed a crooked smile. "Lonnie, get in the Jeep."

"Don't I get to kill him?" Lonnie asked, sounding disappointed.

"No. Get in the Jeep, and strap yourself in. We're leaving."

"But I want to smash him."

"Now!"

Lonnie pouted and tossed the limb to the ground. He opened the back door of the Jeep, and stuffed his enormous body into the backseat. He fumbled getting the seat belt to work.

"Start backing up," Mouse said.

I glanced at Sara, and saw tears flowing down her cheeks. All I could think of was poor Naomi Dunn, and how I'd let her down eighteen years ago.

"I'm sorry, Sara," I whispered.

I clicked my fingers for Buster. He came to my side, and I hooked my finger through his collar. Together, we backed up out of the forest.

Once Mouse was out of eyesight, I heard him get into the Jeep, and start up the engine. Then he and the giant and Sara were gone.

CHAPTER 35

SOMEONE once said that the most pitiful sound in the world was a man crying. Karl Long certainly proved that to be true.

He cried as Mouse and Lonnie drove away. He continued to cry when I cut him down, and laid him on the ground. His foot was a bloody mess, and I searched the campsite for something to turn into a bandage.

"I fucked up," Long sobbed.

I wasn't going to argue with him. Left to do my job, I would have rescued Sara and brought a pair of killers to justice. Instead, I was back to square one.

I did not find anything resembling a bandage. Not wanting to see him bleed to death, or go into shock, which a loss of too much blood would bring on, I took off my shirt, and ripped it in two.

"Hold still, this is going to hurt," I said.

I made the bandage good and tight. Long stopped the waterworks and gritted his teeth. Buster plopped down beside him, and Long rubbed my dog's head.

"Okay, now you have to get up," I said.

"I don't think I can walk," Long said.

"I'm not asking you to walk. Just stand up. I'll help you."

I pulled Long to his feet. He leaned against me, and hopped on his good leg. The blood was draining from his face, and I knew his wound was starting to hurt.

"What now?" Long asked.

I took out my cell phone and handed it to him. "I'm going to carry you to the chopper. While I'm doing that, I want you to call nine-one-one, and tell them what happened."

Long powered up my cell phone and made the call. I threw him over my shoulder in a fireman's carry, and hiked out of the forest. The sun was blinding, and I crossed the property with my head bowed, listening to Long talk to a 911 operator.

"Tell the operator the Jeep is probably heading north on Twenty-seven," I said.

"Right," Long said.

We were approaching the pasture where the chopper was parked. Long was a load, and I found myself gasping for breath. Buster ran ahead of me, barking loudly.

"Oh, Jesus," Long suddenly said.

My cell phone fell out of his hand, and bounced on the ground.

"Karl, are you all right?" I asked.

Morris jumped out of the chopper and came running toward us. I laid Long on the grass. He had passed out and looked like death warmed over. Morris took his pulse and shook his head gravely.

"He's going down fast. I have to get him to a hospital," Morris said.

"His daughter's abductors are getting away. We have to look for them."

"Look, mister, my priorities are different from yours," Morris said. "Karl Long is my boss, and I'm not going to let him bleed to death. That's my call. Now help me get him into the chopper."

"Just do one sweep north," I pleaded. "That's all I'm asking. It's what Karl would have wanted."

"You're not listening. Get out of my way."

Morris gathered up Long in his arms and hustled across the pasture to the chopper, where he poured Long into the backseat. I started to follow, then heard a woman's voice. Grabbing my cell phone off the ground, I pressed it to my ear. The 911 operator was still there.

"This is nine-one-one. Please tell me your emergency," the operator said.

"This is Jack Carpenter," I said. "There's a navy Jeep Cherokee heading north on Twenty-seven. The vehicle is carrying an abducted woman named Sara Long. Are there any cruisers in the area?"

"Hold on," the dispatcher said.

I watched Morris get into the chopper and shut his door. A sickening feeling filled my stomach as the chopper began to rise into the air.

"Hey!" I screamed, shaking my fist.

Morris lowered his window. "I'm taking him to Broward General. I'll come back for you later!"

"You son-of-a-bitch!"

"Sorry, man!"

I cursed Morris, but the chopper's blades drowned out my words. The chopper rose into the sky, and I watched it float away. The 911 operator came back on the line.

"I'm sorry, sir, but there are no cruisers in the immediate area."

"How about police choppers?" I asked.

"I'm sorry, but there was an emergency on the other side of the county, and they're all taken."

My head felt ready to explode. I sat down in the grass and stared at the ground. "I used to be a cop. Can you please tell me what's going on? I need a chopper."

"I thought your name sounded familiar," the operator said. "There was a drug bust on the median of I-95 earlier today. The car was filled with cocaine and automatic weapons. The guys running the drugs made a run for it, and the choppers are being used to track them down."

"So I'm screwed," I said.

"Give me a description of the vehicle, and I'll send an alert to the neighboring counties. If you'd like, I can also send a cruiser to where you are."

"How long will that take?"

"Fifteen, twenty minutes."

A horrible laugh escaped my lips. Mouse and Lonnie had already gotten a good head start. Worse, they were driving into central Florida, which had hundreds of unmarked roads and practically no cops. With that much more time, they would be impossible to track down.

"Why not," I said.

I folded my phone and rose to my feet. Sitting still was not an option. I had to do something or I'd go crazy. Mouse and Lonnie had departed in a hurry, and hopefully left some clues as to where they'd gone. I headed back to the clearing in the forest.

I did a quick search of the area. It was filled with crudely made animal traps, which I quickly disarmed.

Mouse and Lonnie had left the tarp, a couple of half-finished cans of soda, and a bag of trash. I dumped the trash onto the ground and poured through it. A receipt from a florist named Nell's caught my eye. They had spent thirty dollars for flowers, and I wondered what they were for.

I checked the time. Twelve minutes had passed since I'd called 911. I needed to walk down the dirt road to 27, and flag down the police, who wouldn't be able to find this place otherwise. As I started to leave, I called for Buster. No response.

An uneasy feeling came over me. Had Buster stepped into another trap? I called again. To my relief, I got a loud *Yip!* in response. Buster only yipped when he found something that he didn't want to part with.

I followed the sound through the forest to another clearing. My dog lay on his belly in the dirt. He was clearly pleased with himself, and his tail thumped the ground.

"What did you find, boy?"

Next to Buster's feet was a bouquet of freshly cut carnations. Half were red, the rest white. I picked them up, and saw they were resting on a pile of small white rocks. Someone had put the rocks there, and I wanted to know why.

I took the top rock off the pile. Lying beneath it was a thin gold chain. I gently pulled the chain free from the pile. Hanging from it was a gold crucifix.

I swept the remaining rocks aside. Lying at the bottom of the pile was a laminated card covered in dirt. I cleaned the card on my pants leg and stared. It was a Florida driver's license for a woman named Kathi Bolger.

"What the hell," I said.

Bolger's head shot was on the card, as was her weight, height, and DOB. Born June 9, 1969, she stood five foot ten, and weighed one hundred and sixty pounds. The photo showed a pretty blond with expressive eyes, and sun streaks in her hair.

My hand shook. Bolger's profile was the same as Mouse and Lonnie's other five victims. Young, pretty, and of good size.

I looked at the gold crucifix hanging in my other hand, and the white rocks spewed across the ground. Then it clicked what Buster had found.

It was Bolger's grave.

CHAPTER 36

As I WALKED toward 27 to meet the police, I realized who Kathi Bolger was.

Kathi Bolger was the oldest open missing person case in Broward, and had gone missing in 1990. I'd reviewed her file as many times as Naomi Dunn's. Like Dunn's case, the details of what had happened to Bolger were etched in my brain.

Bolger had lived by herself in an apartment near Bonaventure. Enrolled at the local community college, she'd held down several part-time jobs to pay tuition. She had a boyfriend, and got along well with her family. Her life was normal, except the fact that one day she'd vanished off the face of the earth.

The Broward cops had conducted an extensive manhunt. Dogs, horses, choppers, and an army of volunteers had searched for Bolger. Not a trace of the young woman had been found. Not even her car had been located. In that regard, her case was different from Dunn's. There was no evidence in the Bolger case to suggest foul play. She had simply vanished, something that happened to dozens of people in south Florida every year. Because of that, I had not considered her a possible victim in this case, but now I knew better. Bolger had been Mouse and Lonnie's first victim.

I came to a padlocked gate at the end of the road. I hoisted Buster over, and climbed over myself. Standing next to Highway 27, I looked both ways. Not a car in sight.

I took Bolger's license from my pocket, and studied her photo. She'd gone missing at the same time Daybreak had been shut down. Maybe a coincidence, only I didn't believe in those. The solution to her disappearance was right in my hand.

My skin started to tingle. A story was taking shape in my mind. Nineteen years ago, Mouse and Lonnie had escaped Daybreak. They'd abducted Kathi Bolger and brought her to this remote farm. Something terrible had happened, and Bolger had died. Needing a replacement, they'd sought another woman similar to Bolger. That woman had been Naomi Dunn. And the cycle had continued, right until a few nights ago.

A flashing light caught my eye. A police cruiser was racing down 27 from the south. I hailed it down.

Although I'd left the force in disgrace, some cops considered me a hero for what I'd done. The one who responded to my 911 call belonged to that club. Officer Riski shook my hand, said it was a pleasure to meet me. He grabbed a T-shirt from the gym bag in his cruiser, and said I could keep it.

I put the T-shirt on, and found it was a perfect fit. It had the words *Broward County's Finest* stenciled over the pocket. The irony wasn't lost on me.

Riski cut the padlock on the gate to the farm. I loaded Buster into the cruiser, and we took off down the dirt road. By the time we'd reached the cracker house, I'd told Riski everything that had happened.

"You're sure this is the woman's grave," Riski said.

"Yes," I said.

Riski called CSI on his radio. Normal response time was twenty minutes. Riski would have to go back to 27 to meet them, just like I had for him. It gave me an idea, and I said, "With your permission, I'd like to look inside the house."

"Think it might contain some clues?"

"Yes. I think the woman in the grave might have been kept there."

"Go ahead. Just don't touch anything," Riski said.

I got out of the cruiser with Buster, and Riski drove back to the highway.

The cracker house was made of cinder block and had a pitched metal roof. As I shouldered open the front door, sunlight flooded the interior, followed by the scampering of little feet. I gave the critters a good head start, then let Buster loose.

I followed him inside. The front of the house was a combined living room/dining room, the few pieces of furniture covered in mold. I noticed the walls in the room were shifting. I had seen this phenomena before. The house was so thick with cockroaches that they made the wall panels move.

I stuck my head into the kitchen. The linoleum floor and countertops were coated with dust, which lifted eerily into the air whenever I exhaled.

In the back of the house were two small bedrooms. The first bedroom looked like a man cave, and contained a pair of twin beds, a boxy TV sitting on an upturned orange crate, several unopened crates of beer, and a pile of adult men's magazines.

The second bedroom was more feminine. It had a queen-size bed, a dresser, and a vanity. Rifling the dresser drawers, I discovered an assortment of women's clothes, including a see-through nightgown and several pieces of filmy lingerie.

From outside the house I heard a noise. A vehicle had pulled in, and I heard the CSI team get out of the van. I wanted to be there when the CSI team exhumed Bolger's grave, and decided to leave.

I headed back to the front of the house. Buster had trapped a rat beneath the dining room table. I hooked my finger in his collar.

"Enough of that," I said.

I noticed a stack of yellowing Polaroids lying on the table. Blowing away the dust, I picked up the photos by the corners. The photographs were so old, the subjects were starting to fade away. I placed them in a row on the table. The deeper the photograph lay in the stack, the sharper the subjects became.

The last photo was the clearest. It was of Lonnie and a young woman, whom he held lovingly against his chest. Lonnie was much younger, and had a full head of dark hair. I studied the woman's face. She was smiling through clenched teeth. A fake smile, probably done for the camera. Her eyes told another story. I had seen that look in the faces of abducted children I'd rescued who'd thought they were never going to be found. It was the look of hopelessness, of dread. Taking Kathi Bolger's license from my pocket, I compared it to the photo.

It was the same person.

CHAPTER 37

I WALKED outside the house. Officer Riski stood beneath the shade of a tree, talking with the driver of the CSI van. I handed Riski the stack of Polaroids I'd found.

"I told you not to touch anything," Riski said.

"They jumped into my hand," I said. "May I have your permission to watch the CSI team exhume the body?"

"Promise me you won't get in the way," Riski said.

"I won't get in the way," I said.

"You're a lousy liar," Riski said.

Soon I was sitting on a tree stump in the forest, watching the exhumation. The CSI team consisted of three men and one woman. Each member wore a plastic Tyvek suit that tied around their necks, goggles, a paper mask, and rubber gloves. Tyvek suits were the newest thing in preventing crime scene contamination, and reminded me of homemade Halloween costumes that kids used to wear.

Bolger's grave had been marked off with white string. Using hand shovels, the CSI team dug up the earth and dropped it into a metal sifter. When something of interest was found, it was cleaned, put in an evidence bag, and tagged. It was tedious work, but I was determined to see it out. The way a killer disposes of a victim can tell an investigator many things, and I wanted to see Bolger's body when it came out of the ground.

Three hours later, I got my wish.

A shovel hit bone. The team got on their knees, and removed the remaining dirt with their hands. Bolger's body slowly became visible. It had been wrapped in plastic garbage bags, the tops tied together with wire. The team lifted Bolger out of the ground, and laid her gently down on blankets a few feet away.

The team's captain was a soft-spoken detective named Christine Jowdy, who I'd worked with when I was on the force. Jowdy pulled a bottle of cheap cologne from her pocket and unscrewed the top.

"Who wants some?" Jowdy asked.

The other members of the team removed their surgical masks. Jowdy sprinkled cologne into each of the masks, then glanced up at me.

"Want to rub some over your lip?" Jowdy asked.

"No thanks," I said.

"This could smell pretty bad."

"I'm used to it."

Jowdy shrugged and put the cologne away. She took a Swiss Army knife from her pocket and delicately cut away the plastic. To everyone's surprise, Bolger's body was swathed in blankets, and resembled an Egyptian mummy.

Bolger was photographed from a variety of different angles. It was starting to get late, and someone suggested getting lights to illuminate the grave area.

"If we move fast, we can beat the darkness," Jowdy said.

Jowdy began to carefully cut away the blankets, which tore like paper. Bolger's white shoes were the first thing I saw; then the skinless bones of her ankles; then her dress. *White shoes*. I inched closer as the rest became visible.

"You need to back up," Jowdy said.

I was standing directly behind Jowdy, my feet glued to the ground.

"Did you hear what I just said?" Jowdy asked.

"Just let me see the rest," I said quietly.

She glanced up at me, pissed. "What if I say no?"

"Come on. I found her."

Jowdy let out an exasperated breath and cut away the remaining blankets. Bolger's skeleton stared up at me. I tried to avoid looking at her face. She'd been buried in a white, ankle-length dress, and had her arms crossed in front of her chest. A plastic name tag was pinned to her shirt pocket. It said *Daybreak Nurse*.

Riski gave me a ride back to my Legend. He was one of the good guys, and went out of his way to call the police in the neighboring counties to see if the getaway vehicle had been spotted. So far, nothing.

Soon I was driving on 595 in my Legend. It was growing dark, and rush hour was starting to wane. The police department parking lot was empty as I pulled in.

I parked below Burrell's office. The light was still on. Candy was like me in that regard. She lived the job. I called her on my cell.

"I was starting to worry about you," Burrell said.

"It's been a shitty day. I heard you scored a major drug bust."

"We stepped in horseshit on that one. Any luck finding Sara Long?"

"I got close, but no cigar. I need a favor."

"Name it."

"I don't want to ask you this over the phone."

"Where then?"

"I'm parked just outside."

"Give me a minute."

Sixty seconds later, Burrell emerged from the police station and slipped into my car. Her clothes were starting to look like she'd slept in them. I rolled up the windows.

"Why the secrecy?" Burrell asked.

"I want you to weasel your way into the police department stockade. There's a section that houses the department records archive. Each year has its own box of records. Take out the box for 1990."

"What am I looking for?"

"A file on a mental health facility called Daybreak."

"Why do you want to see that?"

"The two guys who abducted Sara Long were patients there. The giant is named Lonnie. He's six-foot-ten, and one of the scariest people I've ever seen. Yet somehow no one I spoke to would admit to knowing him."

"Why would they lie?" Burrell asked.

"I'm guessing a superior told them to."

"You make that sound routine."

"That sort of thing used to be routine. My rookie year, the chief sent out a 'No one dies during spring break' memo. He ordered the cops and the coroner not to report any student deaths to the media until after spring break was over. And we didn't."

"Did any kids die?"

"A couple did. They got drunk and fell off hotel balconies."

Burrell stared at the empty building and didn't speak for a while. She came from a family of cops, and liked to think that cops were different.

"Okay," she finally said. "I'll go to the stockade, and get the box. You want to come by, and look through the files with me?"

"I have to go to Broward General and check up on Karl Long," I said. "I'll call you when I'm done. Maybe we can hook up then."

"Dinner's on you," she said.

CHAPTER 38

I ENTERED Broward General Hospital through the main lobby. I had visited here enough times to be on a first-name basis with most of the staff and doctors. The receptionist was a tanned woman in her late-thirties named Dextra.

"Hello, Detective Carpenter, how have you been?" Dextra asked.

It had been a long time since anyone had called me detective. I didn't see any point in correcting her. "I've been fine. I'm here to see a patient named Karl Long. He was flown in by chopper a few hours ago."

Dextra tapped her keyboard and stared at her computer screen. "Let's see. He's not showing up on the new patient registry. Do you know what happened to him?"

"Gunshot wound."

"Oh. Did you nail another bad guy?"

"I didn't shoot him. Really."

Dextra gave me a sly wink, and made a call on her phone. I drummed my fingers on the countertop and avoided her stare. Flirting with Dextra was the last thing I wanted to be doing right now. Hanging up, she said, "Karl Long is still down in the emergency room. You can go see him, if you'd like."

"Thank you. Take care."

I started to back away, and Dextra held up a manicured finger.

"I get off at eight," she said. "Maybe we could go out, get something to eat."

I swallowed the rising lump in my throat.

"Or maybe you could invite me over to your place," she said.

I could tell that Dextra liked to fantasize about cops. I'd met women like her over the years. I'd never understood what the attraction was, and I decided to level with her. "I don't have a place. I got thrown off the police force last year, and I just got evicted from my apartment. All I've got is my fifteen-year-old car, a mean dog, and a trunk full of old clothes. Still interested in going out with me?"

Dextra shrank in her chair, her bubble burst.

"No thanks," she managed to say.

"Have a nice night."

I found Karl Long lying on a bed in the emergency ward. He was hooked up to every machine in the place, plus an IV drip. A cutie a few years older than his daughter sat in a chair beside his bed, holding his hand. The glazed look in Long's eyes told me that the nurses had given him a strong narcotic to ease the pain of his wound.

"Jack . . ." he muttered.

I knelt down so our faces were a foot apart. I had thought about Long flying back in the chopper, knowing he'd let his daughter down. It had to have ripped him apart.

"How are you feeling?" I asked.

"Great since they shot me up with painkillers. This is my friend Heidi."

Heidi and I exchanged nods. She had waist-length blond hair and fake tits. Young enough to be his daughter and old enough to know that was why she was here.

"Jack and I need to talk," Long said.

"I'll go to the cafeteria and get a drink," Heidi said. "Nice to meet you, Jack."

Heidi left. I took her chair and leaned on the arm rail of Long's bed.

"Any luck finding those guys?" Long whispered.

I shook my head.

"I heard you yelling at my pilot. We lost our chance, didn't we?"

I nearly said yes, but bit my tongue instead. The pilot had made his choice, and talking about it was not going to change anything.

"We'll get another," I said optimistically.

Long nodded and shut his eyes. He looked asleep, and I considered leaving. Then his eyes snapped open, and he placed his hand on my arm. "There's something I need to tell you about Sara," he said. "I think it's important."

"Go ahead."

"When Sara was a little girl, a man tried to kidnap her from a school playground. Sara bit him on the arm, and got away. She's always been like that. Once my daughter sees an opportunity to get away from these guys, she'll take it."

I felt a sharp stabbing in my gut. Lonnie and Mouse

weren't playground perverts. They were sociopaths, and would kill Sara if she tried to escape. I needed to step up my search before that happened.

"That's good to know," I said.

Long eventually shut his eyes and fell asleep. Going outside to the parking lot, I took Buster for a walk on Andrews Avenue when my cell phone started to ring. It was my old pal, Sonny. Our last conversation hadn't been friendly, and I wondered what he wanted.

"What's up," I answered.

"You want your room above the bar back?" Sonny asked.

I stopped walking. That was exactly what I wanted; a familiar place to rest my head, and have a burger and a beer with people that I knew. The skeptic in me held back.

"What's the catch?"

"No catch. I talked to Ralph about it this afternoon, and he agreed."

"What about Buster?"

"Buster, too."

"What about the subpoena?"

"Ralph made it go away."

Cars whizzed past me on the street. I should have been happy to get my old place back, but it didn't feel right.

"You still haven't told me what the deal is," I said.

"We got held up this afternoon," Sonny said. "A Hispanic junkie came in, and stuck a gun in my face. Made me clean out the till and give him my jewelry and then the little prick robbed the guys sitting at the bar. Then he grabbed a bottle of Jameson's off the bar and waltzed out."

"I'm sorry. You okay?"

"I thought I was going to have a heart attack. Went to the hospital, and they got me calmed down. Then I called Ralph, and told him what happened. I reminded him that as part of your rent, you used to sit at the bar when it got busy, and make sure the place didn't get robbed. I told him that if he didn't hire you back, I was going to quit."

"And he said yes?"

"What the fuck else was he going to say? You want your room, or not?"

Buster got excited when I pulled into the Sunset's parking lot. I popped the trunk and took my stuff back up to my room. Then I found a washed-up stick by the shoreline, and engaged in some serious quality time with my dog.

The Sunset was quiet when I entered. The Seven Dwarfs sat at the bar, nursing their drinks. Sonny sat behind the bar on a stool, channel surfing. He made eye contact with me, and nodded without speaking. He looked shook up. So did the Dwarfs.

"What are you having?" Sonny asked.

"The usual. What did this guy take besides the cash?" I asked.

Sonny pulled down the neck of his T-shirt. An ugly red line circled his throat. Sonny's father had died when he was young, and Sonny had taken his father's dog tags from Vietnam, and gotten them gold-plated. The junkie who'd robbed the place had ripped those tags right off Sonny's neck.

"What about you guys?" I asked.

The Dwarfs rattled off their losses. Four gold wedding

bands, three watches, a black onyx ring, and several gold class rings. Their social security checks had just come in the mail, and they'd lost all their money as well.

"I can't do anything about the cash, but I can get your jewelry back," I said.

Sonny nearly came over the bar. "You can?" he said.

"Yes. Write it all down so I don't forget anything."

The Dwarfs made a list of the stolen items on a cocktail napkin. Sonny plopped a foaming draft beer down in front of me. I raised it to my lips, and saw the Dwarfs lift their glasses in a toast.

"Here's to Jack getting our things back," one of them proclaimed.

"Here's to Jack," the others chorused.

I drove to Hollywood, and took Sonny with me. There was a pawnshop on the main drag whose owner was doing five years in the state pen for fencing stolen goods. Not long after his arrest, the owner's son had gone down for the same crime. A second son had taken over the business, and was cut from the same cloth. I went there first.

A bell rang as we entered. The shop was jammed with electronic equipment and wide-screen TVs. Electric guitars hung from the ceiling that looked like throwbacks to the Jimi Hendrix Experience. Behind a glass-topped counter filled with Rolex watches and glittering diamond rings sat son #2. His name was Burton, and he was eating a big wet sandwich wrapped in wax paper. His sleeveless shirt was unbuttoned to his naval, and was dotted with mustard and bits of cabbage.

"What can I do for you gents?" Burton asked.

"We're looking for some jewelry," I replied.

Burton spread his arms to indicate the assortment of items for sale. Sonny stuck his face to the glass in search of his father's dog tags. Burton couldn't watch us at the same time, and I turned around, and stared at the surveillance camera above the door.

"Something wrong?" Burton asked.

"Your surveillance camera is unplugged." I turned back around. "Learn that trick from your old man? Or did your brother teach you?"

Burton put his hand under the counter. "You want trouble? I'll give you trouble."

"Your father used to keep a Smith and Wesson back there. Ever have it cleaned?"

"That's none of your business."

I drew my Colt and aimed it at his chest. He quickly brought his hand up.

"Please don't shoot me," Burton said.

I put my Colt away. "A junkie came in here and pawned some jewelry he stole from my friends. By law, you're supposed to record all sales on a video camera. You get around the law by unplugging the camera whenever you want to fence something."

"You want the stuff back?" Burton asked.

"Yes. Then we can all go back to being friends."

Burton opened the store safe. From it, a black felt bag was produced, its contents poured on the counter. "That's all of it," he said.

I took out the napkin, and checked off the stolen items. Everything that had been stolen from the Sunset was accounted for, except Sonny's father's dog tags.

"Where are the dog tags?" I asked.

"I threw them out. They were garbage."

Sonny leapt over the counter and laid a punch on Burton's chin.

"I want my fucking tags," Sonny said.

Burton pulled himself off the floor and led us outside. Four garbage pails sat by the back door. Burton said, "I threw the tags into one of these pails."

Sonny kicked him in the ass and lifted him off the ground. "Find them."

Burton pulled off the lids and started looking. It took awhile, but he eventually found the tags stuffed inside a wad of receipts. He wiped the tags on his shirt, and gave them to Sonny, then tried to shake Sonny's hand to show there were no hard feelings. Sonny growled at him, and Burton lowered his arm.

"See you around," I said.

CHAPTER 39

I AWOKE the next morning feeling like I'd stepped back twenty years. My rented room above the Sunset looked like my old college dorm room. A few sickly pieces of furniture, and a mattress on the floor. Buster lay beside me, head resting on my chest.

I hit the beach and took my dog for a long run, followed by a hard twenty-minute swim. I was sucking down my second cup of java when my cell phone rang. Sonny moved down the bar, and I took the call.

"I thought we were having dinner last night," Burrell said, sounding pissed.

"I'm sorry. I had to help a friend recover some stolen goods."

"How many times did you hit the guy?"

"I didn't lay a hand on him, Your Honor."

"I've heard that line out of you before."

An elderly couple came into the bar and inquired about breakfast. Seven in the morning and they were both dressed like they were going to church. I was soaking wet from my swim, and saw them stare at me. I headed outside.

I stood in the building's cool shade. The tide was up,

the crash of waves as loud as a passing train. I lifted the phone to my face. "Sorry about that. How did your search for the file on Daybreak go?"

"Not good," Burrell said.

My spirits sagged. If I couldn't identify Lonnie and Mouse outside of their first names, I'd never find Sara. "What happened?"

"I went to the police stockade like you suggested. The Daybreak file was stored in a box from 1990. It's pretty thick—maybe a hundred pages long. I took it home, and read through it over cold Chinese."

I made a mental footnote to take Burrell out to dinner someday soon. Otherwise, she'd probably never speak a civil word to me again.

"What did the file say?" I asked.

"I couldn't read half of it. The pages were blacked out with Magic Marker. There was a memo in the front of the file that said the information had been censored from the file to protect the rights of the patients."

"Was there a roster of patients' names?"

"Yes. It had been blacked out as well. I took the page to the lab, and had a tech scan it with ultraviolet light. Unfortunately, the Magic Marker had wiped out the writing. The tech said it was hopeless."

I leaned against the building. *Hopeless.* It was a word that rarely slipped into my vocabulary, yet it was exactly how I felt right now.

"I scanned the pages that were legible into my computer, and e-mailed them to you," Burrell said. "Maybe there's a clue hidden somewhere in those pages."

"How many pages did you send?"

"All of them."

That had probably taken Burrell a few hours. I felt like a real heel.

"I'll go look at them right now," I said. "I'm sorry I didn't call you back last night. I owe you dinner."

"Yes, you do," Burrell said.

She was gone before I could say good-bye.

Dogs do not know failure, at least not any I'd been around. They treated each day like a new adventure, their spirits never wavering. This was especially true for Buster. He rode to my office with his tail wagging, ready for whatever challenges the day held. I wanted to share his enthusiasm, but it was hard. I was running out of road.

I parked by Tugboat Louie's front door. Thirty seconds later, I was in my office, booting up my computer. I went into e-mail, and opened Burrell's missive. The pages she'd sent to me were hard to read, but that didn't stop me. I was determined to read every line on every page, no matter how long it took.

Several hours later my cell phone rang. I had a splitting headache from staring at the computer screen, and I pulled myself away and looked at the face of my phone. It was Jessie, the light of my life. I turned away from the computer to speak with her.

"Hey honey, how's it going?" I answered.

"I'm okay. How are you? I hadn't talked to you in awhile, and wanted to see how things were going. Mom called me this morning, and I filled her in. I thought you were going to call her. You said you would."

Another broken promise. I'd left a trail of those recently. But the fact was, my job was the reason Rose and I were no longer together. Calling my wife when I was in the middle of a job would only exacerbate the problem, so I hadn't called. I said, "I know this is going to sound like a lie, but I haven't had a moment free."

"Are you still looking for Sara?" my daughter asked.

"Yes. It's consuming every minute of my day."

"Some kids are going around campus saying that if the police don't find a missing person within forty-eight hours, they almost never do. Is that true?"

"No, honey, it's not."

Jessie went silent. Normally, she had more words in her than a dictionary. I guessed the loss of her friend and teammate was starting to sink in.

"I want to help," my daughter finally said.

"What about your classes?"

"I'm done for the day."

I hesitated. I normally didn't get my family involved in cases, only Jessie had already helped me link Mouse and Lonnie to three other abductions.

"You're on," I said.

"Great. What do you want me to do?"

"There was a mental health facility in Broward called Daybreak that got shut down. I want you to go online, and see what information you can find about the place. I'm interested in finding a list of patient names."

"Are these the guys who kidnapped Sara?"

"Yes. Their first names are Lonnie and Mouse. If I can find out their last names, I can contact social security, and learn where they're originally from. It's a slim lead, but I need to have it run down."

"I'll get on it right away."

"Thanks. Please don't tell anyone about this, okay?"

"I won't tell a soul," my daughter said.

I spent the rest of the morning and a few hours into the afternoon pouring over the Daybreak file on my computer. The majority of what I read was medical mumbo jumbo that didn't have any bearing on my search. Whenever I did run across something that felt promising, I was met with the black line from a Magic Marker.

By the time I reached the last page, my brain was fried and I didn't know any more than when I'd started. I needed to take my frustration out on something, and chose the plastic garbage pail beside my desk. My kick sent it clear across the office, where it bounced off the wall and left an ugly bruise. I should have felt better, only I didn't.

My cell phone rang. It was Jessie. Perhaps my daughter had found the information that had so far eluded me, and I excitedly flipped open my phone.

"I hope your morning was more productive than mine," I said.

"I'm pulling my hair out," Jessie said. "I Googled Daybreak, and found over ten thousand places where it's referenced. I went to a few hundred of those places, and tried to find your information. Every time I thought I'd found what you were looking for, the site told me that the information had been deleted."

More bad news. Buster had retrieved the garbage pail and brought it back to me. I pulled open my desk drawer and tossed him a dog treat.

"I did find one thing that looked promising," she said.

I sat up straight in my chair. "What's that?"

"I found a website called browardoddities.com. It's got all sorts of crazy stuff about Broward County posted on it, including some information about Daybreak. I did another search, and discovered that a guy named Ray

Hinst runs the site. I searched his name, got his number, and called him. Hinst lives in Broward, and sounds like a decent guy. He told me that he worked as an orderly at Daybreak. He offered to give you a tour of the place, if you're interested."

"Hinst gives tours?"

"Yeah. He said a lot of thrill-seekers like to go into the buildings, but don't like to go alone. I guessed you'd want to hear what Hinst had to say, so I arranged a tour for you. Hinst agreed to meet you at Daybreak's front gates at three o'clock."

I checked the time. I was going to have to move fast if I was going to make it.

"This is really great," I said. "Thank you."

"Maybe I can be your assistant one day."

Jessie's words sent an icy finger down my spine. Nothing would have made me happier than to have my daughter working by my side. But not at this. I had seen too many bad things to want my only child to follow in these footsteps. Anything but this.

"We'll have to talk about that sometime," I said.

"Is that a promise?"

"Yes, it's a promise."

"Good-bye, Daddy."

CHAPTER 40

I GOT ONTO 595 and punched the gas. My Legend was old but the engine still had some kick. I pushed the speedometer up to seventy, and kept it there.

It occurred to me that I hadn't asked Jessie how much Ray Hinst was going to charge me for a tour of the Daybreak facility. Not that it really mattered; I would give him every bill in my wallet to hear what he had to say.

I weighed calling Rose. She deserved to hear what was going on, especially my two visits to the hospital. Those things mattered to her. But something told me that I shouldn't. We got along great when I wasn't working, but right now I was working. Better to wait until the case was done before we hooked up again.

Soon I was in the western part of the county. Fewer buildings, more farmland and pastures, lots of dirty pickup trucks on the road. It reminded me of growing up, which didn't seem so long ago.

Highway 27 appeared. I headed north on it. A mile up the road I spotted a dead possum on the side. My daddy used to think that roadkill was a sign of a healthy forest.

To me, it just meant that people drove too damn fast.

I found the entrance to Daybreak and turned. The road was unpaved, and my car lurched violently every few yards. Buster was leaning out the open passenger window, and I grabbed him by the collar to make sure he didn't fall out.

Reaching the entrance, I hit my brakes. The guardhouse was boarded up, and had "No Trespassing" signs plastered on its sides. I looked around but didn't see Hinst.

I drove into the facility. The buildings looked more ominous at ground level than they had from the chopper. Vandals had knocked out all the windows and spray-painted black graffiti on the walls. It gave the place a ghostly feel and made me understand why thrill-seekers would come here. I parked in the courtyard, leashed my dog, and got out.

"Are you Jack?" a gravelly voice asked.

I turned around. A man in his early sixties wearing battle camouflage and a safari hat had materialized behind me. Buster curled his upper lip and let out a menacing growl. Hinst was good. I hadn't heard him approach.

"That's me," I said. "This is my dog, Buster."

"I'm Ray. I'm not particularly fond of dogs. Your daughter said you were interested in a tour. My going rate is fifty bucks an hour, paid up front."

I gave Hinst a hundred-dollar bill, hoping it would soften him up. He stuffed the money into his pants pocket while giving me a hard look.

"Something wrong?" I asked.

"You don't look like the people that normally come out here, that's all."

"What do they look like?"

"Weirdos."

"I'm weird on the inside."

"Your daughter said you were interested in the place, but didn't elaborate."

Jessie hadn't told Hinst that I was working on a case, or that I was an ex-cop. That kind of information normally put people on the defensive. Better for Hinst to think that I was some local yokel looking to kill an afternoon. I smiled loosely.

"I always heard stories about this place, figured it was time to come out, and take a look." I took out my trusty pack of gum, and offered him a stick. Hinst's eyes told me that he wanted a piece, yet he shook his head. Still didn't trust me. "I mentioned it to my daughter, and she went online and found your website. You know how kids are."

"Don't have any kids. Where do you want to start?"

"Your call."

"Follow me. We'll go to Building A first. That was where they kept the real crazies. Keep your mutt on a short leash. I don't want him biting me in the ass."

We crossed the courtyard to Building A. Hinst walked with a slight hitch, and seemed to favor his left leg. It looked painful, yet didn't seem to slow him down.

Hinst entered the building, and I followed. We walked down a short hall, and passed a number of windowless cubicles. The ground floor was carpeted with flaking paint that blossomed from the walls and ceiling like rose petals. Hinst produced a flashlight, and pointed its beam at a stairwell in front of us. With Hansel-and-Gretel-like caution, someone had tied the end of a spool of purple yarn to the bannister. The thin purple line unspooled up the flight of stairs and into vast darkness on the next floor.

"Whoever used the yarn was probably coming in here for the first time," Hinst explained. "They didn't want to get lost. You don't want to get lost in here."

"No, sir," I said.

Hinst started up the stairs. "This place used to be a small city. Had its own power plant, fire station, hospital, movie theater, even its own bakery. World unto itself."

"How many patients?" I asked.

"At its heyday, about five thousand. This building held the bad ones."

"Bad in what way?" I asked.

Hinst squinted over his shoulder at me. "This building housed the criminally insane, the guys that were never getting let back into society. We had blood drinkers and cannibals and people that if you let out on the street, they'd kill every single person in sight until you hauled them back in. It was a horror show."

"Did you ever work in this building?"

"Yup. Got out of the Marines in '72 and took a job here working security. Stayed until they shut the place down."

We had reached the top of the stairs. Still talking, Hinst trailed off to my left and went down another hallway. I followed him, feeling my skin tingle. I had finally found someone who could answer my questions.

Hinst entered a room and shut off his flashlight. Sunlight streamed in from a dozen barred windows, revealing a massive kitchen with canopies of an exhaust fan system that stretched across the ceiling like the wings of a giant aluminum bird.

"This was where the grub was fixed," Hinst explained. "Next door was the dining room. It was sort of funny. When we brought the crazies in here and fed them, they calmed down, just like in the army."

Our next stop was the sleeping quarters. The room was large and low-ceilinged to the point of feeling claustrophobic. A number of metal beds had been piled up in the corners, their rusted box springs hanging out like innards.

"What about in here?" I said.

"Nothing happened here," Hinst grunted.

He started to leave. I sensed that he didn't enjoy being in this space. On the other side of the room was a wall covered with drawings done in black ink. The drawings were grotesque; in one, a man was swallowing a woman whole, with her feet dangling from his gaping mouth. In another, a zombie warrior held a sword dripping with blood in one hand, a decapitated head in the other. I crossed the room for a better look.

"That's just some shit somebody drew," Hinst said.

"An inmate?" I asked.

Hinst didn't reply, which only confirmed my suspicion. I got up close to the wall. The drawings were definitely the product of a sick mind.

"You gonna spend all day in here?" Hinst asked impatiently.

I ignored him and moved down the wall, soaking in every image. Drawings told you a lot about a person, and the emotions swirling inside of them. The artist responsible for these images had gone over to the dark side a long time ago.

At the end of the wall, I stopped. Staring back at me was a drawing of a giant. The giant held a man by the throat, and was squeezing him so hard that the man's eyeballs were exploding out of his skull. The giant looked like Lonnie.

I turned around to ask Hinst a question, and found him gone. I crossed the room and went into the hallway. Hinst was leaning against a wall, a cigarette dangling from his lips. He tried to light it with a paper match, only to drop the packet of matches to the floor.

Picking the matches up, I lit his cigarette.

"Thanks," he said, taking a deep drag.

I rested my hand on his arm. Hinst looked like he'd seen a ghost. Or worse, a roomful of ghosts. He lifted his eyes from the floor to look at me.

"Tell me what happened in there," I said.

CHAPTER 41

"Nothing," Hinst said.

I tightened my grip on his arm. "In the other room there's a drawing on the wall of a giant, and he's killing a man with his bare hands. That's Lonnie, isn't it?"

Hinst's head snapped. "You know about Lonnie?"

"Yes. I'm chasing him."

"Jesus Christ. I thought for sure someone would have killed him by now."

Hinst took another drag on his cigarette, went to the barred window at the hallway's end, stared out at the courtyard. "I used to think that I'd never stop having nightmares about Vietnam. Then I came to work here, and had new ones."

"How did Lonnie end up here?"

Hinst looked at me, saw something in my face that made him reach for his pack. He offered me one. I hadn't smoked in years, yet I took the cigarette anyway, and filled my lungs with smoke.

"Lonnie got sent here as a kid," Hinst said. "Mother and two sisters raised him. He was a giant, and he was also retarded. When he got a little older, he started to hump one of his sisters, so his mom made him live in the basement. I guess that changed him."

"Why do you say that?"

"Well, one day he came upstairs when his mother and sisters were eating dinner. Had a sledgehammer in his hand. He bludgeoned his mother and one of his sisters to death. The other sister got away and called the police. They arrested him, and sent him here. Lonnie was thirteen.

"I remember the day they brought Lonnie in. They wanted to put him in a juvenile detention center, only Lonnie was too big. He was six foot six inches tall, and weighed a hundred sixty pounds. Boy was nothing but skin and bones."

"He's plenty strong now. Why do you think that is?" I asked.

Hinst finished his cigarette and threw the butt into the courtyard. Lit up another and offered me the pack. Mine wasn't done, but I took a fresh one anyway.

"You know anything about giants?" Hinst asked.

I shook my head.

"They have something wrong with their pituitary gland, and can't stop producing growth hormones. Unless they get treated by a doctor, they'll keep on growing until they die. But here's the strange thing. They're not very strong. They're so big, their bones have a hard time supporting their muscle mass. As a result, they cramp a lot. Something to do with all the sodium in their bodies."

"So what happened to Lonnie?"

"The doctors fucked with him. They did a procedure that stopped his pituitary gland from producing hormones. By then, Lonnie was six-ten and still skinny as a rail. The doctors decided to beef him up."

"How? By feeding him?"

Hinst shook his head. The expression on his face was pained. My mind flashed back to the bloody cotton ball and plastic syringe I'd found in Lonnie's motel room.

"Don't tell me they gave him steroids."

"That's exactly what they did. And boy, did he get strong. Put on a hundred twenty pounds of muscle in a few months. I used to go into that room and see him doing push-ups for a half-hour straight. He was a monster."

"Weren't people afraid of him?"

"Sure they were afraid. But the folks running this place didn't care. Lonnie was an experiment to them, not a person. They didn't care about him at all."

"When did Mouse enter the picture?"

"You know about Mouse?"

"He and Lonnie are still together."

Hinst swallowed hard. Again he shook his head. "Mouse was a criminal. Can't say I ever heard his real name. He convinced a judge he was crazy, so he got sent here. But he was crazy like a fox. He used Lonnie. They were a team. Even the guards were scared of them."

"Do you know this area well?"

Hinst nodded. "Sure. I grew up around here."

"There's an abandoned farm a few miles north of here. Lonnie and Mouse hid there with a nurse they abducted from this facility. A woman named Kathi Bolger."

I thought Hinst was going to hit the floor.

"You mean Kat Bolger? Oh, my God. She used to take care of Lonnie."

"I need for you to tell me about her."

Hinst ground the tiny butt of his cigarette into the floor, and made a *Follow me* motion with his hand. Together we walked down the hall to the sleeping quarters.

"This was the last place I saw Kat Bolger," Hinst said, standing in the room's center. "Right in this very spot. She was helping push a patient on a gurney."

"When was this?"

"It was the last day, right before Daybreak was shut down. The state medical examiner had made a surprise visit, and saw all the shit the doctors were pulling. You know, doing experiments on patients without their permission. Like with Lonnie."

"So Lonnie wasn't the only one they messed with."

"No. It was widespread. Later the state went and blacked out all the records, just so no one would find out what the doctors were doing."

"What happened the day Daybreak was closed?"

"The place was a madhouse, and that's no joke. The patients were screaming and refusing to leave. This was home for most of them, and they didn't know where they were being sent to. Bad thing to do to a crazy person."

"You said Nurse Bolger was pushing a gurney."

"That's right. There was an orderly with her. A buddy of mine named Grady. Grady and Bolger were pushing a patient out of the ward."

"Who?"

Hinst gave it some thought. "Oh, shit. It was Lonnie.

Lonnie got sick, and passed out. Grady was sent up to help Bolger move him out."

"You're sure this happened on Daybreak's last day?"

"Yeah. People were flying around everywhere."

And in all the confusion, Mouse and Lonnie grabbed Bolger and escaped.

"I need to find Mouse and Lonnie," I said. "Do you remember their last names?"

Hinst scratched his chin. "Let me think. Lonnie's began with an R. I think it was Polish. I never heard Mouse's last name."

"You've got to try. It's important."

Hinst shut his eyes and attempted to dredge up their names from his memory. After a moment his eyes opened, and he shook his head.

"I'm sorry, mister," Hinst said.

My spirits sagged. Another dead end.

We started to leave. Walking out, Buster's nose twitched. He'd picked up a scent. I let him lead me across the room to a closet. He scratched at the door, and I tested the knob. It was locked.

"What's in the closet?" I asked.

"It was used for storage. Why?"

"My dog thinks there's something in there."

"We shouldn't be messing around in here."

"I'm going to see what's inside."

"Well, I guess I can't stop you."

I got a tire iron from the trunk of my car, and used it to pry open the door. Inside the closet were rusted bed frames and a steel drum spray-painted with the word *Daybreak*. Hinst helped me roll the drum out into the center of the room, and I popped the lid with the crowbar. The smell nearly knocked me off my feet.

"What the hell is that odor?" Hinst said.

I looked inside the drum. Lying on the bottom was a corpse dressed in a green orderly's uniform. The corpse's body was broken in several places, and had been folded together like a bunch of sticks. The name tag above his pocket said Grady.

CHAPTER 42

I HAVE SEEN the dead more times than is healthy. One thing I've learned from the experience: The dead don't talk, but they do scream.

Hinst and I sat on a concrete bench in the cool shade of the courtyard. Hinst smoked cigarettes until his pack was gone. Looking at his profile, I could tell that finding Grady's body inside the drum would haunt him for a long time.

I had a general idea of what had happened the day Daybreak shut down. Lonnie had played sick. Bolger and an orderly tried to move him. Lonnie killed the orderly, and held Bolger against her will. Mouse put on a stolen orderly's uniform. Then they forced Bolger to come with them, took her car and escaped, never to be seen again.

"His name was Grady York," Hinst said after awhile. "We used to go out for beers. He'd been over in 'Nam, too. I talked to him the morning the place was shutting down. He agreed to meet me after work for a cold one. When he didn't show, I figured he'd just blown me off. You know how it is."

"Sure," I said.

Hinst scratched Buster's head. My dog had parked himself at Hinst's feet, and was leaning against his leg, like he knew how much Hinst was suffering and wanted to comfort him.

"I need to find Lonnie and Mouse," I said. "Is there anything else that you remember about them? Anything at all?"

Hinst gave it some thought. I listened to the wind whistle through the empty buildings. It didn't sound like any wind I'd ever heard before.

"Come to mention it, yeah," Hinst said. "Mouse used to bum smokes off the guards. We talked a few times. I think he knew that I knew he wasn't crazy. He kind of got off on that, you know?"

"Like you were a co-conspirator," I said.

"Yeah. Mouse told me something once that stuck in my head. He said that if he ever got out of Daybreak, he was going back home. I said something like, 'Why go home? The police will just arrest you.' And Mouse smiled and said, 'The police don't arrest people where I'm from.' That always struck me as odd, you know?"

"Did he mention the name of the town?"

"No. But he was definitely from Florida."

"How do you know that?"

"Mouse called himself a cracker. Only Floridians do that."

"I need to call the police. They're going to ask you a lot of questions."

Hinst blew the smoke out his lungs. He dipped his head, and started to weep. It was an anguished sound, filled with the remorse that comes from wishing you'd acted differently than you had. Finally, it subsided, and he rubbed his face with his sleeve.

"Grady was my buddy," he whispered.

"I know he was," I said.

A cruiser showed up, and the uniform took our statements. Officer Riski again. Riski cracked a joke, and said that wherever I went a dead body usually followed. Riski was trying to be funny, only there was nothing funny about finding a dead man stuffed into a drum.

I sat in my car and tried to shake the images from my head. A couple of songs on the radio didn't help. Nor the AC blasting in my face. Buster lay on the passenger seat, and I pulled his head into my lap, and buried my face in the soft fur of his neck.

After a while I started to feel better. Not a lot, but enough to chase away the dark clouds circling around me. Deciding to take advantage of my weakened state, Buster rolled over on his back. I obliged him with a tummy rub.

My cell phone beeped. I went into voice mail and retrieved the message. It was from Tony Valentine, the casino consultant whom I'd helped nab the gang of cheaters at the Hard Rock. Valentine had sent a text message along with an attachment. I read the message first. It said, "Is this the guy you're looking for?"

Valentine had impressed me as a smart guy, and not someone who'd waste my time. I opened the attachment. It was a mug shot of a white male with sandy brown hair and a loopy grin on his face. The photo wasn't great, and I brought the phone a few inches from my face, staring for what felt like an eternity, but was probably only a few seconds.

Mouse.

I got so excited, I hit the horn with my fist. Across the

courtyard, Officer Riski jumped a few inches in the air. I rolled down my window.

"Sorry. My mistake."

Riski shot me a dirty look and resumed questioning Hinst, who still sat on the concrete bench. I rolled the window back up, and called Valentine.

"Grift Sense," Valentine answered.

"This is Jack Carpenter. You got him."

"Good. I owed you one."

"Tell me how you found him."

"All it took was a phone call to Chief Black Cloud at the Hard Rock. The Native American casinos keep a national database of people who cause trouble in their casinos. They call the database American Eagle. Most of the people on it are card counters and cheaters, but there's also plenty of scum.

"Something told me this guy you were chasing had done this before. So I asked Chief Black Cloud if he'd take the guy's photo off the Hard Rock's surveillance tape, and run it through the American Eagle database."

"And a match came up."

"You bet. His name is Andrew Lee Carr, nicknamed Mouse. He got backroomed at the Hard Rock's Tampa casino three years ago. A coed from the University of South Florida claimed Mouse was following her around the casino, and trying to film her. Security pulled him off the floor and questioned him. Carr claimed the girl had flirted with him, and that he hadn't broken any laws. They eventually let him go."

"The casino didn't call the police?"

"Unfortunately not. I also ran a background check on Carr. He was arrested in 1985 for robbing two convenience stores in central Florida and shooting the cashiers at point-blank range in the face. One of the cashiers died. Carr was eventually caught, and charged with first-degree manslaughter. His defense attorney convinced the judge that he was insane. He helped his cause by smearing his own feces on the defense table during the jury selection at his trial."

"That's a new one," I said.

"Tell me about it. The judge sent him to a mental institution called Daybreak. I tried to get some information on the place, but there was nothing out there."

I leaned back in my seat and took a deep breath. My wife was fond of saying that everything in this world happened for a reason. There had been a reason why I'd met Tony Valentine, and now I knew what it was.

"You just made my day," I said. "Let me ask you something. Did the report mention Mouse's hometown?"

"Hold on, let me take a look."

Valentine put me on hold. I rolled down my windows, and let the hot air invade my car. Every tired bone in my body felt refreshed. I'd found the bastard.

Valentine came back on the line. "Your friend is from a small Florida town called Chatham. I just looked it up on my computer. Chatham is about ten miles north of St. John's River, in the central part of the state."

Mouse had boasted to Ray Hinst that the police in his hometown wouldn't arrest him. What better place for Mouse and Lonnie to hide than Chatham?

PART 4

NUB CITY

CHAPTER 43

I LEFT DAYBREAK feeling better than I had in a long time. I knew the name of one of Sara Long's abductors as well as the name of the town he and his partner were hiding in. Mouse and Lonnie were in my sights.

But rescuing abduction victims was never easy. And there was the matter of dealing with the sheriff of Chatham. Before I went charging in with guns blazing, I needed to figure out what his deal was.

It took an hour to reach my office. During the drive, my cell phone rang several times. I kept my phone on a Velcro strip attached to my dash, letting me see who was calling without taking my hands off the wheel. Burrell was trying to track me down.

I thought I knew what Candy wanted. She'd caught wind that I'd unearthed another corpse and wanted to know how it fit into my search for Sara Long. Being the lead investigator on Sara's case, Burrell had a right to know *everything* I knew. Not telling her what I'd learned was against the law and could land me in real trouble. Only right now, the last person I wanted to be talking to was a cop.

I didn't take her call.

Tugboat Louie's parking lot was jammed, and I parked on the road. Kumar was checking IDs at the front door when I entered. Inside the bar, wild women were dancing on tables while drunk men stood and cheered. Party time had begun.

"A police detective has been calling for you," Kumar said.

"Detective Burrell," I said.

"Yes. She asked me to give you a message."

"Just pretend you didn't see me come in," I said.

Kumar's eyebrows went up in alarm.

"I hope you're not in trouble," he said.

Back when I was a detective, I'd learned that you weren't doing your job right if you weren't causing trouble. The trick was learning how to deal with it.

"Don't worry about it," I said.

Kumar covered his eyes with his hands. "Very well. You were never here."

I went upstairs to my office. The commotion from the bar was so loud that my office furniture was vibrating. I sat at my desk and tried to block out the noise.

I booted up my computer and logged onto the Internet. It was hard to remember what detective work was like before high-speed computers. A great deal of time had been spent on the phone, trying to track down leads and information. Now most of what I needed was a few clicks away.

On Google, I did a search of Chatham. I was not familiar with the town where Mouse was from, but that didn't mean much. There were thousands of small towns in Florida, many not big enough to be included on a map.

Chatham didn't warrant a lot of ink. Fifteen miles north of the Ocala National Forest, the town did not have a website, nor was it included in the website of any of the neighboring towns. Outside of a few cheap motels that catered to hunters and fishermen, there was no real information about the place. In the infinite world of cyberspace, Chatham hardly existed.

I did a public records search of Chatham on a county website, and got a better feel for the place. The town was incorporated, and boasted eight hundred residents. There was a mayor, a town clerk, and a sheriff, all of whom were elected officials.

The sheriff was the person I was most interested in. His name was Homer Morcroft. I did a search of his name, and discovered a newspaper article from 1984 that talked about Morcroft having just been elected sheriff. He'd been policing the town for twenty-five years.

A knock on my door broke my concentration.

"We're all friends here," I said.

Kumar popped his head in. "The lady detective just called the bar, and asked the bartender to page you. He told her he thought he saw you come in."

I cursed under my breath. I knew what was going to happen next. Burrell was on her way here, and would confront me. I shut down my computer, and rose from my desk.

"Thanks for the warning," I said.

I got in my car, and fled south on I-95.

I knew what Burrell would do when she didn't find me at Louie's. She'd drive to the Sunset and look there. When that failed, she'd drive to my other haunts and look. We'd worked together eight years, and Burrell knew the places I frequented. The only way to avoid her was to not be at any of them.

It was time to bring Linderman into the fold. I called his office, and when he didn't answer, tried his cell phone. He didn't pick up, so I called his house.

"Hello, Jack," Linderman answered.

"I hope I'm not catching you at a bad time," I said, figuring I had.

"I was just heading out the door with Muriel. We were going to have dinner at our favorite restaurant on the Key. It's our anniversary."

"How many years?"

"Twenty-five."

"Congratulations. I'm sorry to bother you, but I need your help."

"I'm listening."

"I've determined the identity of Sara Long's abductors. The giant is a mentally disturbed killer named Lonnie. His partner is a murderer named Andrew Lee Carr. They're hiding in a small town in central Florida called Chatham. I need you to help me catch them."

There was a short pause. I could envision his wife, Muriel, standing in the foyer of their condo on Key Biscayne, all dressed up and ready to go out.

"Did you contact the police?" Linderman finally asked.

"No."

"Why not?"

"It's complicated. I'll explain everything when I see you."

Linderman breathed heavily into the phone. I had given up many weekends to help him look for his daughter.

I'd never complained, and didn't expect for him to, either.

"How long will it take for you to get here?" the FBI agent asked.

"Forty minutes, tops."

"I'll tell the guard at the front gate that you're coming."

"Thanks. Tell Muriel I'm sorry."

"I'm sure she'll understand," Linderman said.

Muriel Linderman had her brave face on when I entered the condo. She was a tiny woman, barely five feet tall, with expressive eyes and a tender smile. Before her daughter's abduction, she had taught elementary school in Virginia, where she'd lived most of her life. When she spoke, I still heard the accent in her voice.

Muriel gave me a hug, and invited me to join them in eating Domino's pizza on the balcony. I wanted to apologize for the intrusion, and for ruining their anniversary dinner, but the knowing look in her eyes told me it wasn't necessary.

Their condo was on the south side of Key Biscayne, the view of the glittering bay filled with yachts nothing short of spectacular. I ate a couple slices of pizza without saying very much. Linderman sat beside me, sipping an iced tea. His eyes never left my face.

"Tell me why you haven't called the police," he said.

"Because it might lead to Sara Long getting killed."

"I think I hear the phone," Muriel said.

Muriel went inside, and shut the slider behind her. I chugged back the last of my Heineken, and put the bottle down next to my plate. "If I call the police, they'll contact Sheriff Morcroft in Chatham. I'm guessing

Sheriff Morcroft knows what's going on, and will alert Mouse and Lonnie."

Linderman shot me a contemptuous stare. He did things by the book, and did not tolerate wild theories. "Let me get this straight. You think Chatham's sheriff knows he has two ex–mental patients in his town who are abducting young women?"

"That's right."

"Do you have any proof that the sheriff's involved?"

My chair made a harsh scraping sound as I pushed myself away from the table. "No, I don't. But here's my problem. If I contact the police, and tell them what I know, the information will be in the police information system. You know the cops in Florida all talk to each other, even those in small towns. It will get back to Sheriff Morcroft that he's under suspicion. If he is involved, I'll be signing Sara Long's death certificate."

Linderman considered what I was saying. I rose from my chair.

"So now what?" Linderman asked.

"I'm going to rescue Sara Long. Are you coming or not?"

Linderman's eyes flashed. He put down his drink and gave me a harsh stare.

"You're a goddamn loose cannon," he said.

"Funny, that didn't bother you before."

The look on his face made me wonder if I'd lost another friend. At that moment, I didn't care. I was going to handle this my way.

"All right, Jack. Just give me a minute."

Linderman opened the slider and went inside. Muriel was standing at the sink in the kitchen washing dishes. Linderman put his arms around his wife's waist and whispered in her ear. Her knees sagged at the news of his leaving.

I felt bad for her, and for him—only there was nothing I could do about it. I had a job to do, and that job wasn't finished. They could celebrate later, when Sara was safe.

I turned and stared at the bay. The moon had cast a creamy patina over the water's mirrorlike surface. It was a beautiful night, whatever the hell that meant.

CHAPTER 44

LINDERMAN wanted to take his 4Runner to Chatham. I objected. Although his car was in better shape than my Legend, it still had Virginia license plates, and would stand out like a sore thumb when we reached our destination.

"Can your car make the drive?" Linderman asked.

"It hasn't failed me yet," I said.

I pulled my Legend into the condo's covered parking garage, and parked it beside his 4Runner. Linderman opened the 4Runner's trunk, and unlocked the stainless-steel footlocker in the backseat. From the footlocker he removed two Mossberg shotguns, two high-powered rifles with sniper scopes, a pair of Kevlar vests, and several boxes of ammunition, all of which got loaded into the trunk of my Legend.

"That should cover it," Linderman said.

"We also need a pair of fishing poles."

Linderman went inside the building to talk to one of his neighbors. He emerged with a pair of fishing poles covered with cobwebs.

"This was the best I could do," he explained.

I put the poles in the backseat of my Legend so they

stuck out the open window. It made us look like a pair of rubes, which was exactly the image I wanted to create.

"Are these fishing poles our cover?" Linderman asked.

"Yes," I said. "When we get to Chatham, we're going to pretend we're a pair of college buddies spending a long weekend together fishing and drinking beer."

"I don't know anything about fishing."

"Then I guess you'll be buying the beer."

I drove across Biscayne Bay, and headed north on the elevated stretch of I-95 through downtown Miami. Traffic had thinned out, and I stared at the towering office buildings that defined the Miami skyline.

The interstate split at the Broward County line. I went left, and entered the tollbooth that would put us on the Florida Turnpike. Linderman turned in his seat to face me.

"Tell me why you think the sheriff of Chatham is involved in these women's abductions," Linderman said.

The turnpike was quiet, and I flipped on my car's cruise control.

"Because it solves the puzzle of how Lonnie and Mouse have been abducting young women—and keeping them—without anyone knowing about it," I said.

"How does it solve it?"

"I have a theory about serial killers and serial abductors. Despite what people want to believe, these people don't work in a vacuum. Their friends and neighbors know they're doing *something* wrong, but choose not to get involved. I call it the 'He was such a quiet man' theory, because that's what people usually say when a reporter tells them their next-door neighbor has a basement filled with rotting corpses."

"Why would the sheriff of Chatham be looking the other way?"

"That's a good question. Mouse boasted to a worker at the mental institution where he was living that if he ever escaped, he'd go back home, because the sheriff wouldn't arrest him. I'm guessing the sheriff is doing something illegal and that Mouse knows about it. That's Mouse's insurance against the sheriff arresting him and Lonnie."

Linderman seemed comfortable with my theory and leaned back in his seat. From the pocket of his windbreaker he removed a small package wrapped in aluminum foil. He opened the package and passed me several oatmeal cookies.

"Muriel make these?" I asked.

He nodded while he chewed. I bit into one and tasted raisins. Buster popped his head between the seats, not to be left out. Soon the cookies were a memory.

"What do you think the sheriff is doing?" Linderman asked.

"He might be running a prostitution ring, or selling moonshine. Or he's holding dog fights on weekends. Or it could be worse."

"Drug trafficking?"

"That's a possibility. In the old days, drug traffickers brought their shipments in by boat, but the DEA got wise to them. The traffickers switched to small airplanes, and started landing in towns in remote parts of the state."

"So he could be involved with one of the cartels?"

"It's a possibility."

"If that's the case, there are probably other people in Chatham who are involved," Linderman said. "We could be stepping into a hornet's nest."

I stared at the empty interstate. I had been so focused on rescuing Sara that I hadn't considered all the risks. Linderman took out his cell phone and fiddled with the keypad in the dark.

"Who are you calling?" I asked.

"The director of the Jacksonville office of the FBI," Linderman said. "I'm sure he'd be happy to send some agents over to Chatham to back us up, if we need them."

I found myself nodding. I had been in tight spots with Linderman before, and had even seen him kill a man. Linderman wasn't afraid of danger, or putting himself in harm's way. Like me, he didn't believe in backing down.

I'd chosen the right person to bring along.

CHAPTER 45

THE TOWN of Chatham was pitch dark when we arrived on its narrow streets. Like many small towns in Florida, it had seen better days. The main street was lined with potholes, and many of the storefronts needed a face-lift. The info on the web had said there were several cheap motels, but I couldn't find any of them.

I drove back to the highway, and found a place to stay. It was called The Florida Inn, and was built to resemble a log cabin. A light shone inside the manager's office.

My car's tires crunched the pebble driveway. Linderman put down his pencil and looked up from his notebook. He carried the notebook with him whenever he went on a trip. It was small and black, and had a pencil stuck in the spiral binding. I didn't know if it was for work, or if he kept a journal. I didn't think it was my place to ask.

I took Buster for a quick walk around the grounds. Only two cars were parked in front of the rental units. I put my dog back in the car and went inside.

The night manager was watching TV behind the counter. He sprang out of his swivel chair, his watery eyes filled with suspicion. He wore his hair long, and had a metal hook sticking out of the sleeve of his shirt that made him look like a pirate.

"Didn't hear you come in. Can I help ya?" the manager asked.

"I need a room. My buddy and I have been driving all night," I said.

He flipped open the register. "Where you from?"

"I'm from Fort Lauderdale. My buddy's from Miami."

"You don't say. What brings you to Chatham?"

"We heard the fishing's good up here."

"Depends who you ask. Some people think it's better in the next county."

It was the worst damn sales pitch I'd ever heard. I said, "We'll have to check it out tomorrow, and see where they're biting. You have any rooms?"

"Yeah, we got rooms. But we don't take dogs."

I looked at his chair behind the counter. There was no way he could have seen me walking Buster from his vantage point. Which meant he'd been watching me from the window, then slipped back into his chair when he'd realized I was coming inside.

"My dog isn't staying in the room," I said.

"Then where's he gonna stay?" the manager asked.

"In my car."

"I don't know about that."

I took out my wallet, and let him see the cash I was carrying. Money had a way of solving most problems, and I saw his resolve slip away.

"Well, I guess it will be all right." His finger ran down the open register, then stopped. "You can stay in Room Twelve. Two double beds, hot shower. Cable

TV is extra. Fifty bucks a night. No smoking. Pay up front."

I counted the money for two nights onto the counter. The manager held each bill up to the light to make sure it wasn't counterfeit. Satisfied, he put the money into the register, then gave me the key.

"Don't want no trouble out of you and your friend," the manager said.

"No, sir."

"No getting drunk and busting up the furniture."

"Of course not."

"Or bringing in girls from the strip clubs and having sleepovers."

"Wouldn't dream of it."

"Don't get smart with me, boy, or I'll toss you out of here."

It had been a long time since someone had called me boy. I shut my mouth and backed away from the counter. The manager slipped back into his chair, and resumed watching TV. People called Florida the Sunshine State because of the great weather and friendly people. The manager wasn't going to be a goodwill ambassador for us anytime soon.

I found Linderman where I'd left him, Buster in his lap. The dog eyed me and slipped into the back. I started the Legend and drove down the line of rooms until my headlights were resting on the door to #12. It looked small and depressing.

"You were in there awhile," Linderman said.

I killed the engine. "It was quite the welcome wagon. The manager asked me more questions than my first job interview. He wasn't friendly."

"Think he was checking you out?"

"I sure do. He was way too suspicious."

"Did you give him a credit card?"

"I paid in cash."

"Good. He can't put a trace on your card, and do a background check. Of course he could have a check done on your car's license plates."

"The car's in my wife's name."

"So our cover is still intact."

"So far."

I lowered my windows and got out. Buster tried to join me, and I made him lie down in the backseat. He curled up into a ball but didn't shut his eyes. I retrieved our bags from the trunk while looking over my shoulder at the front office. I spotted the surly manager standing by the window, spying on us.

"We're being watched," I said.

"Think he treats all his customers this way?" Linderman asked.

"It bothered him that we were out-of-towners."

"Who else is going to stay here?"

I unlocked the door to #12 and switched on the lights. I'd never been in the army, but the room reminded me of what a barracks might look like, with a pair of lumpy beds, a scuffed dresser with a washbowl, and walls painted a sickly green. The promise of a television set was nowhere to be found. I decided not to complain.

Linderman used the bathroom first. His flush of the toilet sent a thunderous roar through the paper-thin walls. I went next. When I came out, he was gone.

I found him outside, kneeling on the ground beside the car.

"Lose something?" I asked.

"Yes. I can't find my journal. I had it a few minutes ago."

There was a hint of desperation in his voice. I got on the ground and helped him look. The journal was hidden beneath the car. Linderman wiped it clean on his shirt, then checked the pages to make sure none were torn. Satisfied, he went back inside.

I got to my feet, and saw Buster sitting behind the wheel. His ears were sticking up, and he looked mad as hell at being left behind. I ignored my best friend, and went inside.

I lay on one of the beds in my clothes. I was dead tired, and needed to catch a few hours sleep if I was going to be sharp tomorrow. Linderman stripped down to his boxers, got into the other bed, and killed the lights. For a long moment neither of us spoke.

"I've had that journal for five years," he said when I thought he was asleep.

I rolled onto my side to face him. "What do you write in it?"

"I write things that I want to tell my daughter."

There was pain in his voice. My eyes had adjusted to the darkness, and I saw him lying on his back, staring at the ceiling.

"I have a special relationship with Danielle," he went on. "When she was in first grade, she fell off the jungle gym on the playground and broke her arm. I was at work, and felt this sudden jolt of anxiety. I called Muriel, who called the school, and was told Danny had gotten hurt."

"You're on the same wavelength," I said.

"That's it. Is it that way with your daughter?"

"Sometimes."

"After Danny disappeared, I had a hard time adjusting. Even though she was gone, something in my psyche told me that she was still alive. I know this sounds crazy, but I could still feel her emotions, like that day on the playground."

"Is that why you keep the journal?"

"Yes. I write down all the things that I think Danny would want to know about. Like friends from high school who've gotten married, and relatives who've passed away. I want to make it easier for her when she comes back."

Over the years, the parents of missing children had told me the special things they'd done for their kids in their absence. I'd always assumed it was a way of coping.

"Sometimes, I feel like I'm flogging myself," he said.

"You have to follow your heart."

"Not your conscience?"

"No, your heart. It will always tell you the right thing to do."

"Is that what guides you?"

"Yes."

I heard a scratching sound on the door. Linderman heard it, too.

"I wonder who that is," he said.

I rolled out of bed. Out of habit, I grabbed my Colt off the dresser, then threw open the door. Buster lay on the stoop, his tail thumping the ground. I glanced at the manager's office. The light was off, and I let Buster in.

CHAPTER 46

I AWOKE at dawn to the sound of rolling thunder.

I threw off the covers and went outside. The clouds had darkened and it was raining hard. My car's windows were down, and I climbed in, and rolled them up. Then I dried the seats. My Legend had been good to me, and I was going to return the favor.

Back inside the motel room, I found Linderman clothed and brushing his teeth. He was the model of efficiency; his bed was already made, his dirty clothes put away. The only thing that looked out of place was the salt-and-pepper stubble dotting his chin.

"Since we're telling everybody this is a fishing trip, I figured I shouldn't shave," Linderman said. "How's the weather?"

"Crummy. It's pouring rain."

"You're going to have to educate me. Do guys go fishing in the rain?"

"Guys go fishing if the beer is cold," I replied.

"Is that a hint?"

"Only if you're still buying."

We soon hit the road. My first stop was a convenience store a few miles down the highway from our motel. I bought two coffees and a twelve-pack of cold Budweiser. The clerk gave me a harsh look as he rang up my items.

"You new around here?" the clerk asked.

"Visiting from Fort Lauderdale," I said. "My buddy and I are looking to do a little fishing. Any places you'd recommend?"

"Best fishing is in the next county," the clerk said.

Another born salesman. I thanked him and left with my items. Outside it was coming down hard. I got into my Legend, and gave Linderman the coffee, then put the twelve-pack on the backseat. Firing up my engine, I aimed my car toward town.

"What's next?" Linderman asked.

"We need to buy some bait," I said. "Shiners or minnows would be best."

"Where do we go?"

"Normally, we'd go to a feed store, but I'm going to play stupid and visit a couple of different stores in town," I said. "I've got a nasty feeling about this place."

"Besides the sheriff being corrupt?"

We came to a four-way stop. Mine was the only vehicle on the road, and I threw my car into park and pulled the lid off my coffee. "So far, I've spoken to two residents, and both have tried to persuade me to leave."

Linderman sipped his coffee and grimaced. "That could be a coincidence."

I blew the steam off my drink and took a sip. It tasted like engine oil. I rolled down my window, and poured it out.

"I don't believe in those," I said.

Chatham was nothing to write home about. Main Street was a row of flat-roofed buildings with faded brick facades and dirty storefronts. Pickup trucks and old rusted cars were the vehicles of choice. The rain had pushed everyone inside, and I crawled past the buildings looking for a place to park.

"Not much in the way of parking," Linderman said.

"Like I said, it's a real friendly place."

I drove down a side street and found a metered parking lot. I parked in a spot, and dug in my pockets for some change. Linderman produced a quarter.

"My treat," he said.

He got out, and fed the coin into the meter. I saw him pull the rest of the change from his pocket, and start feeding in more coins.

"Damn meter only gives twelve minutes for a quarter," Linderman said as we headed toward town. "Even Washington, D.C. isn't that bad."

We turned the corner with the rain blowing in our faces. Main Street was quiet, and I spied movement in a storefront window a block away. The fleeting image of a man's face. It was gone as quickly as it appeared.

"We're being watched," I said.

"Think your car is safe?" Linderman asked.

I glanced down the street at my Legend. The notion that someone might break into the trunk and steal Linderman's guns felt very real to me.

"Not really," I said.

Linderman took Buster's leash from my hand. "Why don't you go do some snooping? I'll stay here, and make sure no one breaks into your car."

"Sounds like a plan. If you need me, just make Buster bark."

"How do I do that?"

"Nudge him with your toe."

I headed down Main Street. The sidewalks were cracked and uneven, with pools of water everywhere I stepped. I came to a pharmacy and ducked beneath the striped awning. I looked up and down the block, then went inside.

The pharmacy was empty. Along the back wall was an old-fashioned ice-cream counter with a hand churn and a penny lick. It was the first thing I'd seen in Chatham that felt friendly. Behind the counter stood a coarse-featured woman wearing blue jeans and an oversized man's denim work shirt. Her eyes held mine suspiciously.

I can be as charming as the next guy. I flashed her my best smile.

"Good morning."

"Can I help you?" she asked.

"My buddy and I want to do some fishing," I replied, sticking with my script. "I was wondering if you could recommend a place to buy bait."

"Try Reggie's Bait and Tackle," she suggested.

"Is that in town?"

"No. I can show you where it is on a map."

"I'd really appreciate it."

She moved down the counter and fetched a map that was stuck between the wall and the cash register. She walked with a pronounced limp, and used her hands to stop herself from falling. I got up close to the counter, and pressed my belly to the edge. Looking down, I saw that her right foot was missing from the ankle down.

"Aw, hell, this is the wrong map," she said. "Hold on a minute."

She grabbed a cane and pushed open a swinging door to a back room. A towheaded little girl darted out, holding an ice-cream cone.

"Mind your own business, Macey," the woman said.

"Yes, Momma," the little girl said.

The woman limped into the back of the store. Macey took her mother's place behind the counter, the top of her head barely reaching the Formica. Her face was smeared with chocolate ice cream. I'd learned more as a cop talking to kids than I had from anyone else. I pulled a paper napkin out of a dispenser, and handed it to her.

"You've got ice cream on your face," I said.

Macey wiped away the ice cream while licking her cone at the same time.

"How old are you?" I asked.

"I'm not supposed to talk to strangers," she said.

"I'm a nice stranger."

"Momma will spank me if she catches me talking to you. Momma doesn't want me talking to nobody. Says people can't be trusted."

"Some people can be trusted."

Macey eyed me warily. I pulled out my wallet, and removed a crisp five dollar bill. Placed it on the counter, and drew my hand away. Macey glanced back at the room where her mother had gone, then stuffed the bill into the pocket of her dress.

"I'm looking for a couple of friends of mine," I said. "One of them is named Lonnie. The other is named Mouse. They live in Chatham."

Macey shook her head. She didn't have a clue as to what I was talking about.

"Lonnie is a giant," I said.

The little girl's eyes went wide, and she stopped eating her cone.

"Do you know him?"

"Uh-huh."

"I need to find my friend Lonnie. Do you know where he lives?"

"In the woods." Macey was quiet a moment, as if weighing her words. "The kids in school say that if you're bad, the giant will climb through your bedroom window at night and eat you."

"Have you ever seen him?"

"Once. I got lost and ended up where he lived. He was scary."

I heard banging from the back room. I didn't want Macey getting paddled, and I turned my back, and pretended to be looking through a rack of outdated hunting magazines. Her mother limped through the swinging door.

"Found it. Macey, you run along now."

Macey gave me a look that said please don't tell. I smiled and watched her leave. Her mother slapped a map onto the counter and pointed.

"This here's Reggie's Bait and Tackle. I can give you directions, if you like."

I looked at the map. The place where the woman was recommending that I purchase my fishing bait was in the next county.

"Isn't there anything closer?" I asked.

"Afraid not."

The woman crossed her arms in front of her chest. Her body language was anything but friendly. Outside, I heard Buster barking. I thanked her, and hurried to the door.

CHAPTER 47

I LEFT the pharmacy and ran down the street. Linderman and my dog were nowhere in sight. Turning the corner, I saw the FBI agent standing in the metered parking lot, checking out my car. Buster was not with him.

I get nervous when I lose sight of my dog. My legs picked up speed, and did not stop running until I was standing beside Linderman.

"What happened?"

"Buster saw a guy trying to jimmy the door of your car, and took off after him," Linderman explained. "The leash flew out of my hand."

I could have been angry with Linderman, only Buster had done the same to me many times. "Where'd he go?"

He pointed at the stand of pine trees adjacent to the parking lot. The trees were so thick that I couldn't see through them. Cupping my hands over my mouth, I let out a yell. From inside the pines came a happy yelp. I felt myself calm down.

"Your car took a hit," Linderman said. "There's some paint missing by the door."

I gave it a quick inspection. The trunk was still

locked, and so were the doors. The missing paint around the window wasn't pretty, but I could live with it.

"Did you see the guy who did this?" I asked.

"Just his back," Linderman said.

Buster emerged from the stand of pine trees walking on three legs. Stuck in his mouth was a rectangular piece of cloth. Whoever had tried to break into my car had gotten a real ass chewing. I checked his paw. There was a thorn stuck in the pad.

"I need some help," I said.

Even the best dogs will bite you when in pain. I held Buster's mouth while Linderman removed the bloody thorn from his paw. He didn't flinch.

"Any luck at the pharmacy?" Linderman asked.

"I'll tell you in the car," I said.

I got the hell out of Chatham, and drove toward the highway and our motel. On both sides of the road I saw broken-down farm buildings and unworked land. Florida had more cattle and horses than Texas, yet none of it seemed to be here.

"Lonnie and Mouse live somewhere nearby in the woods," I said.

Linderman turned in his seat to stare at me. If anything defined our relationship, it was my ability to surprise him.

"Who told you that?" he asked.

"I bribed a little girl with five bucks, and she told me. Little kids go cheap."

"If a little kid knows they're here, then probably most of the townspeople do."

"That would be my guess."

Linderman fell silent, and stared at the rain-slicked road. I sensed he was still having a problem with my Chatham conspiracy theory.

"I have a friend at the DEA's office in Miami," he said. "I was on the phone with him while you were inside the pharmacy. My friend works all the major drug cases in Florida. He said Chatham isn't involved in trafficking drugs."

"How about manufacturing crystal meth? That's big in these parts."

"Nope."

"Could they be growing marijuana?"

"I asked, and he said the town was clean."

Most of Florida's crime problems over the past thirty years were drug-related. The fact that Chatham wasn't involved in drugs only deepened the mystery. A convenience store appeared up ahead, and I tapped my brakes.

"Well, they're doing something bad," I said.

The store was called Shop & Save. Half grocery, half hardware store, with a rack of cheap clothes thrown in for good measure. I grabbed three prepackaged sandwiches and some cold drinks and went to pay up. The teenage kid working the register had shoulder-length hair and red-laced eyes. He rang up my items without making eye contact.

"You always smoke your breakfast?" I asked.

The kid lifted his head. I could have knocked him over with a feather.

"I don't know what you're talking about," he stammered.

"I smelled the reefer on your breath when I walked in."

"I'm not stoned."

"It smelled like homegrown."

The kid's face turned wet with fear. Linderman shouldered up next to me, and opened his wallet in front of the kid's face. The gold FBI badge was hard to miss.

"Shit Daniels," the kid said.

"Take a deep breath, and tell me your name," I said.

"Tucker. My friends call me Tuck."

"Are you from around here?" I asked.

"Next town over."

"We're interested in what you can tell us about Chatham," I said.

Tuck swallowed the rising lump in his throat. I didn't like scaring the daylights out of adolescents, but we needed some answers, and he looked like a good subject.

"Folks in Chatham have always been unfriendly," Tuck said. "It got worse a couple of years ago."

"What happened?" I asked.

"Some guys from Jacksonville showed up, and started asking questions. Then the townspeople started fighting with each other. Couple buildings got burned down, and I heard some folks disappeared."

"They disappeared?" Linderman said.

"That's what I heard. Can I ask you guys something?"

"Go ahead," I said.

"You're not going to arrest me, are you? I only took a couple tokes."

"Whose buildings got burned down?" Linderman asked.

"Old Man Kaplan lost a barn and a bunch of animals," Tuck said.

"Think he'd be willing to talk with us?" I asked.

Tuck saw his opening. He came out from behind the counter, and pointed at the road outside the store. "Go back the way you came. Four miles, you'll see a dirt road. Drive down it, and there will be a big farm on your right. That's Kaplan's place. I'm sure he'd be willing to tell you what happened."

Tuck had given us plenty of information to work with. I patted him on the arm. "Thanks a lot. One last thing. Don't tell anyone about this conversation."

Tuck walked us outside to our car, and shook both our hands.

"I won't tell a soul," the boy said.

CHAPTER 48

WE GOT BACK on the road. Four miles later, an unmarked dirt road appeared, just like Tuck had said it would. We bumped along it until a farm came into view. There were acres of corn and tomatoes, plenty of cows, and a large pasture filled with chestnut-colored horses. The property was surrounded by a three-board fence topped with barbed wire. Yellow signs warned trespassers that they'd be shot on sight. In one pasture, I spied a man riding a tractor. I wanted to speak to him, and flashed my brights. Instead of slowing down, the man drove to the opposite side of the field.

"Is that what they call Southern hospitality?" Linderman asked.

"This is one spooky place," I said.

I pulled off and parked in the grass. We got out of the car and stood by the fence. Several minutes passed. Finally the man on the tractor drove over and killed his engine. It made a whistling sound as it shut down. He wore a long-sleeved shirt and a straw hat, and had olive-colored skin. The brim of his hat was pulled down, shielding his eyes.

"Mister Kaplan?" I asked.

"Mister Kaplan's away." The man had a thick Mexican accent.

"Can you tell us when he'll be back?" I asked.

"Can't you read the signs? No trespassing."

Linderman took out his wallet and let the man see his credentials. The Mexican climbed down from the tractor to look at his badge. The front of his shirt came out of his pants, revealing the black pistol tucked behind his belt.

"Mister Kaplan went to Orlando," the Mexican said. "He'll be back in a couple days. That's all I know."

"What can you tell us about the fire on his property?" Linderman said.

"Mister Kaplan don't want us talking about that," the Mexican said.

"I'm with the FBI," Linderman said.

"I can read," the Mexican said.

"You can get in trouble by not talking to us," Linderman said.

"I lose my job if I do," the Mexican said.

The Mexican climbed back on his tractor. Clearly, the FBI didn't carry much weight in his world. He started up the tractor's engine.

"We're just trying to help," I yelled in Spanish.

The Mexican looked down at me. I held my hands up in a pleading gesture. He pointed to the rear of the property, then drove away.

We drove around the property. Kaplan had a big spread of land, and had a dozen people working for him. It was the first working farm I'd seen in Chatham, and it looked prosperous. As I came around a curve, Linderman spoke up.

"Over there. Look."

I followed the direction of his finger. In the rear of the property sat the charred remains of a burned-down building. The concrete footprint suggested a large structure. A hay barn perhaps. Or horse stalls.

We got out to have a better look and pressed our bodies against the fence. The remains appeared to have been there for a while. The cinders were old and gray, and the grass around the building had grown back. I spotted a wood sign stuck in the ground. Handwritten, the letters had long since faded.

"Can you read that?" I asked.

Linderman shook his head. We were on the same wavelength, and both hopped the fence. We crossed the property with an eye out for trouble. We stopped in front of the sign and still had to squint. The sign read, "To the varmints who torched my barn and killed my horses. Unlike the good Lord, I will not forgive you."

"What do you think is going on here?" Linderman asked.

"I wish I knew," I said.

The sound of gunfire snapped our heads. The shots had come from the forest behind Kaplan's property, and sounded like a small-caliber rifle.

"More trouble," I said.

I drove down the dirt road to a small pond nestled behind Kaplan's farm. About an acre in size, the pond's water was brackish, the surface as smooth as glass. A pair of bamboo fishing poles were stuck in the ground by the pond along with a cooler. The owners of the poles were nowhere in sight. The rain had stopped and the sun was out.

I parked beneath the inviting shade of a tree, and we both got out. Linderman removed the shotguns from the trunk of my car, and tossed one to me. The shotguns were called Mossbergs, and had gained wide popularity with law enforcement after quelling several prison riots in the late nineties.

"How many shots did you count?" Linderman asked.

"I heard two," I said.

"Same gun?"

"I think so."

We walked down to the pond with the Mossbergs. In the soft ground I spied two pairs of footprints. Buster had taken a liking to the cooler, and with his nose popped the lid. I let out a soft whistle. The cooler was filled with flathead catfish resting on ice.

"Are they good to eat?" Linderman asked.

"They're a local delicacy," I said.

"Looks like we stumbled upon a good fishing hole," he said.

I started to agree with him. Then I spotted the rifle poking out of the trees on the other side of the lake, and knew we were in trouble.

CHAPTER 49

I HAD BEEN in my share of firefights. Ninety percent of the time, no one got shot. The reason for this was simple: The target usually ducked.

I tackled Linderman to the ground. A split-second later, a gunshot rang out, the bullet flying over our heads. Either the shooter had lousy aim, or was trying to scare the daylights out of us. Buster, who'd been sniffing the catfish, took off running.

We lay with our stomachs on the soft ground, staring across the top of the pond. A pack of crows had exploded out of the trees and turned the sky black.

"Where are they?" Linderman whispered.

"On the other side of the pond."

"How many rifles?"

"Just one."

"Show me where they are."

I pointed at the spot where I'd seen the rifle poking through the trees. Linderman took aim and squeezed the trigger of his Mossberg. The shotgun's pellets ripped through the branches and echoed across the forest. Screams followed, accompanied by Buster's frantic barking. I jumped to my feet. Linderman was right beside me.

"I'm going to my right. You go to the left," the FBI agent said.

Linderman took off in a crouch. I did the same, the two of us moving around the pond at the same speed. I could hear Buster ripping something apart behind the trees. A pair of high-pitched voices screamed for mercy.

As I drew closer, the voices became more distinct. Two boys, maybe a few years past puberty. Out of the corner of my eye, I saw Linderman aim high into the trees, and fire another shell. One of the boys screamed for his life.

"Don't shoot me . . . please!"

Linderman halted when he was twenty feet from the trees. "Both of you come out with your hands in the air. Right now!"

"Get your dog away from us," the second boy pleaded.

I hollered for him. I heard a yip, followed by Buster exploding out of the trees. He came over to my side with a wild look in his eyes.

"Now come out, and do it slow," Linderman ordered.

Two adolescent boys walked single file out of the trees. Each wore green camouflage clothing and a baseball cap with the visor pointing backward. One of the boys' pants legs had been ripped to shreds by Buster. They were so scared that both of them had started bawling.

"Are there just two of you?" Linderman asked.

"Yes, sir," one answered.

"See if he's telling the truth," Linderman said to me.

I skirted around the boys and entered the woods. I came to the spot where they'd been hiding, and found a pair of .22s in the leaves. I brought the rifles out and showed them to Linderman.

"Keep your eye on them," Linderman said.

I kept my shotgun trained on the boys. Linderman took the .22s and emptied them of their ammunition. Then he tossed the rifles into the middle of the pond. He watched them sink, and turned back to me.

"Let's find out what they're up to," he said.

We separated the boys, with Linderman taking one to the other side of the pond, while the boy with the ruined pants stayed with me. Buster had not calmed down, and several times I told him to lie down, afraid he might again go on the attack.

"What's your name?" I asked.

"Clayton," the boy mumbled.

"Look at me when I'm talking to you, Clayton," I snapped.

He lifted his gaze. He had muted brown eyes and peach fuzz on his cheeks. Sticking out of his baseball cap were several wisps of curly black hair.

"How old are you?" I asked.

"Thirteen."

"You live in Chatham?"

Clayton vigorously nodded his head. Fear has a powerful effect on people, and often cleanses their consciences. He looked ready to confess.

"Why'd you shoot at us?" I asked.

"We thought you were the Bledsoes."

"Who are they?"

"They're a family that lives in town. They come out and steal our fish."

"Do you know Mister Kaplan? He owns the farm down the road. Someone burned down his barn and killed his horses. Was that you and your friend?"

Clayton stared at the ground and didn't respond. My

heart was racing from being shot at, and I wasn't willing to put up with any of the kid's crap. I nudged Buster with my foot, and my dog emitted a vicious bark. Clayton jumped back in alarm.

"Don't let him bite me!"

"Did you set that fire?"

"No, sir. It wasn't me."

"But you know who did, don't you?"

Clayton glanced at his buddy on the other side of the pond. Satisfied his buddy wasn't watching him, he said, "Yes, sir. I know who did it. It was the Bledsoes."

"Tell me why they did that."

"Some men from Jacksonville came to town and started asking questions. Word got out that nobody should talk to them. Only Mr. Kaplan did, and his place got burned."

"Who else talked to them?"

"The Webber family did. They ain't around anymore."

"The men who were asking questions . . . were they policemen?"

"No, sir. They were private investigators. They worked for some big insurance company. I don't know what they wanted."

I had heard enough. Clayton had answered my questions without hesitation, a sign that he was probably telling the truth. Linderman and Clayton's friend came around the pond toward us. I pulled Linderman to one side, and we compared notes. Their stories were the same, and we decided the boys were telling the truth.

"What do you think?" I asked.

"Outside of the fact that they shot at us, I think they're harmless," Linderman said. "I vote for letting them stay. Maybe we can pull some more information out of them."

I agreed, and turned to the boys.

"Grab your poles," I said.

We let Clayton and his friend fish the pond with us. They stood a good distance away, and kept to themselves. Had we let them run into town and tell everyone about the strange men with the shotguns, I knew our chances of saving Sara Long were doomed. Better to keep them around, and let them enjoy the afternoon.

Using the boys' bait, Linderman and I caught six of the prettiest flathead catfish I'd ever seen, and stored them in their cooler. As the sun started to set, I called the boys over. They reluctantly joined us, and glanced nervously at the shotguns lying in the grass.

"Here's the deal," I said. "Each one of you gets to pick a fish. We're going to take the rest. I'll pay you for the cooler. Deal?"

The boys nodded woodenly. Clayton picked the largest of the catch, while his friend took the next biggest fish. I handed Clayton a twenty-dollar bill, which was more than enough for the cooler and the ice.

"You boys have a nice day," I said.

Clayton had a funny look on his face. Like he'd come to an understanding about what had happened, and needed to get it off his chest. He took off his baseball cap.

"I'm sorry we shot at you," Clayton said.

"Mistakes happen," I replied.

"Thank you for not killing us," Clayton said.

"Yeah, thanks for not killing us," his friend echoed.

"You're welcome," I said.

I watched Clayton and his friend walk away with their fish. It was a strange thing for a couple of teenagers to say, but I thought I knew why they had. Chatham was filled with dark secrets. And when the townspeople broke those secrets, they paid for it, sometimes with their lives. I picked up the cooler and carried it to my Legend. Linderman grabbed the shotguns and joined me.

"I want to go back to town, and find out what's going on," I said.

"Do you think that's wise?" Linderman asked.

If wisdom was my guide, I'd never have become a cop, or did the work that I did now. The fact was, I wasn't leaving Chatham until I found Sara Long, and discovered what the hell was wrong with these people.

"Time will tell," I said.

CHAPTER 50

IT WAS DUSK when we pulled into Chatham. The streets had come alive, with cars and pedestrians and signs of life not seen that morning. An eatery on the main drag called The Sweet Lowdown looked promising. I parked beneath a sign that warned the space was for restaurant loading only. As I got out, an overweight man wearing a grease-stained apron came out the front door, and started to berate me.

"Sweet Christ, can't you read the sign? You can't park your car there," the man said angrily. "Find another spot, or I'll have you towed."

"You the owner?" I asked.

"Damn straight I am," he replied.

I went around to the back of my Legend and popped the trunk. Curious, the owner followed me. I proudly showed him the cooler filled with flathead catfish. Before my eyes, the owner's hostility melted away.

"Would you look at those. You fixing to sell them?" he asked.

"Heck, no, I want you to cook them," I replied.

"You boys don't think you can eat all of these, do you? There must be thirty-five pounds of meat here."

"Whatever we don't eat, I was going to let you keep," I said.

"That's mighty generous of you," the owner said.

"My friend and I are only in town for a couple of days," I explained. "It would be a crying shame to see these beautiful fish go to waste."

The owner wiped his hands on his apron, then stuck out a meaty paw. "I'm Gabe. It's a pleasure to meet you."

I shook his hand, and so did Linderman. If Buster had been standing there, I had a feeling Gabe would have shaken his hand as well. Free food did that to people. I grabbed the cooler and followed Gabe inside the restaurant.

Gabe treated us like kings. We were seated at a table by the front window, where we could eat our dinner and watch the world pass by. Our catfish were put on ice and displayed in the restaurant's other front window. A waitress put a pitcher of beer on our table, and said it was on the house. She asked us how we wanted our fish cooked.

"Fried," I said.

"The same," Linderman said.

She filled two glasses with beer and left. The beer looked tempting, but I wasn't in a partying mood. I looked around the restaurant. Mounted deer heads hung from the walls, along with old Florida license plates and sepia-toned photographs of the town from years ago. I glanced out the window at the street. Pedestrians meandered by, as did cars on the main drag, no one moving particularly fast. It was the quintessential picture of small-town life. Only I knew it wasn't. Something was terribly wrong here.

Our dinners came. Our plates overflowed with fried

catfish, hush puppies, and fried okra. To wash it down, our glasses were poured with all the sweetened iced tea we could drink. Linderman tried each item on his plate hesitantly. Deciding the food wasn't poisoned, he dug in.

"Giving him the fish was a smart idea," Linderman said.

"It bought us a few hours," I said.

"What do you think is going on?"

"I wish I knew."

I ate my meal. Knowing that I'd caught the fish myself made it taste that much better. As I raised my fork to my mouth, I stopped. A white-haired couple had entered the restaurant, and stood by the hostess stand waiting to be seated. Both wore leather pants and leather jackets, and were carrying motorcycle helmets. They were normal-looking, except that the man's left arm was missing, the sleeve of his shirt tied in a knot. The woman was missing her right foot, and walked with a carved wooden cane. They returned my gaze, and I lowered my eyes to my plate.

"Something wrong?" Linderman asked.

"See that couple at the hostess stand?"

"What about them, besides the fact they're both missing limbs?"

"The manager at our motel is missing his hand, and the woman who waited on me at the pharmacy this morning was missing her foot."

The couple walked by our table with a hostess. The armless man stopped to kick the leg of my chair. I lifted my eyes, and was greeted with a look of pure, unadulterated hatred. The armless man was tall and broadchested, with a flat face and shoulder-length yellowing hair that was more nicotine than ivory.

"You got no right to stare at us," the armless man said.

"Sorry if I offended you," I said.

"If I was you, I'd finish my dinner and move on."

"I'll do that," I said.

"And don't come back."

"No, sir."

The armless man joined his wife on the other side of the restaurant, and sat down at a table. I caught my waitress's eye, and she hurried over.

"Everything okay?" our waitress asked pleasantly.

"I'd like to buy that fellow and his wife a drink," I said, pointing to where the armless man and his wife were sitting.

"You mean Travis Bledsoe and his wife? Sure," the waitress said.

She crossed the restaurant and spoke to the Bledsoes. I'd never liked people who burned down property and killed harmless animals, and I gave Travis Bledsoe a hard look. Bledsoe returned my gaze with a dark, burning stare.

The waitress came back to our table.

"He's not interested," the waitress said.

"Thanks for asking," I said.

"You're welcome. You want some dessert? We've got delicious homemade blueberry pie."

"Sounds like a winner," I said.

She took our plates and left. Linderman leaned in close, and lowered his voice. "Bledsoe is carrying a gun around his ankle. I spotted the bulge."

"Anyone else in the restaurant armed?" I asked.

"Two guys up at the bar are carrying as well."

I glanced at the pair of good ole boys holding up the

bar. They'd been drinking boilermakers and talking college football since we'd come in.

"Ankle holsters?" I asked.

"Uh-huh."

Our desserts came. The blueberry pie was as good as advertised. I ate mine slowly, watching the room while Linderman watched the action outside. I felt like I'd stumbled onto something, yet still didn't understand what it was.

"How about some coffee?" our waitress asked.

She stood next to our table, holding a pot and two cups. I glanced across the room at the table with Bledsoe and his wife. He was watching us with murderous intensity. I wanted to buy some more time, and I said, "Do you have decaf?"

"I can brew you a pot," she said cheerfully.

"That would be great."

"Two cups?"

"Please."

She left. The restaurant was starting to fill up. A line had formed by the hostess stand, and I spotted a big man wearing coveralls who was also missing an arm. That made five limbless citizens of Chatham and counting.

Our waitress returned with a fresh pot of decaf. She poured two steaming cups with a big smile on her face.

"Those catfish in the window are sure drawing them in," she said.

"I'm glad they're not going to waste," I said.

I blew the steam off my drink and looked at Linderman. The FBI agent had stopped eating his dessert, and was staring out the window at the street.

"See something?" I asked.

"This is really sick," Linderman said.

I craned my neck to have a look. The sidewalk outside The Sweet Lowdown was filled with people out for an evening stroll. Over a third of them were missing an arm, a leg, or a hand, with some even missing two limbs. They all seemed to know each other, and had stopped to chat or to have a smoke. It was a parade of the maimed.

I quickly counted the number of dismembered standing outside. There were thirty-five. That made forty limbless citizens so far.

"At least half these people are carrying a concealed firearm," Linderman said.

"Want to leave?"

"Whatever gave you that idea?"

"At least the food was good."

"You're a funny guy, Jack."

I waved our waitress over to the table. She acted sad to see us leave. I had to think she was the only person in the restaurant who felt that way. I asked for the check, and she informed us that the meal was on the house. I threw down a fat tip.

"Ya'all come back," the waitress said.

We headed for the door. The hostess nodded as we passed, happy to see a table free up. Something about her looked vaguely familiar. Tall and dark-skinned, she was pretty in a reserved way, her eyes lowering when she realized I was gazing at her. My eyes fell on her plastic name tag. V. Seppi.

Linderman and I went outside. The crowd standing outside the restaurant was three deep. I tried not to stare at those who were missing limbs. It was hard. They were everywhere I looked.

Going to my Legend, I popped the trunk. I found the

file on Lonnie and Mouse's victims that I'd been carrying around, and beneath the trunk's tiny interior light, I poured through the pages.

I came to the missing person reports that my old unit had given me two days ago. My eyes locked on the victims' photos. Then I knew.

Victoria Seppi had been Lonnie and Mouse's fourth victim.

CHAPTER 51

I DROPPED THE FILE into the trunk, and slammed it shut.

The dismembered townspeople of Chatham were staring at Linderman and me. They were in their late forties to late fifties, white, and decently dressed. Many of the women wore expensive jewelry, and several men sported fancy wristwatches. Not a single one of them looked poor.

"Have a nice night," a man in the crowd said.

The words had an ugly ring to them. A number of men in the crowd were resting their hands on the guns concealed behind their shirts. It felt like a posse. I had been in hostile environments before, but nothing like this.

Linderman and I climbed into my Legend. Buster had tuned into the bad vibes and was standing up on the backseat, growling at the crowd. As I pulled away, he started barking. I didn't slow down until the town was in my mirror.

"Pull off the road and kill your lights," Linderman said.

I pulled down a darkened side street, and turned off

my headlights. Moments later, a car filled with men cruised past.

"Think they're looking for us?" I asked.

"Probably want to make sure we leave town," Linderman said.

I drew my Colt from my pocket, and stuck it between my legs.

"Did you see the hostess?" I asked.

"Just in passing. Why?"

"Her name's Victoria Seppi. She was Lonnie and Mouse's fourth victim."

"Are you sure?"

I retrieved the file from the trunk, and got back into the car. I removed Seppi's missing person report from the file, and passed it to him.

Linderman read the report with a flashlight so as not to illuminate my car's interior. He clicked off the light when he was done.

"We need to nab her and find out what's going on," Linderman said. "Her case is still open. She's committed a crime by not contacting the police. I have every right to detain her."

His voice was strained, and I could tell he wanted to get to the truth as much as I did.

I called information, and got The Sweet Lowdown's number. Then I called the restaurant. Victoria Seppi picked up, and I asked her how late they stayed open.

"Kitchen stops serving at eleven o'clock," Seppi said.

I thanked her and hung up. We had several hours to kill.

Driving to the outskirts of town, I parked behind an abandoned factory that had once manufactured cardboard boxes, and let Buster run loose. I leaned against my car, and tried to calm down. Knowing that Sara Long was somewhere nearby did not help my mood. Nor did the fact that Chatham was filled with people who might try to kill us if we tried. If we didn't handle this right, it was going to blow up in our faces.

At a few minutes before eleven we drove back to Chatham. The town's streets had cleared out, the restaurants and bars closing up for the night. I parked two blocks away from The Sweet Lowdown, and killed my headlights.

We watched the restaurant's employees leave through the front door, then saw the neon sign go off. Finally, two figures emerged. Gabe, the owner, and Seppi. Gabe locked the front door and went to his car, while Seppi walked around the building.

Linderman reach into his coat, and removed his wallet. He took out his FBI badge and pinned it to his windbreaker. "Follow her," he said.

I turned on my headlights and drove down the street toward the restaurant. Gabe drove past me, his eyes half shut. I punched the gas once his vehicle was out of sight.

"Hurry," Linderman said. "I don't want Seppi getting into her car."

I took the corner with a squeal of rubber, my headlights catching Seppi as she entered the metered parking lot behind the restaurant. She turned instinctively, and looked directly at us. Fear shone in her eyes. She fumbled with her purse, and its contents spewed out onto the ground. She cursed and began to run.

I pulled up alongside her, and Linderman rolled down his window.

"Victoria Seppi. I'm with the FBI. I order you to stop," Linderman said.

Seppi looked sideways at us. The fear in her eyes had turned to desperation. Instead of slowing down, she kicked off her shoes, and tried to outrun us.

"Hit your brakes," Linderman said.

I did as told. Linderman jumped out of the car, and gave chase. Seppi was fast, but Linderman was faster. He quickly caught up, and grabbed Seppi from behind by the waist. They both went down to the ground.

I pulled the car up alongside them. Buster was standing up in the backseat, barking furiously. I calmed him down and jumped out.

Linderman and Seppi were still on the ground. Seppi struggled helplessly beneath Linderman's weight. Not a sound came out of her mouth. I had seen that with victims of abductions before. The screaming was only on the inside.

"Do you want me to handcuff you?" Linderman asked.

"No," Seppi said through clenched teeth.

"Then cut the nonsense. We just want to talk with you."

"They're going to kill me," Seppi said. "Do you understand that? They're going to kill me, and my mother, and then they'll kill both of you."

"Not if we have anything to say about it," I said.

Seppi looked up at me for the first time. She must have seen something in my face that told her I was one of the good guys. She stopped struggling, and almost at once began to cry. Linderman climbed off of her.

"Here. Let me help you," I said.

I pulled Seppi to her feet. Her hostess uniform was covered with dirt, as were her face and hands. She looked terribly vulnerable, and I felt sorry for her. She glanced up and down the street, and I saw something resembling anger flash across her face.

"Don't tell me you came here by yourselves," Seppi said.

I nodded, and so did Linderman.

"Oh, Jesus Christ," she said.

CHAPTER 52

THE THREE OF US piled into my car. Linderman sat in the backseat with a shotgun lying across his lap, while Seppi sat in the passenger seat next to me. When I told her to fasten her seat belt, she let out a nervous laugh.

"You're funny," she said without humor.

I turned my Legend around, and drove back to the town's main drag. I stopped at the intersection, and looked both ways. The streets and the sidewalks were deserted, the stores shut down for the night. I glanced in my mirror at Linderman.

"Which way?" I asked.

"What's the closet city?" Linderman asked.

"Daytona Beach. It's about a thirty-mile drive."

"We'll go there. I'll call my counterpart at the FBI's Jacksonville office, and have him meet us."

I pointed my car east. A part of me wanted to floor the accelerator, but I knew that it was better not to run when you weren't being chased. We reached the edge of town without any problems, and I felt myself relax.

"We're not going to make it out of here," Seppi suddenly said. "Sheriff Morcroft comes by my house every night to make sure I'm home. If he doesn't see my car in the driveway, he'll know something's wrong, and he'll come looking."

"What time does he usually come by?" Linderman asked.

"Twelve-fifteen on the nose. Sometimes he even knocks on the door, and makes me come outside."

"How long has he been doing that?" Linderman asked.

Seppi started to answer, but the words wouldn't come out. Her hand wiped away the tears running down her cheeks. The questions were tearing her apart, but we needed to know.

"Since you escaped from Lonnie and Mouse?" I asked.

Her head snapped. "Who told you about them?"

"We've known about Lonnie and Mouse for several days," I said. "They recently kidnapped a young woman in Fort Lauderdale, and brought her back here. She was a nursing student, just like you were."

Seppi's chin fell on her chest, and she fought back a sob. I stared at the darkened road in front of me. An uneasy silence fell over the car. For a few minutes, no one said anything. Buster stuck his head between the seats. Seppi broke out of her funk, and started to pet him.

"I wanted to tell someone about them—I swear to God, I did," Seppi said. "But Sheriff Morcroft threatened me. He said that if I contacted the police and told them about Lonnie and Mouse, he was going to the nursing home where my mother lives, and put a pillow over her face. I couldn't let him do that. Do you understand? I *couldn't*."

"How long did they hold you prisoner?" I asked.

"Two and a half years," she said.

"I'm sorry," I said.

"You want to know something? It felt like ten."

I had a dozen more questions I wanted to ask Victoria Seppi, and I'm sure Linderman did as well. But I never got the chance to. Five miles outside of town, I spotted the outline of a car parked behind some pine trees by the side of the road. It could have been an abandoned vehicle or a pair of lovers, but my gut told me it wasn't. Moments later, a pair of headlights appeared in my mirror, and I knew it was trouble.

"We've got company," I said.

Linderman turned around in his seat and looked behind us.

"Pickup truck. Could be anybody," he said.

I was doing sixty-five. I punched the gas, and my Legend spurted ahead. The pickup quickly caught up.

"Better lose them," Linderman said.

"I'll try."

Seppi clasped her hands together and started to pray. I did not want to die in this little podunk town, and I floored the accelerator. My Legend was old, but still had some pep. Within moments the speedometer was clicking a hundred.

The pickup was up to the challenge. It caught up to me, and started to hang on my bumper. I couldn't make the Legend go any faster without blowing the engine. Seppi turned around, the seat belt pulling at her throat. She let out a horrible shriek.

"They're going to kill me!"

"We're not going to let that happen," I said.

"You can't stop them!"

The pickup flashed its brights. I felt like the driver was playing chicken with me. I glanced to either side of the road. I was surrounded by empty farmland, most of it fenced. I considered going off the highway and trying to escape across a field, but quickly discounted the idea. It would buy us time, but the ending would be the same.

Instead, I pushed my foot down to the floor, and kept it there. The Legend found new life, and within a few seconds, I was clocking a hundred and fifteen mph. A sign appeared warning me that a steep curve lay ahead.

"Hold on," I said.

Seppi grabbed the "Aw shit" handle over the door. In my mirror, Linderman grabbed Buster, and held him protectively against his chest.

I hit the curve in the road without slowing down. I had been involved in enough car chases as a cop to believe that I was good enough to do that. The driver of the pickup didn't have the same faith in himself and slowed down.

I came out of the curve like a rocket. The road ahead was perfectly straight, with not another car to be seen. I heard a loud, throbbing sound, and realized it was my heart pounding in my ears.

Ten seconds later, the pickup appeared in my mirror. There was a good quarter of a mile separating us. Just enough distance to give me a momentary respite. The sound of a bullet hitting my car quickly dispelled that feeling.

I looked straight up. A bullet had ripped across my roof, and left a seam directly above where I sat. Five inches lower, and it would have blown my head clean off.

"They've got a high-powered rifle," I said.

Seppi brought her hand up to her mouth like she was going to puke.

"We're sitting ducks as it is," Linderman said. "Slow the car down, and put on your emergency lights. I want them to think we're pulling over."

"We're not?"

"Just do as I say."

I let my foot off the gas, then flipped on the emergency flasher. The Legend quickly lost speed, and the pickup caught up to us.

"What now?" I asked.

"Just watch."

In my mirror, I saw Linderman roll down his window. He was crouching low in his seat, so as not to be seen by the pickup's driver.

"How close are they?" Linderman asked.

"About a hundred yards back," I said.

"Are they directly behind us?"

"Yes."

"Put your indicator on, and slow down some more."

I did as told. The pickup drew dangerously close. At any moment, I expected another bullet to hit my car, and my life to be over.

"How far back are they now?" Linderman asked.

"About three car lengths," I said.

"Perfect."

I stared at my mirror. Linderman stuck his body through the open window, and aimed the Mossberg at the pickup's windshield. Flames spit out of the shotgun's barrel as he fired. I heard three shots in rapid succession followed by the sound of the windshield imploding. The pickup veered off the road, and took down a fence. It rumbled across a barren field before abruptly disappearing.

I pulled off the road and parked in the grass. The three of us got out. The wind was blowing from the north, and I could hear the strains of country music in the distance. I pulled Buster out of the car, and went to where the pickup had taken down the fence.

"What are you doing?" Linderman said.

"I want to find out what happened to them," I said. "If they're still alive, they're going to call for reinforcements. We're twenty-five miles from Daytona. We're not going to be able to run away from them."

"We need to leave, the sooner the better," Linderman said.

I was holding my car keys. I threw them to him, and they hit Linderman squarely in the chest.

"You go," I said.

I followed the tire tracks across the field with Buster beside me. The sound of Garth Brooks grew louder with each step I took. The ground seemed to fall away, and I stopped. Down below was a large, man-made hole, what locals call a borrow pit. The pit was filled with uprooted trees and piles of debris. The upside-down pickup lay at the bottom, its wheels still spinning and music coming out of its cab.

"Next to me," I said.

Buster glued himself to my side, and together we climbed down. Nearing bottom, we both started to slide. I righted myself, and drew my Colt.

"Get out and show me your hands," I said loudly.

There was no response from the pickup. I approached in a crouch, my gun held with both hands. In the moonlight, two men hung upside down in their seats. One had a hunting rifle with a sniper sight clutched in his hands, while the other held a pistol. Their faces had been blown clean off.

Reaching in through the open driver's window, I killed the pickup's ignition. I didn't like killing people without knowing who they were, and I searched the driver's pockets, and found a wallet along with a handful of loose change.

I pulled out a driver's license. Holding it up to the moonlight, I read who the dead man was. I cursed loudly.

Walking around to the other side of the cab, I picked the other dead man's pockets. I found his wallet, and read his ID. I cursed again.

I hurried back to the highway with my dog. Linderman and Seppi stood next to my Legend, waiting for me. Linderman threw my keys back to me.

"Find anything?" the FBI agent asked.

"You just killed the sheriff of Chatham and his deputy," I said.

CHAPTER 53

I DROVE to Daytona without seeing another car on the road. It was a welcome relief, considering what had happened.

Daytona had more cheap hotel rooms than probably anywhere else in Florida. Many were located near the speedway where the Daytona 500 was held each year. Linderman chose the Holiday Inn across the street from the speedway, and rented a suite in the rear of the building, which let me park away from the road.

We took Seppi to the suite on the hotel's second floor, and fed her black coffee and doughnuts and let her watch TV. The sheriff and his deputy's killings had done a number on her, and she flipped through the channels aimlessly, unable to focus on any one program. I asked her if she wanted us to send someone to the nursing home to make sure her mother was all right, and she shook her head.

"No one's going to hurt my momma now," she told me.

A few hours later, the director of the FBI's Jacksonville office, Special Agent Vaughn Wood, arrived, along with his female assistant. Wood wore a black turtleneck and black cargo pants that made the dark rings beneath his eyes much more pronounced. His assistant wore a blue pantsuit and looked like a soccer mom. They'd brought a tape recorder with them, which they set up in the suite's living room in order to interview Seppi.

Seppi sat on the couch and chain-smoked cigarettes. Linderman sat in a chair facing her, and did the questioning, while Wood, his assistant, and I stood against the wall. Seppi started by talking about her background. She was a native of Chatham, as were her parents, and had had a normal upbringing. Then, she described her abduction from Daytona Community College, and why she'd never gone to the police.

"I love Chatham," Seppi said, feathering the smoke of her cigarette through her nostrils. "But my town has a dirty secret that I was raised not to talk about. So this is hard. You understand?"

Everyone in the suite nodded.

"In the late 1980s, the paper mill shut down, and Chatham hit the skids," Seppi said. "There were no jobs, and times were tough. One day, some locals were sitting around a bar getting drunk. One of them was a guy named Travis Bledsoe.

"Travis had a few drinks, and accidentally cut his hand with a knife. Travis looked at the wound, and started talking about his hand's earning potential, and its value on his insurance policy. That's how the whole thing got started."

"How what got started?" Linderman asked.

"How the townsfolk in Chatham started losing limbs to collect on the insurance," Seppi replied. "It was sick, but that was what a whole bunch of them did."

"You mean they purposely amputated their limbs?"

"Yeah. One guy sawed off his hand at work; another shot off his foot while protecting his chickens. One dumb ass cut off his hand *and* his foot with his tractor because he thought it would get him more money. In two years, a hundred people filed claims for accidents."

"Didn't the insurance companies catch on?"

"Not right away. The people were smart about it. Some went into the next county and had their accidents, while others did it on vacation. It took the heat off the town. I heard they collected twenty million dollars."

"And no one caught on," Linderman said.

"Not right away," Seppi said. "Then two years ago, a couple of the big insurance companies in Jacksonville merged, and their books got audited. Some smart accountant saw all these claims that had been paid to Chatham. The company got suspicious, and hired a pair of investigators to snoop around."

"Did they find anything?"

"Three people in town tried to talk, but they got silenced. Travis Bledsoe and his four sons did the dirty work. They burned Kaplan's barn, and killed his horses. They also paid a visit to an old couple named Webber who used to be missionaries. The Webbers refused to shut up, and they disappeared."

"What was the sheriff's involvement?" Linderman asked.

"Sheriff Morcroft figured out what was going on twenty years ago. He extorted the people who'd cut off their limbs, and got them to pay him protection money."

"How many people in town know about this?"

"Most of them, I guess."

"Explain to me how Mouse and Lonnie fit into this scenario," Linderman said.

Seppi grew silent and crushed a cigarette in an ashtray. I stood across from her, watching her facial expressions. She'd been composed up until now. But I knew from past experience that this was going to be the hard part. Mouse and Lonnie had kept her prisoner for a long time. Getting her to talk about it was not going to be easy.

The suite had a minibar. I pulled out a bottle of overpriced spring water, and filled up a glass. I brought it to Seppi, and suggested that she drink it. She smiled at me with her eyes, and drank the glass until it was empty.

"Mouse and Lonnie showed up in Chatham in the early 1990s," Seppi said. "They lived on a dairy farm that Mouse's uncle owned. People in town knew they were up to no good, but didn't say anything."

"Why not?" Linderman asked.

"Mouse knew about the insurance scam. He was part of the club."

"So Sheriff Morcroft left them alone."

"That's right. Sometimes Mouse came into town to buy things. Outside of that, nobody saw them much."

"Did the townspeople know that Mouse and Lonnie were keeping young women in the compound against their will?" Linderman asked.

Seppi grew silent. I refilled her glass and earned another smile. I mouthed the words *Take your time*. She nodded, and lit up a fresh cigarette.

"People knew they had girls," Seppi finally said. "Mouse would buy tampons at the CVS and make jokes about it. But the people in town discounted it."

Linderman drew back in his chair. "How did they discount it?"

"A gang of Hells Angels once lived in Chatham. Their girlfriends would wear patches that said 'Property of Big Frank' or 'Property of Crazy Al.' The girls were slaves, but they went along with it. People in town treated Mouse and Lonnie's girls the same way. They assumed the girls were there because they wanted to be."

"How did you end up with them?" Linderman asked.

Seppi's eyes grew distant. "I was a cashier at the supermarket one summer. Mouse came in one day, and saw my schoolbooks. He asked me what I was going to college for. I told him I was studying to be a nurse.

"Two weeks later, I was back in school in Daytona, hanging around my dorm room one weekend. There was a knock on my door, and I opened it. Lonnie rushed in and knocked me out. I didn't remember very much, except how that giant son-of-a-bitch kept smiling at me.

"I woke up inside their farm. Mouse had soldered metal bracelets around my ankles. The bracelets had bells on them. I couldn't move without them hearing me.

"Mouse explained the deal to me that night. He told me that I was a substitute for a nurse who Lonnie had fallen in love with when he was in a mental institution. My job was to give Lonnie his medicine, and shoot him up with steroids. I also had to measure him every few days to make sure he wasn't growing anymore. I also had to cook, and keep the place clean. If I did my job well and kept Lonnie happy, Mouse said nothing would happen to me."

"Were you sexually assaulted?" Linderman asked.

Seppi sucked hard on her cigarette. "No. Mouse

wanted to sleep with me—he said so a bunch of times—
but Lonnie wouldn't let him. I was Lonnie's girl."

"Did Lonnie rape you?"

"The steroids shrunk up his balls."

"How did you manage to escape?"

"They screwed up. One day Mouse went into town,
and Lonnie stayed behind. It was hot outside, and
Lonnie had been lifting weights in the yard. He came
inside, and told me he wasn't feeling well. I gave him a
cold drink and suggested he lie down on the couch. He
went and lay down, and fell asleep. I walked past him a
couple of times, and rang my bells. He didn't wake up."

"Is that when you ran?"

"Not right away. I was scared. I knew what had happened to Mouse and Lonnie's other victims. But when I
realized this was probably my only chance, I left."

"Where did you go?"

"I went straight to Sheriff Morcroft. He listened to
my story, then put me in his cruiser, and took me to my
momma's nursing home. He told me he was sorry about
what had happened, but because of the insurance
claims, he couldn't draw attention to the town. When
we got to the nursing home, he told me he'd kill my
momma if I made any trouble."

"What did you do?" Linderman asked.

"I went home and cried for two weeks. Then I took
the hostess job at The Sweet Lowdown, and got on with
my life. It was strange. Folks in town just acted like
nothing had happened. After a while, I started doing the
same thing."

Lying on the coffee table was a folder containing the
missing person reports of the other victims. Linderman
spread the reports across the table.

"What happened to Mouse and Lonnie's other victims?" Linderman asked.

Seppi looked at the reports, and the color drained from her cheeks. The victims' faces stared up at her. Seppi's expression turned strangely vacant, and she turned sideways on the couch, and stared at the wall.

"They died," she muttered.

"Did Lonnie kill them?" Linderman asked.

"Yeah. There was a small cemetery behind the house where he buried them. He liked to put flowers on their graves."

"So the other four victims are buried at the compound?" Linderman said.

"There were five," Seppi said.

The suite grew silent. I saw Linderman's jaw clench.

"Tell me about the other victim," Linderman said.

"She was right before me," Seppi said. "They kidnapped her down in south Florida. I saw her sneakers lying around one day."

"Running sneakers?" Linderman asked.

"I think so. They were blue Nikes."

"When would this have been?"

"About five years ago."

"Is she buried . . . with the others?"

Linderman's voice had cracked. He switched off the tape recorder, and rose quickly from his chair. Wood and his assistant looked at him in alarm.

Linderman did not respond to their stares. Instead, he walked to the living room's glass slider. Opening it, he went onto the balcony.

"Excuse me," I said.

CHAPTER 54

I WENT onto the balcony to check on Linderman. He was holding the railing with both hands, listening to the night sounds. I placed my hand on his back.

"You doing okay?" I asked.

"Not really," he said.

"You can take a break, you know."

"I'll be all right. Just give me a minute."

I lowered my hand and stared into the darkness. Many times I had tried to imagine the torturous existence he and his wife had led since their daughter's disappearance. Each time I had come up short.

"I've thought about this day for a long time," Linderman finally said. "In the beginning, I prayed that I'd find Danny alive, and I'd bring her home and our lives would go back to normal. Then, as it dragged on and on, I just prayed for it to be over."

Linderman took his hands off the railing, then turned and stared at me. His stony expression had melted. I could not remember ever seeing him look so vulnerable.

"And now the day is here," he said.

We went back inside, and returned to our spots. Seppi fired up a cigarette, and the questioning resumed.

"How do we find the dairy farm?" Linderman asked.

"I can draw you a map, if you want," Seppi said.

A piece of notepaper and a pencil were produced. Seppi took her time drawing a map of Chatham. When she was done, she showed us where Mouse and Lonnie's dairy farm was located in relation to the town. It was due north and adjacent to a national forest, with a single road going in and out.

"The farm is a couple of acres, and has a house and a barn," Seppi said. "It's surrounded by a high fence, and there are security lights."

"Any dogs?" Woods asked.

"No—Lonnie's terrified of dogs."

"What kind of firearms do they have?" Linderman asked.

"From what I remember, Mouse had a pistol, which he shot sometimes. He kept it in a safe. He was always afraid of me getting ahold of it. The real threat is Lonnie. He's the strongest person I've ever seen. And he's not right in the head."

There was a knock on the door. We all jumped. Wood said, "I ordered pizza during the break," and went to answer it. A chubby pizza delivery boy stood outside. Wood handed him money, and brought two pizza boxes into the suite. The smell filled the suite, and soon we were all eating slices of pepperoni pizza.

"Who in Chatham will put up a fight when we go in?" Linderman asked.

Seppi had taken to the food, and answered with her mouth full. "With Sheriff Morcroft and his deputy gone, the people in town will lean on Travis Bledsoe. Travis was in Special Forces. He's missing an arm, but he'll put up a fight."

"Show us where Bledsoe lives," Linderman said.

Seppi drew Travis Bledsoe's house on the map. It was outside of town, on the same road as Mouse and Lonnie's farm.

"Bledsoe lives with his wife and four sons," Seppi said. "They keep assault rifles in their house, and plenty of ammunition. They're militia."

"Is Bledsoe the only one we should be worried about?" Linderman asked.

"Everyone else in Chatham is old or crippled," Seppi said. "If you put Bledsoe and his clan down, the town is yours."

The questioning ended, and the tape recorder was shut off. Wood, Linderman, and I went onto the balcony to talk, while Wood's assistant stayed with Seppi.

"This isn't good," Wood said. "If Bledsoe and his sons put up a fight, we'll have a mess on our hands. I want to assemble a large group before going in."

"How large?" Linderman asked.

"At least fifty men," Wood said. "I'll pull all the FBI agents out of my office, and also use SWAT teams from the Daytona Police Department. They'll need to be briefed on what to expect."

I cleared my throat. This wasn't my rodeo, but I still wanted my voice to be heard. Wood shot me a disapproving look.

"You want to say something, say it," Wood barked.

"The sheriff of Chatham and his deputy are lying dead in a pickup truck outside of town. Someone is going to find them, and realize things are going sideways. We don't have the kind of time you're talking about."

Wood frowned. Like most FBI agents, he didn't like being challenged. He looked to Linderman, more interested in what Ken had to say than me.

"Jack's right. We're running out of time," Linderman said.

Wood's frown grew, and he crossed his arms in front of his chest. "What do we do? Go in there with guns blazing, and hope for the best?"

"Draw Bledsoe and his sons out of the house and arrest them," I suggested. "We'll get Seppi to call them."

"You think she'll do that, after what she's been through?"

I had dealt with countless victims of abductions. Some fell apart after their ordeals were over, while others grew stronger from the experience. Seppi was a survivor, and I felt certain I could get her to help us.

"Yes, I do," I said.

Wood looked to Linderman for the final word.

"It's worth a shot," Linderman said.

The FBI agents left me alone with Seppi in the living room. I sat in a chair across from her, our knees nearly touching. While I'd been gone, she'd taken to feeding Buster the crusts from our slices of pizza, which my dog practically inhaled.

"He's a nice dog," she said. "Is he a pure breed?"

"I think so. I got him from the pound."

"I hear they're the best kind of dogs to have."

"I need your help," I said.

Seppi tossed Buster the last crust and turned to face me. Her expression was cold, almost defiant. I chose my words carefully.

"We need to set a trap for Bledsoe and his sons so we can arrest them."

"Is that where I come in?"

"Yes."

Seppi leaned back on the couch. She had finally escaped Chatham, and the sheriff who had threatened her mother's life was dead. There was no *need* to go back.

"Can't you figure out another way to do this?" she asked, growing angry.

"We need to do this right now," I said. "Mouse and Lonnie are holding another young woman hostage."

Seppi sat up straight. "They have another girl?"

"Yes. She's a college student studying to be a nurse, just like you were. They abducted her three days ago."

"So they haven't ruined her yet."

Ruined. I didn't know what Seppi meant by that. Yet hearing the word told me that what had to be done couldn't wait any longer.

"Please help us," I said.

Seppi punched one of the pillows on the couch. The resolve that had allowed her to survive her ordeal rose to the surface, as I had hoped it would.

"Tell me what I have to do," she said.

CHAPTER 55

WITH AN HOUR of darkness remaining, we put my plan into action.

We began by driving back to the town of Chatham. Our procession consisted of four vehicles. The first two were unmarked black vans containing the Daytona Police Department's ten-man SWAT team. Then came Wood and his assistant in their black Audi. I was last, with Seppi sitting beside me, Linderman and Buster in the back.

Five miles outside of Chatham, we found the spot where Sheriff Morcroft's pickup truck had taken down the fence. Everyone pulled over, and I led Wood and his assistant to where the sheriff's pickup lay upside down at the bottom of the borrow pit. Wood shone his flashlight on the two corpses. Rigor mortis had set in, and the men's faces were a gruesome mix of purple and red.

"I still think we're taking an unnecessary risk," Wood said.

"Not if we do it right," I said.

"You like to have the last word, don't you?"

I started to reply, then realized I'd be agreeing with him. I heard a rustling sound, and Wood killed his flashlight. In the darkness, a pair of silvery eyes began to circle us.

"Is that a dog?" Wood asked.

"Coyote," I said.

"It doesn't seem to be afraid of us."

"It wants the bodies."

Wood had strapped his gun to his side. He drew and aimed. The gunshot echoed across the field like a solitary clap of thunder.

I left Seppi with Wood, and drove to Chatham with Linderman. The town was quiet, and I pulled into the metered parking lot behind The Sweet Lowdown. Seppi's blue Honda was parked in the rear of the lot, and I pulled up alongside it.

Linderman hopped out of my car. He had Seppi's keys, which he used to unlock the Honda. The Honda was slow to start, but finally turned over. Linderman pulled out of the space, and I followed him out of the lot.

We drove through town. The images from the night before were still vivid in my memory. I was never going to forget the gruesome parade I'd seen outside the restaurant. Only the insane cut off their own limbs. Yet the people in Chatham who'd mutilated themselves were far from insane. They'd let a terrible idea take hold of them, and that idea had taken on a horrifying life of its own.

Buster sat beside me, his hackles standing straight up. People didn't pay attention to animals' behavior, but I'd been raised to look at it as a sign. My dog knew that this was a bad place.

Five minutes later, we'd reached the broken fence, and Linderman pulled off the road, and I did the same. Wood emerged from the shadows. He'd put on a black windbreaker and wool hat, and was nearly invisible. I lowered my window.

"How did it go in town?" Wood asked.

"No problems," I said.

"Good. The SWAT team is ready."

"Where are the other cars?" I asked.

Wood pointed up the road. "Just around the curve. They're hidden behind some trees."

"I'll be right back," I said.

I drove up the road, and parked my Legend with the police vans and Wood's Audi. I started to get out, and Buster tried to follow. I wanted him by my side, but I knew things might get ugly. The last thing I wanted to see was my dog get hurt.

Buster whined as I walked away from my car.

Seppi and Wood were standing by the break in the fence when I returned. Seppi had her cell phone out, and looked at me expectantly.

"Everything set?" I asked Wood.

"We're ready whenever you are," Wood replied.

"Call him," I said to Seppi.

Seppi called Travis Bledsoe on her cell phone. I stood close enough to Seppi to hear the call go through. It rang ten times before Bledsoe finally answered. His voice was thick with sleep.

"This had better be good," Bledsoe said by way of greeting.

"Travis, this is Victoria Seppi," Seppi said.

"Whatta yah want, Victoria?"

"Something bad's happened. I need your help."

"Call the flipping sheriff. That's what he gets paid for," Bledsoe snapped.

"Sheriff Morcroft's hurt, and so's his deputy."

"Hurt? What do you mean?"

"I was driving down Highway Forty-seven, and saw a huge hole in the fence," Seppi said. "I figured a car had gone through it, and went to look. Sure enough, there's Sheriff Morcroft and his deputy hanging upside down in his pickup at the bottom of a hill."

"Are they alive?"

"Yeah, but they're all busted up. Sheriff Morcroft asked me to call you. He said you'd know what to do."

"For the love of Christ, are they drunk?"

"They're hurt, Travis. You've got to help me."

"Fuck it. All right. I'll come out there with my boys."

"Thank you, Travis."

Seppi folded her cell phone. She shivered from an early-morning chill. I put my hand on her shoulder and smiled at her.

"Did I do good?" Seppi asked.

"That was perfect," I said.

I walked with Seppi and Wood across the field. We stopped at the top of the borrow pit, and stared down at the sheriff's upside-down pickup truck. The SWAT team was at the bottom of the hill, and had taken up positions around the piles of debris that were lying around the pickup. Each SWAT team member wore body armor and carried a menacing-looking assault rifle. Linderman was with them. He'd also donned body armor and was carrying a shotgun.

Seppi crossed herself and turned her back on the dead men. She was holding up well, considering the situation.

"I need to talk to the SWAT team," Wood said. "Sound the alarm when the Bledsoes arrive."

"Will do," I said.

Wood started down the hill. The wind had picked up, and the sound of my dog barking could be heard in the distance. Wood halted and looked at me.

"Is that what I think it is?" the FBI agent asked.

"Sounds like it," I said.

"Want me to go shut him up?"

There were three things in this world a person wasn't supposed to mess with, and one of them was a man's dog. I almost told Wood to go to hell.

"He'll calm down," I said.

Wood walked away. The sky was growing lighter and filling with color. Soon the darkness had been erased, and a chorus of chattering birds greeted the new day.

"I used to dream about this day," Seppi said.

Linderman had said the same thing to me earlier. I knew that his dreams and Seppi's were much different.

"What was in your dream?" I asked.

"I dreamed that a stranger came to town. He looked just like Clint Eastwood, and he was carrying a rifle. He shot Mouse and Lonnie dead, then he shot Sheriff Morcroft and his deputy and the Bledsoes. Shot every one of them between the eyes, and killed them. But when I'd wake up, nothing would have changed."

"It *has* changed. Everything has changed."

"I know, but it still doesn't feel real."

I heard the low rumble of thunder. The wind had shifted, and was blowing from the east. Looking in that direction, I saw a line of single headlights rumbling down the road toward us. Motorcycles, moving fast.

"Bledsoe and his sons are coming," I said.

CHAPTER 56

I KNELT DOWN behind the hill so as not to be seen. Seppi remained standing, and waved to the Bledsoe clan.

Lifting my head, I watched the Bledsoes roar up. Travis Bledsoe rode in a sidecar, the empty sleeve of his leather jacket flapping in the breeze. A boy that was his spitting image drove the motorcycle attached to the sidecar, while his three other sons rode behind their father in souped-up Harleys. Each member of the clan wore a black leather jacket and a colorful bandanna to keep their flowing hair tied out of their faces. It was like watching a remake of *Easy Rider*.

"Is that all of them?" I asked.

"There are two others, but they're in prison," Seppi said.

The Bledsoes parked their hogs behind Seppi's Honda. Travis climbed out of the sidecar, hitched up his pants, and had a look around. His leather jacket was unzipped, and I spotted a huge sidearm tucked behind his waistband.

"Call them," I said.

"I'm scared," Seppi whispered.

"You're supposed to be scared. Something bad has happened."

Seppi cleared her throat. "Hey Travis, over here!"

Travis Bledsoe and his sons looked our way. I ducked down further, and began to retreat down into the borrow pit. Seppi stayed at the top, her feet frozen to the ground.

"Are they coming?" I asked.

"Yes, they're running this way," Seppi said.

"Come on," I exhorted her.

Seppi snapped out of it, and scampered down the pit. I grabbed her by the hand, and together we ran to the pickup. The other members of our group had gone invisible, and I felt myself panic. I hadn't asked Wood where we were supposed to hide.

Linderman's head popped up from behind a large mound of brush.

"Jack . . . over here!"

I pulled Seppi over to the spot and we both ducked down. Wood and Linderman were hiding behind the brush along with two of the SWAT team members.

"Good work," Wood said. "Now stay out of sight."

"Yes, sir," I said.

We heard the Bledsoes reach the top of the borrow pit. They were discussing how stupid they thought the sheriff was for wrecking his truck when their voices suddenly stopped.

"There's the sheriff's pickup. Where's Victoria?" one of the sons said.

"I don't know," another son said. "You see her, Pop?"

"No," Travis said. "This don't smell right. Nobody move."

The plan wasn't going to work if Travis and his sons

didn't come down the hill. I looked at Seppi. Her eyes told me she understood.

"Hey, Victoria, where'd you go?" Travis called out.

Seppi's face turned fearful. Then, just as suddenly, her resolve returned. She pushed herself away from me, and scurried around the mound and into view.

"Over here, Travis. I'm over here," Seppi called out.

"There she is," Travis said. "Come on, boys."

I stole a glance around the debris. Seppi stood beside the sheriff's pickup, waiting for Travis and his sons. She glanced my way, and somehow found the courage to smile at me. I prayed it wasn't the last time she did that.

I drew my Colt, and looked at Wood.

"Tell her to get down," Wood whispered.

I stole another glance at Seppi. Travis and his sons had reached the pickup, and were peering inside the cab. The armless man's eyes went wide.

"What the hell—they're both dead!" Travis said.

Seppi started to back away from the pickup.

"Not so fast, you little bitch," Travis said.

Travis grabbed Seppi by the shoulder and shook her. She clawed his face and broke free, and started to run. Travis drew his gun and aimed at Seppi's feet.

"We've been set up, boys," Travis said.

Travis fired several bullets at Seppi's feet. She screamed, and fell facefirst to the ground. Travis aimed at her back, laughing his fool head off as he prepared to kill her. His four sons simultaneously drew their guns.

I came around the mound. I'd gotten Seppi into this, and it was my responsibility to make sure she survived. I aimed at Travis, and started squeezing the trigger of my Colt. I did not stop until I was out of bullets.

My first two shots popped Travis in the chest. The

armless man staggered backward with blood pouring from his mouth. He fell against the pickup and his gun dropped from his hand. Then he just seemed to melt into the earth.

One of the Bledsoe boys rushed to his father's aid. The others aimed their weapons at me. I didn't have anything to fight them with, and lowered my arm. I saw my life flash before my eyes, and all the things I'd yet to do.

"Throw down your weapons!" Wood shouted.

The SWAT team came out from hiding, their assault rifles aimed at the Bledsoe boys. It was an old-fashioned Mexican standoff, and I was in the middle of it.

"Now!" Wood shouted.

One of the Bledsoes had the foresight to drop his gun, and throw his arms into the air. But the others didn't, and started firing.

It was the last thing any of the Bledsoe clan ever did.

CHAPTER 57

I RAN TO where Seppi lay facedown in the earth. The air was choking with the smell of gunfire and death, the sound of the SWAT team's furious assault echoing across the barren fields like a Fourth of July celebration that had gone awry. Kneeling, I looked for any signs of bullet holes on Seppi's body. Her clothing was clean, and I gently touched her shoulder.

"Hey," I said.

Seppi's head twisted in the earth. "Is the shooting over?"

"Yes. Are you okay?"

"I think so."

"Come on. You need to get up."

I helped Seppi to her feet. She came off the ground slowly, like someone rising from a deep sleep. She looked around at the Bledsoes and shook her head ruefully.

"Did any of them get away?" she asked.

"No. That was real brave, what you did."

"I don't know what came over me. I hope I didn't screw up your plan."

"Not at all."

The SWAT team were checking the Bledsoes for signs of life. I guided Seppi past them and up the hill. Reaching the top, she stopped to glance over her shoulder.

"Are they all dead?" she asked.

I looked back as well. The Bledsoes were sprawled around the sheriff's pickup, and didn't have an ounce of life left in their bodies. It wasn't the ending any of us had hoped for, but sometimes justice has a way of catching up to people, and making them pay for their sins. The Bledsoes had gotten exactly what they deserved.

"Yes," I said. "They're all dead."

I started to lead Seppi back to my car. She took a few hesitant steps, then stopped walking. The blood had drained from her face, and she did not look well. I had her lean against me, then took her wrist, and felt for her pulse.

"Your heart rate is high," I told her.

"It's always high," she said.

"You don't look good."

"Just give me a minute to catch my breath. I'll be fine."

Linderman came up the hill and joined us. I'd seen him shoot one of the Bledsoes with his shotgun, the boy flying through the air like he'd been struck by a car. Looking at him now, I would never have known he'd just killed someone.

"That was an awfully brave thing you did," Linderman said.

Seppi leaned against me for support. "I'm glad I could help," she said.

"Special Agent Wood would like you to show us where Mouse and Lonnie's compound is," Linderman said. "He's afraid of getting lost."

"I can do that," Seppi said.

"I'll tell Wood," Linderman said. "He wants to leave right now."

"I'm ready when you are," she said.

Linderman marched back down the hill. I started to protest, and Seppi dug her fingernails into my arm so hard it made me wince.

"Don't," she said.

"But you're not well," I said. "You need to go to a hospital, and get checked out."

"I told you . . . I just need to catch my breath."

"We have your map. You don't need to do this. We can find them."

Seppi glanced furtively over her shoulder. Satisfied none of the others could hear her, she leaned in close, her eyes glistening with tears.

"I lied to you earlier," she said.

"You did? About what?" I asked.

"Mouse and Lonnie used to take turns sleeping with me. I want to see the FBI shoot those sons-a-bitches. Please let me be there."

I swallowed hard. Seppi had told me her darkest secret. How could I deny her?

"All right," I said.

CHAPTER 58

THE ROAD leading to Mouse and Lonnie's farm had been carved through a dense forest of trees, and was barely wide enough for two cars. I drove slow, afraid of hitting one of the many deer that peered out from the shadows.

A Colonial-style house came into view. The paint was peeling and three cars were parked in the front yard. On the front porch sat a woman in a rocker. She was missing her right foot. She looked up from her knitting, and waved to us.

"Wave back," Seppi said.

"Why?" Linderman asked.

"That's Travis Bledsoe's wife, Delia," Seppi explained.

We lowered our windows, and waved to the widow Bledsoe. Wood, who trailed us in his Audi, did the same, as did the drivers of both SWAT team vans.

"How much farther to the dairy farm?" Linderman asked.

"A couple of miles. It's the only place around here. You can't miss it."

Linderman still had his body armor on, and was cradling a shotgun in his lap. There was no hiding his apprehension. He was ready for his nightmare to be over.

The most evil of places looked banal, almost dull. They were never dungeons equipped with torture equipment, or attics where the dead hung from the rafters, but were usually houses or farms that could be found in every community.

Mouse and Lonnie's dairy farm was such a place. It had several overgrown pastures, a red barn with a weather vane on its roof, and a two-story shingle house with lead-glass windows and hurricane shutters. Had there not been a tall fence with razor wire surrounding the property, it might have passed as a B&B.

"That's it," Seppi said.

"Anyone home?" I asked.

"That's their Jeep. It's parked by the house."

I slowed down. Mouse and Lonnie's Jeep Cherokee was parked next to the side door of the house. The backseat was filled with groceries. It made me think that they'd just gotten home, and gone shopping.

I lowered my window and stuck my arm out. I pointed at the farm so that Wood and the drivers of the SWAT team vans would know that we'd arrived.

In my mirror, I saw Wood gesture. Wood wanted me to pull over. I obliged him, and let Wood and the vans pass me.

The vans drove up to the gate in front of the house. The gate had a metal chain and a padlock keeping it closed. Two SWAT team members jumped out of the van. One had a pair of bolt cutters, which he used to cut the chain.

The sound of a clanging bell made me jump in my seat.

"What the hell was that?" Linderman asked.

"There's a bell on top of the house," Seppi said. "Mouse used to ring it when there was trouble."

"They're on to us," Linderman said.

The bell stopped ringing. Then a shot rang out. The man with the cutters clutched his arm, and dropped to the ground. I grabbed Seppi and pulled her head down.

"You said all Mouse had was a pistol," Linderman said to her.

"He's a good shot," Seppi replied.

The other members of the SWAT team slipped out of the van, and took up positions behind him. They began to fire back. Wood and his assistant got out of the Audi with their weapons drawn. I heard Wood telling the SWAT team to be selective with their shots because there was a hostage inside the house.

The firing coming from the house suddenly stopped.

"Both of you stay here," Linderman said.

Linderman got out of my Legend, and took up a position with the SWAT team. The firing from the house resumed, with bullets now hitting the SWAT team vehicle. I was a sitting target. I threw my car into reverse, and floored it.

I kept driving in reverse until I was out of range. Then I sat very still, and clutched the wheel. Seppi was still crouched down, and lifted her head.

"What's happening?" she asked.

"They're shooting at each other. Stay down."

Seppi lowered her head. I continued to grip the wheel. I found myself wondering why Mouse had rung the bell when we'd pulled up. The bell in a farmhouse was used to call to people working outside. Had Mouse rung the bell to alert Lonnie?

"Didn't you tell me the farm backed up onto a national forest?" I asked.

"Yes. There are several thousand acres," Seppi said.

"Did Mouse or Lonnie ever go back there?"

"Lonnie did."

"A lot?"

"Yes. It was his favorite place."

I threw my car into drive and floored the accelerator.

"Show me where the forest is," I said.

CHAPTER 59

SEPPI POINTED and I drove. My wheels tore up the grass as I left the road and drove around the farm. Seppi pointed to the gate at the back of the property. It was open, and swinging with the wind.

"There," Seppi said.

I pulled up alongside the gate, and threw my Legend into park. From the glove compartment I grabbed the box of bullets that I took with me wherever I went, and reloaded my Colt.

"Show me where the path into the forest starts," I said.

Seppi led across a short field to the path. It was recently trampled, with two sets of footprints clearly visible in the dirt. Buster sniffed the path and started to whine.

"I left the keys in the ignition," I said. "Go back to the farm, and tell Special Agent Linderman what we found."

"I want to stay here, and help you," Seppi said.

I grabbed her by the shoulders. Seppi had shown a lot of courage, but sometimes bravery got people killed. I said, "Do as I say. It's for the best."

"Please don't let Lonnie get away."

"That's not going to happen."

She left, and I ran down the path with Buster. The forest was dark and foreboding, the air cooler than out in the sunlight. Lonnie had a big head start, but he also had Sara with him, and hopefully that had slowed him down enough for me to catch up.

"Find the girl," I told Buster.

He sprinted ahead. Soon I couldn't see him. My breathing grew labored, and my legs felt like lead. I thought back to the night I'd gone to the Sunny Isle apartments, and confronted Lonnie as he'd come out the door carrying Naomi Dunn over his shoulder. Had I stopped him then, none of this would have happened. But now God was giving me a chance to redeem myself. I told myself not to blow it.

A scream pierced the air. It was the voice of a man, but childlike. The scream was followed by a harsh tearing sound. My dog had found Lonnie.

I went off the path and tore through the woods. I heard Buster's frantic bark, and followed it into a clearing. It was the most beautiful of places, with golden sunlight filtering through the trees and blooming sunflowers everywhere I looked. A barefoot Sara Long stood in the center of the clearing, wearing a white nightgown and a band of flowers in her hair. A rope was tied around her waist that Lonnie was holding on to.

"Bad dog! Go away!" Lonnie said.

Buster had taken a bite out of Lonnie's pant leg, and was circling his prey. Lonnie was trying to swat him away with a tree limb while continuing to hold the rope. Lonnie was shirtless, his muscles so huge they didn't look real. He was so preoccupied fighting off my dog that he didn't see me approach.

"Sara," I whispered.

Sara jerked her head and let out a gasp.

"Oh, my God," she said.

"Duck," I said.

Lonnie suddenly realized I was there. He roped Sara in, and used her body as a shield. He tossed the tree limb at Buster, knocking him to the ground.

"Go away!" Lonnie demanded.

I moved sideways to get a clean shot. Lonnie moved sideways as well, keeping Sara between himself and me.

"Let her go," I said.

Lonnie laughed wickedly. He grabbed Sara from behind by the neck, and lifted her clean off the ground. Sara struggled helplessly, her legs flailing in all directions.

"I'll kill her!" Lonnie shouted.

I instinctively started backing up.

"Don't leave," Sara begged me.

I glanced at Buster. My dog was dazed from getting hit with the branch, and slow to get up. I wanted him to make another run at Lonnie, and distract him. Lonnie had enough intellect to understand what I was thinking, and he shook Sara like a rag doll.

"*Now!*" the giant said.

Lonnie was going to break Sara's neck. I lowered my gun, and continued my retreat. A look of burning hatred filled Sara's eyes.

"Don't you dare leave me!" she shrieked.

She sounded just like her father. Bringing her hands up, she grabbed Lonnie's arms, and pulled herself into the air. She stuck both her legs straight out like a gymnast doing a split.

"Shoot him!" she ordered me.

Sara wanted me to shoot through her nightgown and take Lonnie down. Only I couldn't tell where her nightgown ended, and her body began.

"Do it!" she screamed.

I told myself that it was her life, not mine. Raising my Colt, I aimed a foot below her outstretched legs. My arm was trembling, and I grabbed my wrist with my other hand, and squeezed the trigger.

A black gunpowder hole appeared in Sara's nightgown. Lonnie howled, and staggered backward. He released Sara, and she rolled on the ground next to Buster.

"Freeze," I said.

With a puzzled look on his face, Lonnie examined the bullet hole in his pant leg. A flesh wound. Realizing he was not badly hurt, he charged me like a mad bull.

I didn't like shooting an unarmed man, but I had no other choice. I fired again. The bullet went into the center of Lonnie's chest, but did not slow him down. I got off two more rounds and saw the bullets smack into his body, yet somehow he kept coming forward. It was as if he didn't know he was dead.

There are people who don't believe in evil. I am not one of them. Lonnie was filled with evil, and killing him was the only way to stop his murderous ways. I waited until he was right on top of me before firing again. The shot went straight into his heart, what cops call a kill shot. This time he went down for good.

I sat on the ground with Sara and let her cry on my shoulder. Buster began to lick her face, and Sara pulled him into her chest and hugged him. Lonnie lay nearby with a childlike grin on his face.

"You're very brave," I said.

"Lonnie wanted to marry me," she said. "I'd rather get shot than let that happen."

Lonnie had killed four women that I knew about. I wondered how many of them had shared Sara's sentiment. My cell phone rang and I pulled it from my pocket. It was Linderman. I answered it, and over the line heard heavy gunfire.

"I've got Sara Long," I said.

"She's not in the farmhouse with Mouse?" Linderman asked.

"She's sitting right next to me. Would you like to speak with her?"

"I'll take your word for it."

I heard Linderman tell Wood that the hostage was not in the house. Wood responded by telling the SWAT team to open fire. Over the phone I heard an explosion of bullets as the SWAT team's assault rifles riddled the building.

I'd had enough killing for one day, and folded my cell phone. In the trees, the birds were chirping; next to me, Buster wagged his tail. It was the way things were supposed to be. Quiet, serene, beautiful. I glanced at Sara, and saw the beginnings of a smile.

"What's that sound?" she asked.

I didn't hear anything, and shook my head.

"It sounds like a cell phone."

Sara got to her feet and walked over next to Lonnie. "It's coming from him."

I stood up and moved next to the dead man. A chime was coming from his pants pocket. Kneeling, I stuck my fingers into his pocket and extracted a cell phone. There was a call coming in, and I looked at the cell phone's face. It said MOUSE.

I let Sara see the phone. Then I put my fingers to my lips.

"Don't say a word," I said.

I flipped open the phone and we both listened.

"Lonnie, it's me. I'm coming out through the tunnel. Meet me by the old outhouse behind the property."

The line went dead. Sara said, "Mouse showed me the outhouse when we got here yesterday. He said he'd make me go to the bathroom there if I didn't behave."

"Think you can find it?"

"I sure can."

CHAPTER 60

WE LEFT the clearing and headed down the path toward the house. I tried to reach Linderman and tell him that Mouse was escaping but had to leave a message on his voice mail. As we drew closer to the farm, the sound of gunfire became more pronounced.

Sara stopped at the fence that surrounded the property. She pointed at a building the size of a phone booth that sat outside the fence. It had a half moon carved into the door and a wash basin with a dripping faucet.

"Get behind me," I said.

Sara slipped behind me. I aimed my Colt at the outhouse and started walking toward it. Buster ran in front of me with his nose stuck to the ground. Reaching the outhouse, I walked around it with my eyes peeled to the ground. I didn't see any hidden trapdoors in the earth, but that didn't mean there wasn't one there.

A few feet away, the ground started to shift. I made Sara stand behind a tree, then went into a crouch and aimed my Colt at the spot. Buster was kneeling a few feet away, not knowing what to make of the situation. I heard a man's voice.

"Fuck, this thing is heavy."

It was Mouse. As I watched, a round piece of earth came out of the ground, and was tossed aside. Then a man popped out of the hole with his back to me. He was covered in shit and smelled like the devil. At his trial, Mouse had played with his own feces to convince a judge he was crazy. It was a perfect metaphor for who he was.

Mouse crawled out of the hole. I couldn't see his pistol, but felt certain that he was carrying it. I got up right behind him, and pressed my Colt to the back of his head.

"Freeze."

Mouse stuck his arms into the air. He looked over his shoulder at me, saw Sara and my dog, and knew it was over. He turned around slowly. His pistol was tucked down behind his belt buckle. I reached for it, and he took a step back.

"Where's my buddy?" Mouse asked.

"Give me your gun," I said.

"You shot him, didn't you?"

"Right now."

"Did you kill him?"

I didn't answer. But it was answer enough. A look of sadness spread over Mouse's face. Taking a step forward, he jumped back into the hole.

Sara came out from behind the tree. "Aren't you going to go after him?"

I shook my head. There was no reason to chase a man who's run out of road.

A gunshot ripped through the air. I went to the hole and had a look. Mouse lay on the bottom with the pistol stuck in his mouth and the back of his head gone.

It was over.

CHAPTER 61

AN AMBULANCE took Sara to a hospital in Daytona for a series of tests. As she was taken into the emergency room, I heard Sara tell the doctors that she was fine, and asked if she could be released. Abduction victims often suffered post-traumatic stress, and I talked her into staying at the hospital until the tests were completed.

A few hours later, Karl Long arrived at the hospital, and came into the hospital's emergency room hobbling on a cane. I was sitting in the visitor area thumbing through a magazine. I rose from my chair, and Long hugged me like a long-lost brother.

"How's my baby?" Long asked.

"Your baby is doing fine. We got her just in time," I said.

"Can I take her home? My private plane is at the airport."

"You'll have to talk to the doctors, but I don't see why not."

Long made a check appear out of thin air. Something told me that he'd been practicing doing that on the ride up, just to impress me. With a smile he stuffed it into my shirt pocket. "Thank you, my friend," he said.

I waited until Long had gone back to see Sara before looking at the check. It was for more money than we'd agreed upon. A *lot* more.

Hey, I'd earned it.

Sara was released a few hours later. She was good to go, and I drove her and her father to the airport, and waved good-bye as they stepped on Karl Long's private plane. Then I drove back to Chatham.

The dairy farm was swarming with police and FBI agents when I returned. I was cleared to enter, and took a walk around the property. Mouse and Lonnie's bodies had been brought back to the farm, and lay beneath a pair of white sheets on the ground. The police did not appear to be in any hurry to take them away.

I found Linderman standing by a garden behind the house. He'd taken off his body armor, and had an empty coffee cup in his hand. His clothes were streaked with sweat and hung lifelessly off his body.

"Where are they?" I asked.

Linderman pointed at the garden. It was a small plot of land choking with weeds. I hopped over the small fence that surrounded it. The victims' graves were in the corner, with piles of white rocks for headstones, just like Kathi Bolger's grave. I checked the rocks, hoping the women's IDs were there, but there was nothing.

I studied the graves. Four contained the bodies of young women whose identities we knew. The fifth was a mystery. Was it Danny Linderman or someone else? I had worked with medical examiners' offices before, and knew it could be awhile before we found out.

I went back to Linderman. His eyes had not left the

graves since I'd found him. I took the coffee cup from his hand. He looked at me with dead eyes.

"You okay?" I asked.

"No," he whispered.

I spent the next three days taking long swims in the ocean and playing with Buster on Daytona Beach. At night, I visited the local haunts that served fresh seafood, and ate my fill of fish and crabs and washed it down with cold beer. I talked to Rose several times, and got caught up. I told her everything that had happened, but left out the money I'd earned from the job. I wanted to surprise her with that the next time we got together.

Muriel Linderman drove up to be with her husband, and they spent most of the time in their motel room, waiting for Daytona's chief medical examiner to contact them.

On the afternoon of the third day, the ME finally called, and told Linderman she had made positive identifications of the five bodies that had been exhumed from the garden. She asked Linderman to come to her office.

Linderman called me, and told me the news. I offered to drive him and Muriel to the ME's office. Linderman agreed, and we arrived at the medical examiner's building on the west side of town a few minutes past closing.

The ME met us in the building's lobby. She was a short, pleasant woman, dressed in a lab coat, with bifocals that hung around her neck. She was aware of the Lindermans' situation, and went out of her way to be kind.

She led us to her windowless office. The autopsy reports for each victim lay in a pile on her desk. She offered us seats, which we declined. Picking up the files, she explained how the victims had been identified through dental records. As she named each victim, she placed their file on her desk, until only one file remained in her hands.

"I'm sorry to inform you, but the fifth victim was not your daughter," the ME said. "Her name was Clarissa Santiago. She was a Nicaraguan nursing student enrolled at Nova University in Miami. Santiago disappeared five years ago. Her friends told the police she'd been homesick, and thought she'd gone back to Nicaragua. That was why the Miami police never filed a missing persons report."

Muriel Linderman covered her mouth with her hand. Linderman lowered his head and did not speak. He tried to stop the tears, but could not. In all the time I'd helped him look for Danny, I'd never seen him cry. I wanted to tell him that things would be all right, but that would have been a lie.

"Let's go," I said.

I drove them back to our motel and walked them to their room. I wanted to leave, but I stayed long enough to tell them the words I thought they both needed to hear.

"I'm not going to stop looking for your daughter," I said. "Danielle didn't just disappear off the face of the earth. There are answers to what happened, and I'm going to help you find out what they are, however long it takes."

I put my arms around Linderman and his wife and hugged them. We stood that way for a while, and then I said good-bye.

CHAPTER 62

I DROVE HOME that night with the windows down and the Doobie Brothers' "The Captain and Me" playing on my tape deck. I hadn't listened to their music in a long time, and it took me back to a better place than the one I was in.

It was two a.m. when I walked into the Sunset. The Dwarfs had gone home, and the place was quiet. Sonny poured me a cold draft without being asked, and handed me a bowl of table scraps for Buster. I fed my dog, then took a seat at the bar.

"There's no place like home," I said.

Sonny picked up the remote from the bar and punched a command into the TV. On the screen appeared a women's college basketball game. I raised my glass to my lips, then put it back down. One of the teams was the Lady Seminoles.

"Jessie's team is still in the tournament," Sonny explained. "They played a few hours ago. I thought you'd want to see it."

I sipped my beer and watched the game. The Lady Seminoles were having a bad night and did not play well. With a minute and a half left in the first half, they were down by sixteen points.

A substitution was called. A long-legged blonde sprinted onto the court and got high-fives from her teammates. I could not believe my eyes. It was Sara Long.

"Why are they putting her in?" I asked.

"Just watch," Sonny said.

Sara looked terrible. She threw two air balls, and sent an errant pass into the stands. With the clock winding down, she attempted a three-pointer from midcourt. The crowd seemed to freeze, and I sat up in my chair. The ball went through the net without touching the rim. As Sara came off the court, her team mobbed her.

"The Seminoles won, in case you were wondering," Sonny said.

"Give me the remote."

I rewound the tape to where Sara had entered the game, and watched her play again. This time, I saw how hard Sara was trying, and how that effort had affected the other members of the team. What was broken had been fixed.

Maybe there were happy endings after all.

ACKNOWLEDGMENTS

A NUMBER of people graciously helped me in the writing and research of this book. A big thank-you to my wife, Laura, to Chip Williams for his help on firearms (I will never be able to see a gun dropped on television without thinking of you), and to Rich Dugger, whose knowledge of all things Florida never fails to amaze me. Thanks also to the wonderful folks at Ballantine Books—Gina Centrello, Libby McGuire, and my incredible editors, Dana Isaacson and Linda Marrow.

Special thanks to Andrew Vita, Team Adam Consultant with the National Center for Missing and Exploited Children and former Associate Director/Enforcement for the Bureau of Alcohol, Tobacco, and Firearms. Andy's devotion to finding missing children is a never-ending source of inspiration.